PRINCE OF PERSIA

JACK TAYLOR

PRINCE OF PERSIA
Copyright ©2022 Jack Taylor
978-1-988928-59-3 Soft Cover
978-1-988928-60-9 E-book

Published by Castle Quay Books
Burlington, Ontario, Canada and Jupiter, Florida, U.S.A.
416-573-3249 | info@castlequaybooks.com | www.castlequaybooks.com

Edited by Marina Hofman Willard
Cover design and book interior by Burst Impressions

Printed in Canada

All rights reserved. This book or parts thereof may not be reproduced in any form without prior written permission of the publishers.

Library and Archives Canada Cataloguing in Publication

Title: The Prince of Persia / by Jack Taylor.
Names: Taylor, Jack A., 1956- author.
Identifiers: Canadiana 20220150222 | ISBN 9781988928593 (softcover)
Subjects: LCGFT: Novels.
Classification: LCC PS8639.A9515 P75 2022 | DDC C813/.6—dc23

*Dedicated to good wives everywhere who try to make a difference
in who they are and in whatever they do.*

Shelly,
Thanks for being a woman who brings joy to our world.
Blessings,
Pastor Jack

I

A RAZOR-EDGED BLADE at the throat is a clear attention getter. Nabonidus swallowed as he considered this barrier to finding his roots. Was he descended from king or noble? What matter did it make? He might be decorated with the triumph of champions, but that meant nothing if he was as dead as a rat under the hooves of a warhorse.

Nabonidus gagged as if swallowing an oversized piece of gristle. The stench of decayed flesh, unwashed humanity, and leather-covered beast overpowered his senses. The bloodstained lance remained steady under his chin.

The mounted Parthian warrior opposite him cradled the weapon with intent to use. He was dressed in the garb of the dreaded cataphract, an elite brigade of heavily armed guardians to the Magi and the monarchy. He and his horse were shrouded in scale armor. The scarlet helmet with a black plume out of the top and white streamers from the side marked the warrior's high rank.

The reins burned against Nabonidus's calloused fingers as the lead ox stumbled another step forward. Persian warriors in the gladiator arena in Ephesus had fallen to his skills as the emperor's champion, but he'd always been armed and prepared. His flight from Roman persecution had thrust him from one forum of death into another. The fiery eyes of the assassin with the lance showed no interest in a fair fight. They stayed focused on Nabonidus as he straightened and the lance maintained its distance. Escape would be challenging.

Extracting a leather pouch from inside his tunic, he cradled it in his palm. Then he loosened the cord around the neck of the pouch and held out the offering. An aromatic, musty pine with hints of citrus and an earthy scent like rosemary filled the air. "Frankincense," he said. "I bring the gift of kings."

The cataphract flicked his lance at the offering, leaving the contents of the bag spilling onto Nabonidus's leather legwear. He ignored the unleashed aroma filling the air between them. "Be still!" he commanded.

Charging into view, a dozen archers with bows drawn sealed off the road. Their white pantaloons, baggy blue shirts, and long hair held back with leather headbands gave them freedom of movement on their speedy steeds. The quivers strapped to their backs housed handfuls of metal-tipped missiles. Their black Friesian warhorses boasted powerful, sloping shoulders on compact muscular bodies with long, thick manes like their riders. Lengthy silky tails dropped as the brigade halted twenty strides away.

Two weeks before, Nabonidus had ferried across the Tigris River and made his way toward the lower Zagros Mountains. An hour before being stopped by the cataphract warrior, Nabonidus had crossed the Karkheh River and focused on the king's palace at Susa. His wife, Daphne, was safe with followers of the Way in a village nearby. A sixth sense had warned him danger was close.

They had argued for days prior to the separation. "I need to find out who I am," he said, "before I can share the good news with my people. I'm done with killing. I want peace—inside and outside." Only his uncle could tell him of the family roots.

Daphne didn't want to be left alone in a foreign land with strangers. "Take me with you!" she pleaded to no avail. "I can't do this by myself. All I want is to have a quiet life with you."

He'd been five when an ambush killed his parents in this very area. His sister had been snatched, and he'd been shipped out to become a slave in Palestine. A Roman centurion had sentenced him to a warship's galley for five years and then sold him to a ludus of gladiators in Ephesus. Thirty kills against other champions had won him his freedom. He had helped Yeshua's cousin, John, found a community of faith in the city. None of that mattered now.

Scattered fragments of his mother tongue fountained to the surface of his mind as the warrior shouted at Nabonidus. In the arena, ice had flowed through his veins as he prepared to strike. That sense grew now, but he fought it off, staring directly into the eyes of his challenger. The cataphract drove his lance through the back and into the heart of one ox. The beast buckled at the knees while its partner bawled in protest. Nabonidus remained stiff as a marble statue.

The warrior motioned to one of the archers, who trotted forward. The man probed Nabonidus in Greek, Egyptian, Syrian, Aramaic, and Latin. "Who are you?"

Nabonidus understood each probe but answered in Hebrew. "I am Nabonidus of the family Maimonides."

At the mention of the Maimonides family name, another archer walked his horse closer. He spoke in Hebrew. "The Maimonides name is a royal title. To claim such a name is a death sentence for an outsider. Step down from your cart."

Nabonidus did so, standing with arms crossed over his chest. The midday sun glistened off his forehead and rivulets of sweat streamed down his back. He clenched his fist and controlled his breath. In. Out. In. Out.

The cataphract lanced the second ox in the heart. It buckled onto the first dead one. An archer dismounted, sparked a flame with a flint and lit the cart on fire. The gifts Nabonidus had brought for his uncle sizzled and singed. Nabonidus looked straight ahead.

The Hebrew-speaking archer drew his dagger and stepped in front of Nabonidus. "My grandfather visited Palestine to honor one who the stars said was the King of kings. Are you that one?" The rest of the warriors dismounted and stepped forward.

"I know of the one you speak," Nabonidus said. "He was crucified by the Romans, was buried, and then resurrected."

The archer's brow wrinkled. "This King of kings—you say He died and came alive again? The Romans could not destroy Him?" The men moved into a circle with daggers drawn.

Nabonidus shook his head. The circle around him was now complete.

The interrogating archer stepped closer. "Has this royal son sent you to call us as His army to destroy the Romans and to take His place on the throne of our empire?"

Another head shake. "The King of kings does not need help to win His throne."

"Then why have you come? And why have you come now?"

"I come in His name, not for war, but for peace. I also come because it was in this place that my family was ambushed and I was taken as a slave for the Romans."

"So you seek the throne for yourself?"

"I seek it for no one. I only come in peace to see my uncle."

"And who is this uncle?"

"His name is Ardeshir of the family Maimonides."

Within a flash, the group was on him, kicking out his feet and laying him facedown in the dirt. The fall winded him, but he fought his instinctive reflexes and lay still. Leather straps appeared and were used to bind his hands and feet. A cloth covered his eyes. In a moment, he was manhandled and dumped across a horse saddle. His hands were tied to his feet under the belly of the animal. This was not the welcome he imagined.

Daphne waited patiently by the village well where Nabonidus had left her. She rubbed her abdomen knowingly and smiled at what would come to be. Her husband wanted to get to his uncle's place in Susa before nightfall but hesitated to leave her alone. She had assured him that all would be well. They'd been traveling for six months by camel, horse, and donkey cart, and she was happy to embrace the thought of arrival.

The donkey stood guard like a dog looking down the road where its master had vanished. Perhaps feeling betrayed by the pair of oxen which had taken its place. The beast turned and nosed at the folds of her earth-toned tunic. Her husband always kept a carrot for the animal, and she expected the gesture. She pulled out the treat and fed it to the appreciative donkey. The hairy lips tickled the palm of her hand.

With the blanket off, the black cross down the donkey's brown neck and back stood out strongly. Yeshua had ridden a beast exactly like this a week before his crucifixion. The only difference was that this donkey's cross was strangely broken. Halfway down its spine the cross broke off in a jagged portion toward its right side. She rubbed her hand along the cross and traced the edge of the broken stripe.

People-watching stimulated her mind into storytelling. As she watched the butcher carrying the six white hens by their feet, the scene in Daphne's mind became a loving father with six children who couldn't decide what to get them for Nowruz—the Persian New Year. The old woman feeding corn husks to five large hogs in a pen filled with mud became a Zoroastrian fattening them up for her special pudding to feed her grandchildren on Yalda—the feast to celebrate the winter solstice and light's triumph over darkness. People everywhere lived to celebrate.

A red hawk circled over a nearby field much like hawks circled fields near Ephesus, Tarsus, Damascus, Nineveh, Babylon, and every place in between where she and her husband had rested and replenished their supplies. Women arrived with their vessels, drew their life-sustaining liquid, and attempted to chat. She smiled and nodded until they realized she was a foreigner, void of comprehension.

At last, two young women, nearing twenty years of age, skipped into view chattering and laughing. The elder one wore a crimson pleated skirt gathered at the ankles. A large cape flowed over her chest and elbows, and a raised headpiece of intricately woven beads nestled in her coal black coiffure. The younger wore a simpler version of the same design in an emerald hue. Both the women wore numerous jeweled bangles on their wrists.

Nabonidus had said there might be two. They prodded a donkey loaded with four large clay pots tied on by handles embedded in the molding. When they saw her, they stopped, whispered to each other, and then approached. The younger twisted the bangles on her wrist and then rubbed her hands together. In hesitant Greek, the older one asked, "Are you the one?"

There was no thought of suspicion on her part. "Nai! [Yes!]" she answered.

The two girls bowed before her. "We are the two daughters of Anoshiruvan—the immortal soul who knows. I am Adrina—the flaming lights, and this is Atossa—the free flowing one. We are honored to provide hospitality for followers of The Way."

"And I am pleased to accept it," Daphne said. "I remember you from Ephesus. I am glad you were rescued and sent safely here."

"Where is the gladiator?" the younger asked.

"He went to Susa to see his uncle."

"Who is his uncle?"

"I think the family name is Maimonides."

Both girls grew wide-eyed and gasped as they covered their mouths. "But no! This is not a good time. The king was assassinated, and the guards are out looking for anyone they can find to blame. Any Maimonides is high on the list."

Daphne jumped to her feet. "We must send someone to warn him! Hurry, who can go?"

Adrina turned like an army commander on her sister. "Hide her! I'll send our guardian. No one must know she belongs with the gladiator." Small puffs of dust were the only witness to her wild dash across the plaza.

Atossa removed her own smoke-singed shawl and threw it over Daphne's head. "Hide your face. Bend low as if you're old. I will help you until we find our way home." The younger girl took the ropes of both donkeys and led the way.

By the time the pair had circled the village numerous times and found a hidden way into the clay bricked home, her back, neck, and shoulders were tight. A searing stab into her right shoulder with a twin pain in her lower back only increased as she flopped onto a stool. Atossa brought water for her feet as she handed the head covering back to its owner. "I am sorry to bring you trouble."

Adrina arrived as night fell. Atossa set out the evening meal. "This is our favorite food, which we prepared for your husband. Our mother taught us while she lived." The pungent aroma of spices, nuts, and roasted meat filled her senses.

Seeing Adrina's tight jaw line and creased eyebrows, Daphne turned back to Atossa. "What is it?" she asked.

Adrina took over the explanation. "This is a food called fesenjan. We use it in weddings. It includes pomegranates, walnuts, duck, onions, saffron, cinnamon, and sugar, plus some family spices to make it our own."

Atossa took the covering off of the other clay pot. "This is bademjan. You can see the golden-red tomatoes that we grow. There is also turmeric, lemon juice, eggplant, onions, lamb, and seasonings, and we eat it with rice."

Accepting a healthy proportion of each, Daphne noticed the small helping taken by Adrina. "Are you worried they won't find him? How long will it take before your guardian is able to catch up to him?"

Adrina stepped to the door, listening. "There is but a single road to Susa. Oxen are slow. It will not be long if he is okay." A moment later she was back. "A rider is coming our way. This may not be the news we hoped for."

The stars twinkled horizon to horizon by the time Nabonidus had his blindfold removed, his bindings untied, and his feet set on the ground again. The archers were nowhere in sight, but ten cataphract warriors lined the entrance to a high arched building where an old dark-skinned man hobbled along a mosaic floor with a cane tapping ahead of him. His stooped frame made his white beard seem even longer—falling below his knees. The white tufts above his ears looked like nests waiting for birds to come home to roost.

While the warriors all bowed their heads in respect, Nabonidus was left to stand on his own. The elderly man halted an arm's length away and leaned on his cane. Glancing up, he scanned the captive from top to toes. "Maimonides, are you?"

A nod was enough of a response.

The man with the cane pointed it toward a log resting nearby. "You are a head taller than my bodyguard. You look like you've eaten a wild boar and you seem strong enough to lift an elephant. Pick up that log!"

Nabonidus stepped up to the log, nudged it with his foot and then crouched with his hands under one end. Grunting, he hoisted the end four feet off the ground. Holding it in place, he bent low under the center and lifted it on his shoulders. It was an exercise he had done many times in the gladiator school. He carried it ten steps toward the old man, turned and dropped the log.

The old man lifted his cane a fraction and tapped it three times. The cataphract captor who had first confronted him stepped out of line and moved to his side. "Follow!" he said in Greek.

Two of the warriors grasped wrists and linked arms to form a chair that the old man sank back into. As they marched back under the archway and into the tiled building, Nabonidus followed with the cataphracts close behind. Scattered torches provided dim lighting through the hallways until the band arrived in a large open space with sand covering the ground. A woman, shielded with a golden cape, stood on a dais surrounded by hundreds of large clay lamps.

The old man alighted from his "chair" and stood alongside the woman on the dais. The top of his head was even with her waist as he pivoted in place toward the cataphracts. "The Egyptian!" He turned away, climbed two stairs to a raised seat, and settled in surrounded by pillows. The woman in the golden cape straightened them around him.

The sound of crashing metal behind Nabonidus sent a chill up his spine. He glanced at the old man who jutted his chin out and motioned for him to look around. When he did rotate slowly, the pile of swords was impossible to miss.

The chief cataphract approached and pointed toward the pile. "Choose two weapons. Today, you will prove yourself or die. You will prove your royal blood or set it free in this sand."

It had been seven months since he had defeated the giant German gladiator in the arena at Ephesus. The followers of Yeshua he had helped to save in that bout had scattered. The life of bloodletting was a path he no longer cherished or embraced. This might be the time to bend the knee and expose his neck to end it all. What then would become of Daphne and their unborn child?

Daphne's ribs ached from the convulsing sobs that had wracked her body once the horseman delivered his message. "Rebels and assassins captured your man and took him away. These men live and die by the sword. No one escapes the cataphracts."

What had they done, thinking that they would bring the good news of Yeshua to the Persian and Parthian peoples? That perhaps Nabonidus might have been part of a royal family—perhaps even a prince of Persia waiting to be discovered? Six months of discomfort and blistering sunshine, for this? What would become of the child still to be born?

A cool breeze filtered in through the open window and caressed her cheek like a passing feather. She instinctively touched the place, remembering the many nights when her new husband ran calloused fingers tenderly from her ear to her chin and back again. Being together, alone, refashioned Ephesus as a nightmare to be forgotten. The future would be a haven of peace, wealth, honor, hope, and numerous sons. A new assembly of eager hearers would cherish the beauty and wonder of being loved and cared for. They had laughed together, relishing the goodness of the Almighty in His favor over them. How could this nightmare be true? Perhaps the messenger was mistaken. Perhaps the morning would bring different news.

Before dawn, Daphne rose and waited as birdsong took over from night sounds. Voices echoed off the brick walls and passageways. Perhaps if she walked to the edge of town, she would see someone who had different news.

She was ten strides past the well when a firm grip on her arm stopped her in her tracks. She spun and stared at Adrina's guardian. A rat's nest of hair perched on his chin but his upper lip was bare. A striped head covering pulled tight accentuated the large nose and tight dark eyes. "No!" he said in Greek. "Hide! Hide!" He pulled her along a nearby passageway and twisted through several small alleys before arriving back at the home of the two young women. "Stay! Hide!" he said, quick-stepping back the way he came.

As the messenger scampered away, Adrina stepped out the door. "Did I hear Mishuvan? What was he doing here so early?" She stood aside and motioned with her chin for Daphne to move inside. "You really shouldn't be out here. If someone finds out that you might be related to a Maimonides, we could all hang from the gallows by sunset."

At that moment, a pair of young eyes appeared at the corner of the compound gate. When the lad noticed that he had been seen, he ran.

Adrina yanked Daphne into the home. "Pack your things. That rat will share the news before you could walk past the well." She grabbed a handful of clothing from a cubicle built into the wall. "Atossa, the net is closing—we must swim quickly."

In moments, the younger sister snatched up flatbread, cheese, oranges, nuts, and rice. She stopped to scan the room before turning toward Daphne. "Hurry, grab what you need. The enforcers will be here soon. We will climb out the back window into our uncle Hananel's compound and then take shelter in the cavern."

Daphne scrambled after the sisters as they scaled the wall into an adjoining compound, using carefully dug divots as footholds. By stretching her hand above her head, she could reach the top of the wall. By the time she hoisted herself to the top the two sisters were waiting to help her down. The trio scurried to a rounded hut set at the side of the compound. They pushed through a woven mat doorway, slipped into a room used to store grain and moved aside a small wooden cupboard.

Adrina shifted a carpet, raised a wooden door level with the floor and urged the two others to descend a small ladder. She handed down two small clay lamps, a flint, and a gourd of water. At the bottom of the ladder, she gave a short whistle and shut the door. Soon, a dull thud encouraged them that the cupboard was back in place.

Atossa lit the two lamps with the flint and set about rearranging the space. Sleeping mats, blankets, small wooden bowls, shawls, and a tray of hand-carved wooden cups moved under her touch. "Over there!" She pointed, giving direction to Daphne. "Through that narrow space you will find a larger room where we hold our worship and where we sleep when we need to hide for a while."

"Who was that boy?" Daphne asked.

"The watchman's son," Atossa answered. "He has a love for stories, and a few of his tales have resulted in serious trouble from the governor for some in this village." She pointed toward a small wooden bench in the larger space. "Sit there. This village is nowhere significant, but the watchman loves to dream that someday we will gain the blessing of the governor and that he will be showered with wealth and respect. He will be at our home shortly until my uncle assures him with the right coins that there is nothing to see here."

"Tell us of your journey and we will tell you of ours," Adrina said. "Such wonders our father never told us when we lived in Ephesus. If only you had come in time to see the King of kings. Not even the Roman emperor knows such splendor."

An hour into their exchange, Atossa reached out and grabbed hold of Daphne's wrist. "Shhh! Douse the lamps. Push into the back, and cover yourself with blankets."

Heavy footsteps sounded on the trapdoor overhead.

The Egyptian lay prone on the sand—a spear through his chest and a gash across his neck. Sweat and blood streamed off the sun-blackened chest of Nabonidus as he cradled the sword in his hand. The stench of death was thick. A slash starting at his shoulder was the deepest damage. Welts from the whip the slain warrior had wielded accompanied the puncture wounds on legs and thigh from the trident lying close to his open fingers. The fight had been fierce but not beyond what Nabonidus had faced in the arena as a gladiator.

The white-bearded elder awaited his nod before signaling to a pair of servants to carry the Egyptian to the dissecting rooms. Four white-skirted maidens rushed in and began to treat the wounds of the victor. A cabbage poultice, wrapped over with linen strips, sealed the deepest gashes. The touch and scent of the healers brought back too many vivid memories of the intoxicating culture of adulation in the arena. He gritted his teeth and waited for their departure.

Instead, a cushioned bed arrived and he was coaxed to lie on it. Gentle hands applied oils and massaged away the strain and pain of battle. A singer soothed his soul with the mother tongue he had rarely heard since that horrific day so long ago—the day his parents had been slaughtered and his sister had been snatched. The song spoke of love and rest and then of victory and ravishing. It was not a song designed to satisfy the souls of Yeshua's followers.

When his heart resumed its steady rhythm and his mind released the vivid images of the recent battle for his life, he propped himself up on his elbows and glanced toward the dais. The elder was gone. Only the golden-caped temptress remained. She stepped into the sand and swayed toward him. On reaching his side, she unclasped the cape and slid it over his back. "You are the victor and I am your spoils," she said.

Nabonidus snatched the cape off his back and flipped it back toward her. "Cover yourself," he said. "I have my needs satisfied. Save yourself for another."

She dropped the cape on the bed. "There is no other. Whether you take me today or tomorrow, I am the regent's gift to you until they place you on the throne or until you die."

Hours passed as the three women huddled in the darkness. The dust was thick, musty and almost choking. Overripe fruit shouted its presence from a dark corner. The footsteps above had long subsided, but they had heard no signal that it was clear to abandon the shelter. They had whispered stories of the journey and shared prayers for Nabonidus.

Atossa finally tossed aside the blanket and stumbled to a place under the trapdoor. She listened intently and shuffled back. "There is nothing," she whispered. "I think we can light a lamp and eat something. The boy may be watching, but he won't be able to find us down here."

Daphne got to her knees and stretched. "I don't know how long I can sit doing nothing. Nabonidus needs to know he's not alone."

Adrina reached up and patted her shoulder. "May the peace of Yeshua rest on your shoulders while you carry this cross. He has not left you alone, and He will watch over all His children the same." She reached into a small reed basket and pulled out a pair of ivory dice. "We often use these to fill the time," she said. "If all three of us play, the time will run quickly."

The women shared rice, nuts, cheese, bread, and fruit. Then they settled back in the refuge to wait. It was hours before the thud above signaled them to emerge.

Outside the hut, a quarter moon slipped across a cloudy sky. Hananel stepped across the courtyard and motioned them into his own home. He was tall, slim, and broad shouldered—a man who worked the earth and the wood it produced. His thick, bushy sideburns, merging with a closely trimmed goatee, enlarged the appearance of his head's width while shrinking the length of his face.

Cups of diluted wine and baskets of fresh bread and grapes sat waiting for them. The aroma of baking was heaven enough after the dark, dank space under the hut. The warm water for hands, feet, and face was luxurious.

"News from the guardian," Hananel said. "There's a rumor from a rebel group south of Susa that a new prince has come home. We think this might be about Nabonidus. The Magi have unleashed an army of assassins to locate and eliminate the pretender."

The air rushed out of Daphne's lungs as she fought to breathe. Would the same group of kingmakers who had honored Yeshua at His birth now bring about the death of His followers? Surely, this was all a mistake. There had to be some way her husband could back away from the madness. They could go back to Ephesus if necessary.

Adrina struck a flint and moved from lamp to lamp, lighting the perimeter of the room. "There has to be a way to protect Daphne so she doesn't have to hide." She picked up an orange and tossed it lightly from hand to hand. "What if we smuggled her out of here tonight, changed her appearance, and then brought her back with a big celebration as a cousin?" She looked toward Hananel for response. "Or maybe Daphne could be your cousin."

Hananel rested his forehead onto his two fists, his elbows indenting his knees. "How do you two get me involved with your scandals? You are walking scandals in sandals." He glanced at Daphne and shook his head. "You may yet regret following your husband to this God-forsaken land."

Daphne reached into the fold of her tunic and pulled out the ivory dice they had been playing with. "Every lot is guided by the hand of Hashem—is it not so?" She waited for Hananel's nod. "Evens, I stand as your cousin. Odds, I stand with the girls." She released the dice onto the floor and waited for Hashem to show the way.

The regent's banquet had all the audacity of the feasts thrown by Herod. Only the menu was different. The Roman luxuries of pigeon's tongue, caviar, and pig's feet were missing. Although costumed differently, the same kinds of jugglers, musicians, dancers, fencers, and pugilists filled the space with movement and noise.

Twenty men in loincloths paraded in front of the regent and bowed. They paired themselves at various spaces on the floor and wrestled. Losers were escorted out of the hall while the winners paired up with other winners. At the end there were two men left. They bowed and left together to applause and shouts.

A parade of young women streamed past the head table carrying bronze vessels filled with aromatic oils of agarwood, sandalwood, and amber. The incense chips and oils coming from the bark of trees blended spicy and woody scents into a tantalizing and sensuous aroma.

The cataphract stood to the left of Nabonidus while the regent reclined on the right. Nabonidus raised his chin toward the cataphract. "Why did the two men not wrestle to see who was the champion?"

"They are kept humble so that one day they may wrestle with a true champion."

"What is this incense the women have shared?"

"It is the wood of the gods from the Hindi people and is as costly as gold," the cataphract replied. "The Aquilaria extract is rare and comes from a resin produced by a fungus. It is usually used by our people in funerals or banquets, but the regent honors you today."

"Thank you," Nabonidus said, turning to the regent.

"What do you think of Sasina?" the regent asked, examining the girl in the golden cape as if she were another item on the menu. The elder Parthian reclined on the couch next to Nabonidus at the head of the U-shaped table. Sasina reclined at the far end of the table reserved for women. "Does her touch appeal to your senses? Are you satisfied with your gift?"

"You have an eye for beauty, and I am much too humble a man to deserve anything from you. I would be happy with one request if you would grant it."

The regent lifted up a golden goblet in anticipation. "And what is that one request?"

"Release me to return to my wife and friends. This is all I ask."

The regent slowly lowered the goblet. "Freedom? You seek freedom?"

"Yes, this is my only desire."

The waist length beard began to shake and then the regent lay back laughing until he released his goblet and let it fall onto the marble stones. The music and dancers stopped as the hilarity filled the room. Finally, the elder hugged himself and rolled over until he got to his feet. He steadied himself with a hand on the table as all waited. "The champion has one request. His freedom!"

Laughter broke out around the room as Nabonidus sat up on the dining couch. Madness had filled the place. What was so funny about such a request?

As if in answer the regent reached out and took hold of Nabonidus's wrist. "The warrior who has killed the personal bodyguard of the King of kings thinks he can go free. The champion who is sought for assassination by the Magi themselves thinks he can walk unknown from this den and into the land. The next prince of Persia thinks he can pretend to be a nobody." The laughter continued.

"A tribute to the one who will set us all free." The regent raised another goblet and released a small stream of wine onto the floor. "The only freedom is in death. Victory to the warriors of death." A loud shout sounded and the elder sank back onto his couch. "For the one who carries the name of the son of the great King Nebuchadnezzar, there is only one destiny. My grandfather first sought to ally himself with the Romans against the Parthian rulers, but the Romans have always failed us. Now, you, a Roman champion, will change all our fortunes."

Sasina rose from her place, moved behind Nabonidus, and massaged his shoulders. He stiffened and clenched his fists—at a loss how to respond. Had he not ventured to Persia to discover his destiny? Had he not proved himself again as the people's champion? And yet, what had he done in slaying the Egyptian—the bodyguard for the King of kings? In a single day he had become the enemy of the rulers and a champion for the rebels. If ever he needed Hashem, it was now.

II

IT HAD TAKEN two weeks to complete the ruse. Hananel had slipped away at night with his wife, and Daphne, ferried across the Tigris River at a northern crossing, joined a caravan heading south. Then Hananel made a very public celebration about bringing his cousin to Susa.

Daphne's hair had been dyed and refashioned. Her wardrobe had been adjusted to reflect the Parni peoples with a focus on the wealthier class. She adjusted her speech from Greek to Aramaic and focused on trying to apply an accent.

As the magnificent architecture built by Artaxerxes II loomed in the foreground, Hananel pointed toward the site. "In that city, Alexander the Great married ten thousand Greeks and Persians together to try and unite the two cultures. It has forever changed who we are and how we think."

"Will that make a difference in how people see me?" Daphne asked.

"I don't think anyone will connect you to your husband if they see him," Hananel said. "Your skin is so much lighter than his. He is definitely from the south of the country, and you look as if you could have come from the north."

"We see the beauty of our souls at one with Yeshua," Daphne responded. "Skin is the gift from Hashem as much as our personality and character. My husband has told me many times that he does not look down on me because I am not as dark as he is." She wiped at a tear crawling down her cheek. "I tell him that he has so many scars from whips, knives, and swords that if he had stayed in the arena, we would be like twins. We laugh a lot together."

"It is good we change your name anyway," Hananel said. "Did you know Daphne is the name of a goddess honored by the Athenians for her lusty desires? Why did your parents give you such a name?"

The heat rushed up her neck and cheeks. "It is the name I was called by the priest at the temple of Artemis in Ephesus. The only one I remember. I will be fine with a new name."

The group made a great show of reunion in the market at Susa, where Adrina and Atossa joined them. They danced and sang and showered Daphne with hugs and kisses. "Our cousin has come," they called as shopkeepers, neighbors, and onlookers showed interest. "Our cousin has come from the north." The girls handed over the donkey, which immediately nosed at Daphne's tunic for a carrot. It wasn't fooled by the elaborate ruse. She stroked the broken black cross embedded along its back.

Daphne received little more than an amused glance and a polite welcome from the majority of witnesses. "A special deal for you, my first customer," yelled the carpet salesman.

"Open my business, and receive one fruit free," called the produce vendor.

"Light your way to my shop and save your coins," urged the lamp and pottery dealer. The only thing that seemed to matter is that one more newcomer might be bringing more drachmas into the economy of the city.

Filling their carts with supplies heightened the joy of the day. Flour, honey, lamb, rice, vegetables, and fruits nestled in the front half of the donkey cart while stone and lumber occupied the back half. "What are you doing, building a new room for your cousin?" the carpenter asked when he finished loading.

"Of course," Hananel nodded. "Having one woman under my roof is enough. You know how that is, Haman, right?" He tossed the man a pomegranate and then distributed fruit to the women in his care.

The two men chuckled and waved as they parted. Daphne had been welcomed—mostly by keeping her mouth closed and nodding as others blathered. Her Aramaic phrases were short and to the point. The sense of relief was so great that when they climbed the hill out of the winter capital and began the descent toward home, Daphne chattered in Greek.

She continued freely until Adrina squeezed her wrist hard. "Ouch! What was that for?" she blurted.

Sitting on a camel, not more than a dozen strides away, were the watchman and his son. The watchman sported a grizzled salt and pepper beard stuffed into a star-studded purple head covering. His eyebrows wiggled like giant caterpillars bumping head-to-head. The boy wore a purple-bordered white robe matching his father's. The beast chewed away at a tuft of grass while the pair observed the oxcart. "What is all the excitement about?" the watchman asked.

"My cousin has come to visit from the north," Hananel said.

Daphne had wrapped the blue scarf so that only her eyes showed. She nodded and looked down.

"Is this one from your dead mother's side or your dead father's side?" the camel rider probed. "I've never heard you talk about family in the north."

The boy tugged at his father's sleeve and pointed. "She looks a lot like the woman I told you about the other day who disappeared from their home. Perhaps the governor needs to know about this newcomer."

The father patted his son's head. "A suspicious mind if ever I knew one. Who can blame him? This land is crawling with spies and assassins out to destroy our way of life." He yanked on the reins and nudged his camel alongside the cart. "Perhaps a community celebration to welcome your cousin might be in order. It looks like you've brought the supplies. What did you say her name was?"

Adrina spoke up. "Humaya—the smart one. That is her name. But what is that to you? You have so many things to keep track of that one name is as good as another."

The watchman allowed his camel's nose to snuffle close to the fruit in the cart before restraining him. "Pardon my guardian," he said. "There are many strangers using the silk road from the Orient these days, and we must guard our homes from smugglers and aliens who might steal our daughters and destroy our sons. Even worse are those from the west who come to steal our throne and our culture." He touched his forehead with his fingers and pulled away. "I look forward to your invitation so that we may all get to know this Humaya of yours."

A month under Sasina's touch, and still Nabonidus resisted the direction of her attentions. "What good am I to you if you resist the pleasures I offer?" she cooed. "You are not like other men who desire me with their eyes but dare not cross the boundaries set by the regent. I am your gift, and yet you spurn me as if I am trash. I assure you that I am trained to meet your every wish."

Nabonidus rose from the stool in front of her and brushed her hands away. "If you truly want to meet my wishes, then show me how to escape back to my wife." He stepped into the marble washing pool in the corner of the room and cooled his feet.

Sasina lifted the blue cape she had allowed to fall off her shoulder and wrapped it snuggly around herself. "The regent has been clear. You are with us until you reign or die. You can ask for whatever pleasure you desire except the presence of your wife." She moved closer to him again, drawing his attention. "Am I not the most beautiful of women, prepared for the champion of our people? Do I not have desires worthy of pleasure? Why would you rob me of my womanhood to mourn for what you can never have?"

The former gladiator looked at her briefly as she reached for the belt on her wrap. "No!" He turned, stepped out of the pool into his sandals and reached for a plate of figs and dates. "Yeshua has called us to battle the deepest desires in ourselves if they violate the holiness of the marriage bond. I cannot do this thing before Hashem."

She slid beside him. Close. Caressing his bare arm. Touching his fingers. Reaching for a fig and lifting it to his lips. "Is there sweeter joy than a man and a woman alone? No one needs to know of these moments between us. Everyone already assumes you have played the man with me."

Nabonidus shook her off. "No! I will know. Hashem will know. And when I am back with my wife, she will know."

The temptress slid across the room and flopped on the cushioned couch. "What good am I to you? A complete moon cycle has passed, and I am untouched and unwanted. If the regent knows I have failed in my training, he will feed me to the jackals." She lifted her hands like a beggar. "Is there nothing I can do for you?"

Closing his eyes, he breathed deep. In. Out. In. Out. When he opened them again, her face resembled that of a pouting child. A young woman vulnerable, afraid, confused, uncertain what to do. He moved toward the stool and sat facing her. "Listen to me," he said. "I will tell you stories of a people from the west. A people who fought giants, built temples of gold, and walked through the middle of great seas on dry ground."

She snatched up a small sheepskin and threw it at his feet. Sitting on it, she cocked her head. "This is all you desire? For me to listen to you?"

He nodded. "This is what every man longs for. A woman to listen to him. To respect him. To believe in him."

"And then you will want me?" she asked.

"Then I will tell you more stories," he said.

She draped her shawl over her head in the fashion of a student and waited.

"There once were a people enslaved in a faraway land," he began, "the land of a pharaoh who sought to destroy them. A mighty deliverer rose up to free them..."

She put her hand on his knee. "A deliverer like you," she affirmed. "One who slays the Egyptian."

A pounding at the door stopped them both. "Arise, and present yourself to the regent," the cataphract boomed. "It is time for the second test."

The celebration had gone without incident for Daphne, and even the watchman and his son danced freely with the men. No one openly questioned her presence, and she kept the bottom half of her face covered in the custom of the Parni peoples. She kept her appearance brief, lighting lumps of frankincense around the courtyard as the festivities continued through the night. Shortly before dawn a heavy sheet of rain sent everyone scrambling for their own refuges.

Adrina stepped into the space shared by the three women and peeled off her wet wrap. Daphne had laid out the three bedrolls and covers on the reed mats and sheepskins. "Are you sure you aren't from Parni?" she said, chuckling. "I think the men couldn't get enough of you. I'm glad you're married, or we might have trouble finding husbands." She dropped the wet things in a basket and dried herself off with a cloth. "Now, how do we convince everyone that you have a husband near without betraying him?"

Atossa stumbled through the door laughing. "Uncle thinks you did well tonight. The watchman would like to welcome you again next week. He even offered to give a camel for your riding pleasure if you would join his family for a meal."

Her gut clenched. There was no way she trusted the leering eyes of the watchman. Avoiding the other men had been hard enough. Her years as a young girl serving worshippers in the temple of Artemis in Ephesus flashed in her mind. Hungry eyes, desperate bodies, vicious acts. The throne of the goddess of healing ranked as one of the wonders of the world in its beauty. The priests had taught her clearly. Artemis was the daughter of Zeus, the sister of Apollo, the mother goddess of earth. But one day she had met a true champion who unleashed her from the deceit and destruction consuming her soul. Her pregnancy had been a miracle of Hashem. Even now the fluttering brought a smile to her lips.

A touch on her shoulder shook her out of her thoughts. "Humaya!" It was Atossa. "Daphne, you need to get used to this name, Humaya. Where do you go when your eyes go vacant? Why can't you hear me?"

Daphne inhaled deeply. "Do you remember when the priests in Ephesus killed your father and took you to train as temple maidens for Artemis? I also served as a girl but didn't have anyone rescue me until I was older. Sometimes I remember how good Hashem and Nabonidus have been in rescuing us so we could know the life of Yeshua."

The girls nodded in unison as they dressed in their night clothing. Adrina slipped under her blankets. "Now, if only Uncle Hananel can find us a man like Nabonidus who knows how to love Yeshua and us as well."

Atossa blew out the last lamp and announced the prayer. "O King of heaven, You who call your children to work and then to sleep. Give us the rest we desire so we may serve You and bring Nabonidus home in Your time."

"Amaine!" Daphne murmured at the same moment a yelp sounded from outside the window.

"Who's there?" Adrina called.

The rain had been refreshing as Nabonidus ran. The cataphract had roped the former gladiator to a horse and then forced him to run or be dragged. "Your test is to survive," the warrior said. It had been years since he'd had to endure the strain on his body created through such a test of endurance. His legs burned as with fire, his back throbbed, and his lungs starved for air. Still, he ran, finding the rhythm of the gladiator in training. If only he could catch his captor, strangle him, and escape back to Daphne.

As first light crept over the hills, the run grew harder. He stepped into a dip in the ground and stumbled, surviving only by grabbing the rope to right himself. The cataphract unleashed a whip that sliced into his wrist and his anger unleashed the adrenaline to push himself another hour. And then it was over.

The warrior released the rope, turned, and raced away. He was free. Or was he? In the distance, six mounted archers emerged from a grove of trees. His legs wobbled like rubber, and his feet stood rooted like tree stumps. The nearest refuge was a forest a hundred paces to his right, but it might as well have been a million. The archers were not riding hard to congratulate him on his run.

Looking to the heavens, he called out, "Yeshua, for You I live, and for You I die." With the prayer, his feet found freedom and speed. As he raced into the forest, a swarm of hornets sped overhead toward the archers. Not for a second did he doubt that the insects had come in response to Hashem's answer to his prayer.

The trail opening up for him dipped sharply into a ravine, and he took it without question. Halfway down, the path forked, and he went right, along the edge of a small cliff. He wrestled the rope off of his wrist and tied the ends to two saplings right before the drop-off. He hoped to trip up the horses in a place they couldn't stop.

The screams of the archers behind him spurred him on. Following an impulse he couldn't explain, he turned off the main path onto a narrow animal track. Several hundred paces in, he came upon a cave. He ducked inside and crouched, panting—desperately sucking wind into his air-starved lungs.

The fate of the archers became clear with the panicked screams as several went over the cliff face on their mounts. Others continued to battle the hornets. Only one raced by on his horse, staying on the main trail.

Thirst alone brought him out of the cave. The voices of the archers had long quieted. The lone pursuer who had passed the refuge had retraced his steps and not returned. The quiet of birdsong surrounded him as he limped down a slope toward a small stream trickling at the bottom of the ravine. The bodies of two horses lay still at the bottom of the small cliff where he had tied the rope. Their riders were nowhere in sight.

He cupped his hands and dipped them into the cool water. After sipping some, he dumped handfuls over his head and then cooled his feet. Things grew quiet. Too quiet.

He slipped up the opposite slope and sheltered in a clump of bushes. A cramp in his calf urged him to stretch and moments before he yielded to that urge, a slight movement in the trees opposite caught his eye. Sure enough. It was the cataphract, carefully tracking his footprints along the trail toward the cave. The man signaled, and two archers stepped out of the bush to follow.

When the trio moved out of sight toward his former refuge, Nabonidus turned and headed farther into the forest. The fact that they could track him meant his strategies would have to change. Yet these men were on foot now as he was. Evasive action was the only way to gain time. He worked at stepping on stones, leaping from tree branch to tree branch, stepping deliberately onto false trails. It might not fool an experienced tracker, but it might buy him time.

As the sun slid toward the horizon, thirst again consumed him. He circled back through the forest until he was beyond the crest of the hill where the archers had originally hidden. He crossed a field on his belly, pulling himself with his elbows and pushing hard with his knees. He darted across a roadway and crouched in the tall grasses.

As nightfall descended, a lone oxcart trundled by. He was tempted to beg the driver for passage but was glad when he heard the yells of the archers as they stopped the man. A caravan of camel-riding Arabs strode lazily into view. Another prayer arose.

The leader of the caravan easily spotted him hiding from his perch high above. "You there!" the Arab called. "What are you hiding for?"

Nabonidus pointed toward the archers down the road. "They seek my life. I am only trying to live."

The caravan stopped. "What have you done?"

"I have run away from my captors. I only hope to see my wife on the other side of Susa."

The camel driver searched in his saddle bag until he withdrew a white robe and colored headpiece like the garb he wore. He dropped them to Nabonidus. "Put this on. The last camel has no rider. Climb on and stay quiet. I will handle the men who seek you." He motioned to all the drivers, and the camels collapsed into a kneeling position, complaining as they did.

Nabonidus donned the robe and headpiece and slipped out of the grasses and onto the final camel. A young boy secured him in place and set him in the middle of the caravan. "Keep your head down. Pretend you sleep," the boy instructed. A gourd of water was provided, and he drank greedily. The group waited until dusk and then rose to continue the journey.

As the Arabs passed the cataphract and the two surviving archers, the warrior called out. "Have you seen a dark man wandering along the way?"

The Arab lifted his hands and shrugged. "No speak," he said.

The cataphract took several steps toward the caravan and then backed away. He signaled the two archers and the trio mounted their horses and raced away down the road. Night settled over Nabonidus like a warm quilt. He had survived the second test. Perhaps now he could reunite with Daphne.

As the quarter moon curled into place at the zenith of the heavens, voices sounded on the road outside Susa. The headman of the caravan pulled up his camel and rode beside Nabonidus. "I don't know who you might be, but they have not given up on you. Move your camel to the side of the road, and then drop off the side into the bushes as we continue to walk. The men ahead will not let us pass without a thorough search."

Hananel finished peeling an orange and tossed the fruit to Daphne as she stirred the pot bubbling over a fire. "You're learning fast," he said. "Soon even the watchman will have to believe that you are Parni, regardless of what that rat of a son might say."

"It seems that I need to always be on my guard—even during the night," Daphne said. "There seems to be a spirit of mistrust toward all newcomers around here. What should I know about my people to limit suspicions?"

Hananel broke his own orange into segments and popped one into his mouth. "You don't need to worry. No one will ask a woman about the life and history of her people. They will see it in the way you live and talk and walk."

"Tell me something. Anything." She bit into the orange and wiped the juice running down her chin with a sleeve. "If I am Humaya by name, then I should at least be able to play the part of one who has a mind and is smart."

Hananel nodded. "Okay. I hope you like the stories of a people long past. The Parni are people who have grown in power and influence throughout this whole land. They are loved by some and hated by others."

"Aren't we all?" Daphne said.

Hananel's five-year-old daughter stopped by and giggled when her father popped a slice of orange into her mouth. She scampered away to scatter the flock of pigeons that had descended to peck at the seed being thrown to the chickens by her mother.

"She is a darling child," Daphne said. "I trust my own child will know the love of her father and mother when the time comes."

Hananel watched his daughter. "Yes. She is special. Your child will be loved, no matter who Hashem allows to know him."

Daphne grinned. "So! You are a prophet now. Predicting a son for me."

"Hashem alone knows," Hananel said. "Now, what you should know. Your people worship a Creator without temples or monuments. Our God is above all other gods."

"The followers of Yeshua believe this as well," Daphne said.

A plate of foods was laid on the table in front of them. "Persians brought pistachio nuts and sesame seeds to the west," he said. "We introduced linen from flax. We brought alfalfa for animals. We introduced irrigation."

Daphne chewed on a pistachio, splitting the coating and sucking on the seed. "Let's face it, Uncle. The Persians invented everything. You even invented the riders who deliver manuscripts, and you trained all the pigeons to carry messages."

"Yes!" Hananel nodded. "We are descendants of the Parthians and proud members of the Arsacid dynasty. Under the reign of Mithridates the Second we held the lands east of Rome. Susa has been one of our capitals since ancient times. We defeated the Seleucids who seized power after Alexander the Great swept through these parts. We controlled all the trade along the silk road from the gates of the Han in the east to the plains near where you lived in Ephesus. Only the Romans have pushed us back."

Daphne ladled a portion of the bubbling stew into a wooden bowl and handed it to Hananel. "My grandfather once told me that the Parthians defeated the Romans in a great battle and controlled all the way to Yerushalayim."

Hananel blew on the stew and lifted a mouthful with a piece of flatbread. "Yes, forty thousand Romans died. We have been fighting over Armenia ever since. Mark Antony did push us back. We are awaiting our next great leader to restore our honor."

"And that's why the rebels have taken Nabonidus. They think he may be the next great leader to fight the Romans and restore your honor."

"Yes!" Hananel agreed, using his bread to clean out the last of the stew from the wooden bowl. "The problem is that the Magi have their own idea of who should be on the throne. The chances for your husband are not great."

The regent stroked his white beard at the chin with one hand while brandishing a dagger in the other. Nabonidus knelt in the sand before the dais. He had been stripped down to a loincloth. "So you have survived the test," the elder said. "You only had to evade my men until nightfall.

Killing the Egyptian was a good test result; killing half of my archers was not. Still, you did not violate the rules of survival, so you are still a potential successor to the throne."

The cataphract reached for the ropes that bound Nabonidus's hands behind his back and hauled him to his feet. "We found him with an Arab caravan," the warrior said to the regent. "He slipped away at our stop, but one of our trackers followed him until he lay down to rest. Some training in evasion is still needed. His trail was too easy to follow."

The regent returned to his seat. "It seems it was good enough to avoid your best men for long enough. I will make you responsible for any training he needs, and then if he is unsuccessful, next time it will be your life for his."

The cataphract bowed and pushed Nabonidus out of the arena with a dagger held ready for use. "You had better enjoy every moment you have with Sasina," he growled. "She should have been mine, and I will enjoy carving you up if we are ever put in the arena together. You may think you are a prince of Persia, but to me you are a pretender, and if the Magi don't get you, then know that one of us will."

When the pair arrived at the brick home set aside for Nabonidus, he was pushed in through the door and left. Sasina rushed to him and threw her arms around him, laying her head on his bare chest. He stood still, hands still tied behind his back.

The room was much the same as when he left. Twenty strides from side to side and back to front. Golden curtains tied back over a cushioned couch with crimson satin sheets. It was where the girl slept while he insisted on curling up on a sheepskin on the far side of the fully carpeted room. A tray of nuts, fruits, and cheeses rested on the marble table. A gourd of wine cooled in water. Two ebony stools inlaid with rubies sat near a bench underneath the only window. An oriental fan lay open on the bench. Provocative costumes hung from wooden pegs, lay across woven baskets, and were tucked into alcoves near the bed. He kept his head down.

After hugging him like a statue for several minutes, Sasina backed away and looked at him without hindrance. "Now, it seems I have you where I want you," she smirked. She released her cape and watched his reaction. She moved closer, moving around him, running her hands on his back, his arms, his chest, his face. "Are you no longer a man?" she purred. "Must you be tied like this for me to have my way with you?"

Nabonidus stepped toward the temptress. "Untie me and see," he said.

Every desire in his flesh pulled him to respond to her advances. Who would know? It would serve the cataphract right if he took advantage of the woman and did what they all thought he was doing. She was his gift from the regent. He might never see Daphne again, and what kind of man was he to deny himself for so long?

Sasina ran her fingers along the scars on his back and leaned her forehead against him. His muscles were as taut as the ropes she caressed. He was helpless to resist her advances if she continued to take advantage of his state. Standing in a loincloth before a woman had never shamed him before, but something had changed. He was not the man he used to be. Terror and desire fought for control. Only when he felt her pulling at the ropes did he breathe easier.

"The man who tied you did not want you free," she said. "I will need a dagger to cut the rope. While I cut, I want you to tell me another story. It will take both our minds off of what might happen." She moved away and left him standing alone on the woven carpet.

Before she wielded the dagger, she raised a golden goblet of wine to his lips. "No doubt you have been deprived of food and drink. I would not be a faithful consort if I did not first meet your basic needs. Drink and eat, then tell me your story."

A red hen and a white hen squabbled over a leaf of kale, pecking at the greens and then at each other. Daphne nudged the red hen with her foot. "Get along, you two," she urged. "There's enough for all."

A movement in the corner of her eye drew her attention away from the hens. "I see you, O watchman's son," she said. "Whatever stories you are making up in your mind have no reason to be told. Come out and talk with me."

The boy emerged from behind a hedge. "Who are you really?"

"What is your name?" Daphne asked. "You seem so interested in mine."

"To you, I am Darius."

"Oh, so you are a king? Are you a Mede?"

"That is none of your business." He planted himself, fists on hips. "How do you as a woman know anything about my people?"

She threw another handful of seed to the flock of hens and set down the feed bag on the fence post. "I know you are a man. I have baked some special sweet bread from my people up north. I am willing to share it if you are hungry."

Darius slid his hands off of his hips and cocked his head. "How do I know you're not trying to poison me?"

Daphne turned toward the house. "Do I have a reason to want to poison you? Now, are you hungry, or aren't you?"

The boy took a step in her direction, and she strolled into the house. Within minutes, she emerged with a wooden bowl filled with chunks of sweet bread, orange slices, and nuts. "It isn't much, but perhaps it will help us with our friendship."

The boy took the bowl and stuffed a chunk of bread into his mouth. "This doesn't mean we're friends. You're a woman, and I'm a man. You're a foreigner."

Daphne sat down on a stump. "Tell me about your people," she said. "I think one of the reasons people struggle with each other is because they don't know each other. So who are your people, and what are they hoping to see in this great nation of ours?"

Darius slurped up the rest of the food and lifted the bowl for more. "That was good bread."

"Tell me about your people," she said.

He nodded and rested his back against the pole on the chicken pen. "First, we are people of the mountains from the Ecbatana region. We are descendants of the great Noah and his son Japheth. Our peoples joined the Babylonians to defeat the Assyrians. Under Cyrus, we joined together as one people and overthrew Babylon, and the Persians and Medes became a force to control this whole area. When the King of kings arises again, he will lead us to conquer the Romans so that we reclaim our right as world rulers."

The snowcapped peaks of the Zagros rose to the east and a chilly breeze strengthened to make their presence felt. "So those mountains are your home?" Daphne said, pointing. "You live not far from me? We are of the same heritage?"

The boy's pursed lips and furrowed brows accentuated his silent pause. Then he answered, "Your people are people of the plains, but you still make good bread. You and I need to watch out for strangers. The last King of kings was assassinated, and we must guard this land until the rightful heir arises."

Daphne took the wooden bowl. "Let me get you some more bread. Guardians like us need to stay well fed and ready for anything that comes. Who do we fear might stop the Magi from finding the next ruler?"

Darius stood on the stump and glanced toward the south. "Rebels are rising in Elam. Rome is active in undermining our cause. Smugglers are thwarting the peace of our trade routes. Perhaps from within our own villages the power of the Magi is being twisted."

"You sound like a man carrying the weight of the world on your head."

"I listen to my father. He is one of the elders who sits at the gate of Susa. He reports everything we see in this area. Nothing gets by us."

"It is good to have you as a friend," Daphne said. "I should be well protected while I am here."

Darius smiled. "Perhaps if you can continue sharing your bread, then I can share my protection. If you see anyone strange in the marketplace or around the community, let me know." Darius stretched up on his tiptoes. "Have you seen those camels in this area before? I need to go and investigate. My father will want to know about this." With that, Darius ran toward the small caravan of Arabs.

III

THE MOMENT THE rope fell away from his wrists, things changed between Sasina and Nabonidus. She rearranged the room so she could dress and bathe more discreetly. Her most provocative outfits were tucked away into baskets instead of left hanging in the open. She turned away when Nabonidus changed instead of ogling his muscular torso and making lurid comments. While she continued to massage his neck and shoulders, she didn't push the boundaries of her touch. She settled for stories that would reach her soul.

Over the next six days, a healthy respect grew between them. "I have never had a man value me for my mind before," she said. "You speak of a Creator who cares for me, who knows my fears and joys. You speak of love and purity in the relationship between a man and a woman. You share stories of kings and temples and generals and priests. Tell me again of this Daniel who lived in Susa facing the lions of Darius."

Nabonidus scooped up a handful of nuts and popped one after another into his mouth. "I will tell you of Daniel, but even more important is that I tell you of the Messiah who the kings of Persia came to honor when He was born."

She poured oil in the palm of her hand and set to massaging his neck and shoulders again. "I will listen to whatever you want to tell me."

"As I said before, Daniel's name was changed to Belteshazzar. He was taken by King Nebuchadnezzar from the land of the Jews. He was in perfect health, more handsome than even me, quick to learn all that could be learned, and he was able to serve in the palace not far from here."

"He must have missed his home very much," she said. "I haven't seen my home or my people since I was young. I have served here like Daniel, but I could never be brave enough to face lions. They still have a pit near here, you know."

"What do they use a pit of lions for?"

"It is one of the tests later on for the cataphracts. I have only seen it once."

Nabonidus rose and stretched. "What do you think is next for me?" She sat with her back to him, and Nabonidus was tempted to return the favor of massage. Instead, he turned away and snatched up a cluster of grapes. Popping them into his mouth, one by one, he waited.

"I have never had to care for a prince before. The last one they were training died with the lions. When that happens, they throw the consort in with him." She spoke stoically, without emotion. "I suppose you will still have to face the Magi before the lions. Then perhaps there may be dragons. All I know is that one day the consort of the failure disappears."

She sighed and rubbed her thighs roughly. Standing, she turned to him and held his bicep. "I know that one day when you fall, I too shall die. You may think me empty-headed, but even more than death, I fear that I shall go my whole life without ever knowing the true love of a man. Right now, I would even be willing to settle for one who might pretend to care." She stepped closer and gripped his muscle firmly. "Please, don't fail me now." She closed her eyes and lifted her lips.

At that moment, a pounding on the door interrupted. The pair stepped back from each other. "What is it?" barked Nabonidus.

"Come!" the cataphract ordered.

The marketplace in Susa buzzed with news of the Magi raid on a nearby village. The Magi themselves were the kingmakers, the astrologers, the advisers, the power behind the throne in Persia. They controlled the elite militia responsible for thwarting pretenders, dissidents, assassins, and uprisings among the population. That militia had wreaked havoc on a village considered to sympathize with a rebel faction.

Daphne crouched behind a fountain waiting as a mob chanted and tore down canopies from several of the vendors. A fire started at a carpet dealer then spread to a spice shop. Flaming canopies sent sparks floating across to other flammable spots. Someone upended a pot of oils and then someone's robe caught on fire. A stampede ensued with people, donkeys, sheep, camels, dogs, and chickens adding to the chaos. Her own donkey had run off in the melee.

Security personnel rushed into the frenzy, some trying to douse the flames, some grabbing hold of troublemakers. Daphne noticed a break in the crowd and dashed toward a gate. As she reached the opening, a guard stepped in front of her and knocked her to the ground. The intense pain in her arm ripped through her as she lay winded among the shambles of a carpenter's crafts. Smoke swirled all through the area.

Someone tripped over her legs and fell beside her. As the heat of fire increased, hands grabbed her arms and legs. A scream rocketed from her as she felt herself falling into a deep black hole.

⁂

The instruction from the regent was clear. "Lead my men against the militia that took out the village." The clenched jaw and fiery eyes of the cataphract who had wanted Sasina for himself intensified when Nabonidus was given command.

The warning was also clear. Sasina was tied, and the regent put a dagger at her throat. "If you fail, first Sasina will lose her head and then we will hunt down your wife and place hers on a pole right beside your consort's. I have already sent someone to bring her here. Today, you battle for two women and for your place in the history of your people."

Sixteen cataphracts and twenty-two archers were put at his disposal. A rebel messenger escaping the ransacked village reported that a hundred of the militia had surprised the villagers in their sleep. "Bring the fires of damnation on their heads," roared the regent as best he could. "Decimate them all. Prove you are the rightful ruler."

Nabonidus knelt on the ground and offered a quick prayer. "Yeshua, I desire life but trust You with my death." He turned toward the weapons guardian. "I will need a lance, sword, dagger, and horn."

A trio of trackers dressed in black had been dispatched to locate the militia as they retreated from their night of terror. One of the trackers rode into the camp as Nabonidus's squad mounted. "They've made camp over the hill at the edge of the Tigris. We can cut them off by heading north and across through the second pass."

A war council with the lead cataphract and the lead archer set a plan. The archers would ride into a valley where the militia had to pass. They would flank the group and take the high ground. The cataphracts would charge the militia straight up with their spears set. The archers would rain down arrows on the enemy and charge in from the rear.

The metal-plated warhorses with their matching riders charged ahead as the archers finished loading arrows into their quivers. Bows were restrung, and then the riders were off. Nabonidus rode with the top marksman who would show the way. The archers caught the cataphracts well before the mountain pass and took the lead into the final leg.

A small stream was forged without incident, and Nabonidus followed the lead archer into a small meadow with a raised hill on one side and a forested grove on the other. "Conceal half your men in that forest, and send half to lie on that hill. The cataphracts will wait here out of sight between the hills." He rode to a higher vantage point with the archer following. "When the militia reaches the middle of the meadow, then you will send a flaming arrow into the group. That will signal a charge by the cataphracts. Spend your arrows without mercy. Communicate with your warriors."

"And what will you be doing?" the archer asked.

"I will charge the militia from behind blowing a horn. This will make them think there are more behind and push them into the trap."

"What if they turn on you?"

"Then I will fight until they wish they had faced you instead."

The archer smiled and wheeled his steed away. Instructions were passed, and the troops moved into position. Nabonidus circled back and charged toward the first pass in an attempt to surprise the retreating militia. One loan militia scout riding the crest of a hill saw him and attempted to give chase for a short time before finally falling back and returning to his duty. Nabonidus hoped that the scout would assume that one lone rider was not a threat to a band of trained warriors.

The sun was directly overhead when Nabonidus reached the pass. He slowed and walked his horse through a difficult trail. He glanced briefly toward Susa. It would be easy to race across the hills and find his way back to Daphne. Could he ignore what would happen with Sasina when she had done nothing wrong? Would Daphne be harmed before he could get to her? The regent had left him little choice.

When he broke out into the gulley, near the Tigris River where the militia had camped overnight, the devastation of the site was clear. Trees had been leveled and strung together into tripods where leather wrapping would form shelters. Fires still smoldered. Informal latrines had been dug on the outskirts. No one was in sight.

It took no effort to follow the heavy tracks of the militia as they followed the meandering river valley. Although he had a spear secured to the side of his horse, he had deliberately covered himself with a large cape to look like a pilgrim. He hoped any lingering scouts would ignore him as a threat.

As he neared the second mountain pass, he came over a rise and saw the militia spread out along the river. Some of the warriors had stripped off their armor and jumped into the water, cavorting like children. Some sat in the open, allowing their horses to graze, while others sat with their backs against the few trees in sight eating and drinking. No military band he had ever seen lounged carelessly like this without purpose. Perhaps it was a trick to lure his men into an ambush of their own.

A scout on a hill started toward him and he dropped his spear into some long grass and waited. As the warrior hailed him in Greek, Aramaic, and a local dialect, Nabonidus smiled and waved. The galloping horse slowed to a trot, a canter, and then a walk. The warrior raised his bow and set an arrow.

Nabonidus stepped behind his horse and raised his hands in a sign of peace. "No problem," he replied in Aramaic. "No problem. Horse in trouble." He raised the horse's back foot and held it. "You send blacksmith."

The scout circled and looked around. Everything seemed in order. "No blacksmith. That horse looks too good for a pilgrim like you. What are you doing out here?"

"Going home," he said. "Long journey. No work."

The scout lowered his bow and returned the arrow to its quiver. "Nothing but trouble down here. Stay here until we're gone."

"What about my horse?" Nabonidus asked.

The scout turned his back. "Kill it."

"With what?"

The scout withdrew a dagger and tossed it to Nabonidus. "You can slice its throat with this."

Nabonidus picked up the dagger and in the same fluid motion hurled the weapon into the throat of the rider. The man jolted and then slipped off his horse and lay convulsing on the ground. No one in the camp seemed to notice. He stripped off the scout's outer cape and head covering and slipped them on himself. He stripped the armor off the dead man and heaved him onto the saddle belly down. He tore lengths of cloth from his own robe and tied the man's hands and feet much as he'd been bound by the rebels.

Another scout crested the hill not far away and waved. He waved back and mounted the scout's horse. It appeared that he had taken out trouble and that all was clear. The scout heeled his mount and the horse raced down into the camp where the group was assembling.

Nabonidus led his own horse toward a small stand of saplings and tied it in place. No one seemed to be noticing him. Still, he waited. As the militia began to dawdle back into the valley, Nabonidus pulled out his horn. As they funneled into a narrow section before the second pass, he pushed his mount into a gallop and began to blow. The impact of the horn froze the warriors ahead, and some began to turn.

Nabonidus raced on, blowing. When he got close enough, he started waving frantically. "Run! Run! Run! There are thousands. Thousands! Turn and hide!"

As he raced by the first riders, some continued to stare behind, but others turned and raced with him as he took turns blowing his trumpet and shouting. Soon, a small group of riders raced with him, yelling and waving frantically. As the group neared the ambush area Nabonidus stopped and raced back, urging others to hurry and not get spread out.

A dozen riders charged briefly toward the phantom force, then realized they were being left behind. They turned and raced past Nabonidus, urging him to flee. By the time Nabonidus reached the site of the ambush, most of the militia had faced the wrath of the rebels. Hundreds lay pierced with arrows while others writhed under the hoofs of the cavalry and the cataphract lances.

Fearing the charge of thousands behind them, the militia formed a close rank and stood back-to-back to defend themselves. The archers easily pierced the thin shields with their sharpened arrows until the cataphracts formed a solid line and charged over the group again. Two of the cataphracts fell on that charge.

Dozens of the militia fell to their knees in an act of surrender and mercy but the instructions from the regent had been clear to his warriors. Nabonidus sat and watched as a squadron of elite soldiers was eliminated. Some had escaped into the forest and some over the hills, but the archers were hard on their heels. This battle was done.

Most of the cataphracts rode among the combatants delivering mercy kills. The chief cataphract rode away from the group and faced Nabonidus. "You showed courage today," he said. "The regent may be surprised to hear how you fell in battle charging against the heart of the enemy force."

Nabonidus gripped his sword. "And yet here I am."

The cataphract raised his lance. "I don't like your chances of a sword against a lance. If you try to run, I can tell you I have the swiftest horse in Persia. Why don't I give you a fair chance, and you can try and get away?"

"I've never run from any man," Nabonidus said.

"Perhaps you've never met a man worth running from."

Nabonidus turned his mount and raced down the valley. He would race for his own mount. The cataphract waited until he had gained a good lead and then let out a battle cry that echoed off the hills. Nabonidus felt the shadow of evil closing in on him much, as he'd felt it at times in the arena. He was still a hundred strides away when the pounding of pursuing hoofs sounded off the rocky bluff. He pushed his horse full out, aware now that the cataphract had his lance poised for a strike.

A few dozen strides from his horse, the tip of the lance caught the top of Nabonidus's shoulder. The warrior was playing with him. Enjoying the chase. Certain of his kill. Twenty strides from the trees, Nabonidus launched off the horse and rolled into the tall grasses. The cataphract jabbed at him but rode on by. He turned and set his target on the now stranded usurper of his consort. "I told you she was mine," he said. "Now, she shall be when I take my rightful place."

Nabonidus knelt on one knee and reached for the lance he had dropped earlier when the scout had confronted him. The cataphract charged with lance poised. As he drew it back for the kill, Nabonidus hurled the hidden lance into his chest. The cataphract's look of surprise continued as Nabonidus followed with a dagger to the throat and a sword to the side. The horse raced on as the rider dropped and somersaulted across the turf.

When the rebels arrived back in camp, three cataphracts lay tied on their mounts. Two others had deep wounds from swords and four had arrow punctures in their arms or legs.

The regent examined the bodies of the fallen and looked long into the face of the chief cataphract who had perished in the battle. "He died defending his honor," Nabonidus said. The regent nodded and released the bodies for immolation.

"We haven't found your wife yet," the regent said. "She may have perished in a fire."

"Humaya! Humaya! Can you hear me?"

The gentle shaking penetrated the darkness as Daphne's mind groped for consciousness. Intense burning pain in her right arm got her focused. A cool cloth wiped her brow and a brief stream of water dripped into her ear and down to her neck. A heavy weight pressed on her shoulders and chest, keeping her still.

"Humaya! Humaya! Can you hear me?" Again, the shaking.

A groan was all she could manage, but it seemed enough. The darkness consumed her again.

When light penetrated strongly enough to pull her out of the pit, Daphne opened one eye and peered at the dimly lit room she rested in. Nothing looked familiar. The wooded ceiling panels spoke of an upper-class home. Full-length sapphire curtains bordered the windows, and two engraved clay lamps supplemented the daylight streaming in.

"Dear one," a female voice said. "Your fever is breaking. You are with us again. Ahura Mazda has preserved you, and light has defeated the darkness once again."

"Where am I?" Daphne mumbled.

"Dear one," the voice answered. "You have been delivered to the home of Abdu Zahar—grand priest of all Zoroastrians. He has visited the fire temple with prayers and purified you with holy waters. The great god has deemed that you should dwell once again among the living."

"What happened to me?" Daphne asked.

"You, O Humaya, were caught in the fires of the market. Your arm was broken in a fall. A boy named Darius found you when the carpenter's booth collapsed on top of you."

The name Darius sounded familiar. "Where is Darius?"

"Alas! The fire gods claimed their own." The woman wet the cloth, squeezed it, and replaced it on Daphne's head. "The great priest heard him calling your name and saw him trying to pull you from the flames. A heavy beam fell on him and broke his back. He could not be saved."

An icy chill swept through her bones. Pieces were not fitting into place. "When can I go home?" she asked.

"Dear one, Humaya," the woman said. "And where is your home? The priest has asked throughout the market at Susa, and no one seems to know your name. Your name fits with our people north of here, and so the priest has accepted you as one of his own. He has sent messengers out to see if anyone reports you missing."

Daphne struggled up on her elbows. Rich Persian carpets, embroidered cloths over tables, and ornamented wooden boxes spoke of things outside the realm of familiarity. Several of the carvings depicted a bearded man, one hand outstretched standing above a pair of wings. The woman standing over her was young, covered in a purple linen headpiece embroidered with flames of fire. "You know me," Daphne said, "but what is your name? By what do I call you?"

"I am Vashti, servant of the priests of Zarathustra."

Daphne swung her feet over the edge of the raised bed. "Nothing feels familiar. My name. This place."

"The priest says you received a bad bump on your head from a falling post. It may affect your memory, but do not fear. I will teach you everything you have forgotten about our faith and who your people are."

A fluttering in her belly drew her attention to another issue. "I'm pregnant," she said. "Where is the father? He should know who I am and where I live."

Vashti bowed her head. "I am sorry, but no one has responded to claim you or the child. We can only hope that one day your husband will come looking for you."

Daphne rose to her feet and found her balance. "I think I'm hungry," she said. "What do we Zoroastrians eat?"

The regent showed his gratitude at the vengeance carried out against the Magi militia by releasing Nabonidus with two guardians to search for his wife. The release came with the promise that he would bring Daphne back with him to serve at least until Nowruz—eight months away.

The chilled air from the mountains had a bitter bite and even the birds had vanished from the sky. Nabonidus and his pair of guardians simplified their dress, so as not to attract attention, as they tied their mounts and surveyed the shambles in the Susa marketplace. Vendors were cleaning up and sorting through items that had not been looted or destroyed. Onlookers opined about the cause, source, and purpose of the fire. Nabonidus listened and watched.

"It was the purifying touch of Ahura Mazda," the Zoroastrian priest noted to one of his followers.

"I say it was those cultists from Ephesus trying to destroy our way of life," a clothier said. "They never would buy from me. Probably worked for the Roman emperor to take over our control of the Silk Road to the Orient."

"This is another stroke of terror by the Magi," a carpenter said as he hammered a new post into place under the charred canopy. "They need to focus their battles on the ones who oppose them. In this very place a young boy was crushed. It is all so senseless."

A baker handed out fresh bread to everyone in the area, and Nabonidus gratefully accepted. "You know this is the work of the rebels," he said. "My brother says the regent destroyed the Magi's whole militia because they sacked a village. That old man will do anything in his power to provoke the Magi into open warfare."

"Have you heard of a woman named Daphne in this area?" one of the guardians asked.

"That name isn't familiar," the baker responded. "Ask the women at the vegetable tables. They know everyone."

The trio made their inquiries at the table but changed their tactics. Nabonidus described Daphne until one of the younger girls spoke up. "I think there is someone new to the area who lives at the village down the road," she said. "She often comes with two others who live there."

The two had to be Atossa and Adrina. Nabonidus galloped his horse all the way until they pulled up next to a man sitting at the edge of the village with his head in his hands.

"Honorable sir!" he called. "May we ask you about this village?"

The man rose up and nodded. "I am the watchman. If you have inquiries then I am the right one to ask. Today, however, is not the best day for me."

"And why may that be?" Nabonidus asked.

"My son died in a fire at the market in Susa. He was my only heir."

"We came from the market and saw the disaster," Nabonidus said. "They told us that you might know of a woman, new to the area, who shops with two others. Their names may be Atossa and Adrina. Her name is Daphne."

"I know these two," the watchman said. "But the woman who they know is from up north, and her name is Humaya. These two you seek are cultists who were chased off by a mob two days ago. The woman has likely returned to her area."

An emptiness grow from the inside to fill him. Where else could she have gone? She had vanished as thoroughly as the vapor from his breath. He'd left her near here and the two girls would surely have found her. Perhaps she'd changed her name for protection but where would she be?

The trio spent the next day riding hard from village to village without success. No one had seen a woman matching Daphne's description. As the sun slid toward the horizon during their last opportunity, they passed a Zoroastrian temple. Two women bowed at the door and stepped inside. A strange pull in his gut caused him to yank on the reins. "Stop!" he ordered. He dismounted and strode toward the doorway.

Two sentries blocked his path. "Women only," the leader shouted while Nabonidus was still ten paces away from them.

Nabonidus stopped, straining to see past the two. "I think my wife may be in there," he said. "She just stepped in."

"The two women are servants of the grand priest of Zarathustra," the sentry said. "You will have to look elsewhere for your wife."

The fire dance amid the chanting of whirling dervishes did much to ease the confusion in Daphne's mind and the throbbing in her arm. The fire temple boasted a square brick shelter with identical arches on each of the four sides. Fires burned in the center as worshippers leaped over the flames—whirling and chanting in their white array. She spun in place as Vashti had shown her, and the little one within her seemed to join in the ecstasy of the celebration.

As the music and dancers slowed to a solemn trance, Daphne settled beside Vashti at the edge of the circle. "What is that stone water vessel at the edge of the plaza?" she asked.

"That is a water clock brought from Egypt by the Greek, Alexander." She pointed toward the stone vessel resting at the top of the engineering marvel. "The stone vessel has sloping sides that allow the water to drip in a steady rate through a small hole at the bottom. The twelve columns have evenly spaced markings on the inside to measure the passage of time. The priests use the water clock to determine the right time for rites and sacrifices." She pulled Daphne closer to the object. "See, this mark tells us that the ritual should be over and the feast should start soon. We need to go and serve."

When the feast following the dances had been served and cleaned up, Vashti returned to the priest's home with Daphne. "You have served the worshippers well," Vashti said. "It is clear that you have worshipped the Creator before. You are at one with your people now."

Dishes were put away and the floor swept again. Sweeping proved to be as much therapy as it was work. "I still don't remember the teachings," Daphne said. "You will have to tell me again. My mind does not remember these truths."

"Perhaps your husband was neglectful in teaching you," Vashti said. "Many men consider their women beneath understanding of the sayings of the Ayurveda. Let me tell you once again. Zarathustra was the first to realize the Creator was One."

"Are you sure?" Daphne asked. "Somewhere I remember that the Jews have always believed this teaching. They think their people go back to the beginning of time."

Vashti stood open-mouthed. "Where did you hear such heresy? It was the Jews who stole such an idea from our people when they were captured and kept here."

Daphne dropped onto a stool. "Sometimes the strangest ideas come into my head."

Vashti picked up a brush and began to comb through Daphne's hair, soothing her with her teaching. "Ahura Mazda himself—the Lord of Wisdom—called on the prophet to remind people that there were not many gods, as they believed. There was only one true Lord of all."

"That sounds right," Daphne agreed.

"The Avesta is our holy book, which includes the messages from Ahura Mazda to the prophet in answer to the questions of the early followers. They have been preserved from generation to generation orally but we have captured the wisdom in writing. Our Parthian peoples embraced the light, and we preserve it."

"The Jews have a holy book as well," Daphne responded. "Someone told me the stories in it. I remember one about a man named Daniel who lived in this area."

"Yes, the prophet Daniel is one of our holy men. His tomb is close by. Zarathustra's parents were named Pourusaspa and Dughdova, and they may have built the very temple we worshipped in today."

Daphne ran her fingers through her hair and then cupped her chin in her fists. "Why is everything so confusing? How do we know what is true and who is telling the truth?"

Vashti put the brush away and reached for a clay pot of wine. "Drink something to soothe your nerves. Don't let your mind carry the heavy burdens of men. Focus on the little life that is growing within you, and be at peace with the world."

She settled herself on a cushioned couch and sipped her drink. "Confusion comes through the dark forces of Angra Mainyu. The gods and spirits of light fight for Ahura Mazda and bring us truth. The demons and spirits of Angra Mainyu bring us falsehood and confusion."

Daphne paced the floor. "The fighting in the heavens is played out in the fighting of nations and people here on earth. If there can be no peace in the heavens, how can there ever be peace on earth?" She rubbed her abdomen. "What will my child face when he comes into a world like this?"

Vashti moved to the door. "It is true that every good thing that Ahura Mazda brings into the world is corrupted and thwarted by Angra Mainyu, but Ahura Mazda is wise enough to bring good out of it. You can trust him with your child and with who you are." She picked up a broom and began the therapeutic sweeping of the outside porch. "We are free to choose on which side we will live. One side is life and light, and the other side is death and darkness. Forever."

IV

SASINA WELCOMED NABONIDUS with a special meal of lamb and all the garnishing. He wolfed it down while he paced the floor. The consort tried hard to get him to rest after his feat of victory and flash of failure. The militia lay dead through his display of power, and his wife lay out of his sight through his lack of power. There were some things even a prince couldn't do.

"The Magi have unleashed a militia twice the size of the last to hunt me down," Nabonidus said. "I don't know whether to throw myself in front of their arrows to end this pain or to run back to the arms of Rome and beg for mercy. Either way I lose the woman I love."

Sasina moved toward him and settled him onto a stool. "Ease your mind, my friend. Ease your mind. Together, we will find a way through this."

Nabonidus leaned his head back against her belly and looked up. "We are trapped between the regent and the Magi. There is nowhere to turn. If there is another test, I cannot promise to have what it takes to survive." He rubbed his chin. "Then, I don't know what might happen to you."

She massaged his shoulders and kissed the top of his head. "You have already proved yourself," she said. "I accept what you can give to me while you can. No one runs from the regent, so I have accepted my fate."

His feat had earned them both a chance to roam the grounds. Nabonidus spent his time scouting the perimeter and left Sasina to manage the household chores. It wasn't long before she complained about the lurid comments from the men she met. A protective surge grew in him, and he walked alongside her to the well each day. As he eyed them down, no one approached, and no one made any comments. The water in the well was cool and sweet—especially when she drew enough for him to soak in.

A week went by before the regent called for Nabonidus. The elder reclined on a red cushioned couch under heavy blankets and sipped from a golden goblet as Nabonidus approached him, bending down on one knee. "The militia is destroyed as you requested," Nabonidus said. "The wrath of the Magi is now unleashed like an arrow in your direction."

The old man succumbed to a fit of coughing and then lay flat as two servants massaged him. When he regained his composure, he rose up on an elbow. "I may not be here when they unleash that arrow," he said. "The weather has turned against me. Will you?" He glared intently. "I fear you may run from your calling and responsibility when I am weak. How do I hold your heart and control it when you will not yield to the temptation of a woman?"

He motioned to a cataphract and two others escorted Sasina into the room. The woman was bound and gagged. Her eyes filled with fear. Nabonidus froze in place, refusing to be manipulated. They had dressed her in a most sensuous outfit, leaving little to the imagination.

"Have I not given you the most beautiful of gifts?" the regent barked. "Is this not the woman my own chief cataphract longed for? The one you killed him for? And yet you leave her unwanted like a rat in the garbage." The old man threw off the blankets. "Must I show you the way of a man with a woman?" He rose and pointed at the couch. The cataphracts forced Sasina down onto her back. "If you are going to take the throne, you will need a queen. I declare to you that this is your queen. Now, claim her, or watch her die."

Nabonidus mumbled a prayer under his breath. "My lord," he said to the regent, "if I as your servant have proved my self-control before the greatest of temptations, if I have proved my valor in the face of the greatest enemies, if I have raised your reputation in the heart of this country—then know that I will take what I deserve when the time is right." He got off his knee and bowed his head. "Know that I will guard what you give me as an undeserved treasure, but this test is not worthy of a leader like yourself. Allow me to face the lions, and then leave me to do as I will with my consort."

The elder turned toward the girl being held on the couch. "Get her off," he said, coughing again. "Take her back to her room. If the lions prevail, then she will be their sweet treat in the morning."

As Sasina was dragged out of the room, the elder threw his golden goblet across the room, splattering the red wine onto the Persian carpets. "How dare you defy me in front of my men? Who told you about the test of the lions?" He cinched up his robe and stepped into his sandals. "Never mind. Prepare the lions." Turning to Nabonidus he snarled, "You better hope that whatever gods there be are on your side. I had planned a clear path to the throne for you, and now you cast it aside as if it is nothing but ashes. You have won no favor from me this day, even if you have won the heart of the woman by preserving her dignity."

"Forgive me, my lord!" Nabonidus said.

"Forgive you?" the regent said. "Your own uncle stood in this very place and defied me. He told me that the throne belonged to another whom I would never control. When I sent him to the lions, he dared to say that there would be one of his line who would even overcome the lions." He pulled his blanket tight over his lap as he sat on his throne. "No one overcomes the lions."

"There has been one, my lord," Nabonidus said. "His tomb is near."

"Daniel? You dare to speak of the Magus, Daniel?" He threw off the blanket and stood trembling. "Do not think that the God of Daniel will shut the lions for you. That God has long departed from this land. Now go, and prepare to pray to someone who will listen to you."

Daphne's dreams filled her with dread even during the day—images of gladiators, Roman centuries, hidden caverns, running for her life. Nothing made sense with the life Vashti told her she must have lived. The daily practices from waking to sleeping were laid out for her to follow, and there was no alignment with her emotions, mind, or body to the movements of the life and worship. Yes, the world was a battlefield as good Zoroastrians believed, but was it so uncertain? She reviewed the guidelines daily and tried to memorize what she'd been told.

Vashti had written the guidelines on a parchment posted near the door. Rise and, while the mind is fresh, recite the noble sayings and praise rightness. Set your thoughts on the rut of light. Wash your hands, dress, kindle the fire. Live out your day with the energy of the flames. Pray for true courage in the struggle so you can resist temptations. Strengthen your soul force for victory. Work honestly with all your might so the angels may guard you. Nurture the pure mind and stay busy to protect it from evil and empty thoughts. Embrace independence and industriousness in yourself and others. Be honest in your dealings with others and enjoy peace and wholeness. Care for the poor.

"Before the rooster crows you must train your body to be hard at work," Vashti urged. "If you see nothing to do, pick up a broom and sweep away the dirt. Every day we take the offerings given to the priests and prepare portions for the poor. When you have gained your peace, I will take you to the market with me where we will earn our merits of mercy."

The rituals of morning had their effect, and her body adjusted, but the restlessness in her soul made peace elusive. Each day, when the priest finished his lesson for the newcomers and asked if she was now at peace, she hung her head. "My soul wrestles each night and day with dark thoughts of troubling times, my lord. Perhaps it is the child within, but I will need more time before serving in the marketplace."

"Take up your broom and find your peace," the priest would say. "Chant and recite the noble sayings until they settle in your heart."

One morning, the assistant who often accompanied Vashti lay sick. "Come with me, Humaya!" Vashti urged Daphne. "I need your help. You will find your peace another time, but today we must serve the poor."

Daphne set her broom aside and submissively loaded the donkey cart designated for the marketplace. Fresh bread, vegetables, meat, and grain were placed in their baskets.

"Because the people have been generous to Ahura Mazda, we are able to be generous to those in need. It is the way of righteousness and mercy."

When they reached the Silk Road, the foot traffic multiplied a dozen-fold—traders with ox and donkey carts, horses loaded with baskets, camels striding in caravans. Soldiers boasting bows, lances, and swords charged by it all, ensuring that the peace would last under the iron grip of the Magi.

The two-hour trip to the market in Susa brought a sense of release. The quality of air away from the smoke-filled courtyards near the fire temple made breathing a joy. The mix of cedar, jasmine, grasses, and wildflowers combined with scents of human and animal sweat, curries, and spices in a blend that stimulated a desire to dance.

"You're smiling," Vashti noted. "I haven't seen you smile for weeks."

Daphne laid a hand on her abdomen and nodded. "The babe is moving as if it wants to dance. It feels so freeing to be out here where life is happening without ritual, without rites, without rules and rhythms."

"That is the darkness speaking," Vashti said. "You must train yourself to keep those thoughts under control. Look, we are nearing the gates of the city. Cover yourself and do what I say."

There were six of the beasts—strong, compact golden bodies with black manes, powerful forelegs, and terrifying jaws sporting flesh-ripping teeth. The first hour in the den had set his nerves on fire as the residents of the pit twitched their tails and sized up the large man-beast tossed into their midst. The kings of the beasts bunched together and declared their side of the enclosure.

Nabonidus knew lions from his gladiator days. Stand tall, stay still, face forward, no fear. The largest of the pride crouched in a hunting stance, tail still. Danger was high. A roar from the beast echoed through the space—a sound designed to strike terror into the heart of the bravest warrior. It didn't matter. There was no place to run.

A cataphract above threw large sticks down at the beasts, to rile their fury. He was ignored. Two of the animals moved against the far wall. The animals spread out along the perimeter—attempting to drive Nabonidus into the center where they could jump him from behind. He remained in place, standing tall.

One by one, the great cats sank to their bellies and yawned. They could wait. Their meal was not going anywhere.

Nabonidus eyed the largest feline facing him. He could almost feel their breath on his arms. "Let me tell you a story," he said. "There once was a den like this with lions like you. A prophet prayed to his God, and the king made him spend the night with the pride. His God delivered him, and all was well. In fact, because the lions waited, they ended up with much more to eat than if they ate the first thing on their dish."

The cataphract threw stones and then sticks at Nabonidus, attempting to dislodge him from his refuge against the wall. "Fight, you coward," he yelled. "How dare you kill our chief and pass yourself off as someone worthy of honor. Spend your last hours begging and preparing to be shredded by the beasts. They haven't eaten in three days, and they are ready to enjoy fresh meat."

A stone bounced off the ex-gladiator's jaw, and sharp pain shot into his skull. He moved a step sideways and a lion inched forward. He warded off other sticks and stones until the cataphract ceased and disappeared. The lion yawned again and laid its head on its outstretched paws, eyes never wavering.

The shadows stretched longer and then darker until Nabonidus saw a star break through the canopy overhead. Hundreds and thousands followed, and the carnivores grew restless. They were no longer visible but their musky odor and discharge filled the space. As nocturnal hunters this was their time. The soft padding of their feet hid their movements.

Nabonidus felt the warm breath of one of the cats on his hand as he stretched it out. *Still—don't move a muscle.* That was the key to survival. He prayed inwardly as he stood. "Hashem—God of Daniel, King of beasts and men alike—as You shut the mouths of the lions assigned to destroy the prophet, so shut the mouths of these six. Into Your hands I commit my life. Whether I live or die, guard Daphne and the little one until we meet again."

A flicker of light appeared at the pit opening. It was the cataphract who had thrown the sticks and stones. "So, you magician," he growled. "Mesmerizing the animals with powers not known to men. The gods will lose their interest in you soon. Let's see what happens when they see you holding the fire."

The warrior hurled the flaming torch at Nabonidus and he stepped aside as it fell harmlessly on the ground. All six beasts sprang to their feet, tails twitching, eyes glaring, fangs bared. Nabonidus allowed the torch to burn on the ground. The cataphract hurled another. This one, Nabonidus caught and held out as the chief lion took a step toward him. It was now within six strides. A single leap would down him if it dared. Nabonidus stayed large and motionless until the torch embers burned weaker. He tossed the torch toward the lion and it backed off.

As the torches flickered and dimmed, his eyes adjusted to the darkness again. Moonlight bathed the world above, but only starlight reached into the pit. Glowing eyes stared back at him. His prayers continued.

The marketplace had demanded all her energy as an expectant mother. Daphne packed away the last of the reed baskets and wooden trays used to carry food and goods for the poor. They had successfully dispensed their lot and even accepted offerings of drachmas from devotees who respected their work.

"You worked well today," Vashti affirmed. "The priest will be pleased. Perhaps you will find peace in your own way as the little one grows."

As they prepared to leave, a beggar leaning on a home-fashioned crutch hobbled up. "Please!" he said. "Have you anything to spare? I was caught in a battle through no fault of my own. The physician's amulets and charms have done nothing to relieve my pains."

Daphne sorted through the basket. There was nothing left. "What about the coins?" she said to Vashti. "Surely, we can spare a few." She reached into a box for the money pouch.

"How were you wounded?" Vashti asked the man.

The man's eyes grew wide. "A black demon from Hades rode through our midst blowing a horn and calling down the hordes of darkness on us. I am a farmer who was selling my goods, but they had no mercy on soldier or peasant. I escaped only by lying beneath a dead man."

Vashti turned away. "So you confess that you are a coward. That you are part of the Magi's militia who slaughtered the poor without mercy. You will never get a coin from us." She grasped Daphne's wrist and pulled.

Daphne wrenched away. "Wait! This black demon from Hades. Was he a big, tall warrior?"

The man inched back with his crutch. "He was all that you say and more. One hundred warriors or more were carried and burned because of him. Their spirits haunt me every night, but his haunts me most of all." The man lurched forward and attempted to snatch the money pouch from Daphne. She jumped back, and the man fell facedown at her feet. "Please," he said. "Mercy! I have nothing."

"Where can I find this black demon?" Daphne shouted, surprised at the intensity in her voice. "Tell me, where did you see him?"

The man rolled onto his back. "He haunts the second pass along the Zagros Road."

Daphne dropped a coin and turned. The black warrior. Something powerful filled her soul. He was somehow the secret to who she was. She knew it.

A tongue of dawn light curled into the pit and licked the face of the chief lion. He yawned and slid his own tongue across his nose. Stretching, he rose and nudged the other cats. There was a mix of purrs, groans, and snarls stirring.

The crow of a distant rooster echoed into the cavern, and the dark warrior leaning against a wall pushed himself gently until he was standing erect. The youngest lion leaped, and he batted it across the snout with his forearm. It crashed to the floor and scurried, half-rolling back to the pack.

The disturbance clearly irritated the pride. The other five moved as a unit toward him, snarling. Both hunter and hunted were out of their element. The lions could easily double the speed of the fastest man or gazelle or buffalo, but there was no prey running and no place to gather speed for a spring. The tawny hunter preferred to bring its dinner to ground where it could clamp its jaws over the face and smother its catch while another chewed out the belly and a third crushed the throat.

During the standoff, voices sounded from above. The beasts waited, looking up toward the opening. Within minutes, the regent arrived on the arms of two cataphracts. Dawn had fully come. He looked into the pit and called out, "Prince of Persia, are you there, or have you supplied the lions with their dinner?" Laughter erupted in the background.

Nabonidus stepped forward, keeping a wary eye on the lions. "I am still here, O Regent."

The elder adjusted himself along the top edge to better see the warrior in the pit. "What magic do you hold that even beasts bow to you?" He turned away and commanded, "Get him out, and feed someone else to the beasts."

A rope ladder was lowered, but Nabonidus was leery. The moment he turned his back he would set himself up. "Come down and hold the beasts away while I climb," he said.

The cataphract who had pelted him with rocks, sticks, and torches the evening before looked down. "You should thank whatever gods you serve that I even gave you a way out. I've seen what those beasts have done to a dozen men, and there is no way I am coming down to save you. Use whatever magic you had through the night."

Nabonidus moved toward the ladder, and the beasts understood that their meal was preparing to escape their lair. Now the time had come. They crowded closer, tails stiff in the hunting pose.

"Where's the prince?" another voice called. "The regent wants him now."

The cataphract above turned away. "You'll have to go down and get him. He won't come up."

A second cataphract peered into the pit. "At least lower your lance so he can grab it."

"I'd as soon stick him with it so the beasts smell blood and take him down," the first cataphract said. "Who is this stranger anyway who comes and is exalted when we've given our life to the regent?"

The second grabbed the lance from the first and lowered it. "It's not ours to ask. Only to do."

The first cataphract lunged for the end of the lance at the same moment that Nabonidus grasped the shaft behind the blade. The soldier above tried to yank it away, but his momentum moved him in the wrong direction, and when Nabonidus tugged it hard, the soldier tumbled in on top of the cats.

They were startled, but by the time Nabonidus had taken advantage of the distraction and hauled himself up the ladder, the beasts had fully recovered and pounced on the screaming victim.

Nabonidus rolled across the ground and then bounced to his feet. There was nothing nearby for him to grab except a large boulder, far too big even for him to move. "Quick, give me your spear, we can slay the beasts," he yelled to the cataphract in shock at the edge of the pit. "Go down and fight for him.".

The cataphract glared at Nabonidus, slack-jawed, then turned and fled to the arched building where the regent awaited.

The embers in the fire temple still glowed in the holding pots as Daphne scraped the last of the ashes out of the center of the square worship house. Vashti bowed to the priest as he backed out of the courtyard. The butcher had removed the carcasses of sacrifices, but blood spots remained to be scrubbed from the stone plaza. The sun would be fully down by the time this task was finished.

"I am needed by the priest," Vashti said. "You will have to sleep with the virgin priestesses tonight." She laid her broom aside. "Finish what you can and then get your rest. It's been a long week."

The look Vashti had exchanged with the priest had been unmistakable. This need had nothing to do with a sacred task. Daphne lowered her eyes and continued to sweep. The desire for a man had been strong lately, and with that thought came images of the black demon mentioned by the militia man in the marketplace.

Strong longings grew as she removed her sandals and washed her feet. A powerful image of a tall dark warrior smiling struck her with a force that took her breath away. She sank to the ground and then looked up. The stars in a clear dark sky stretched from horizon to horizon. The moon was emerging from behind the Zagros Mountains with a light that seemed like day.

Her feet found their own path out of the courtyard and onto the roadway. She was barefoot and hardly noticed the cool soil as she quickened her steps. Her middle toe caught a rock, and the pain shot up her shin. What was she doing? Out here, chasing a phantom.

A camel caravan emerged between the hills ahead, and she limped into a grove of trees. The intense pain settled as she rubbed her foot. It was foolish, coming out here without footwear. She rubbed her abdomen and cherished the kick of her little one. It wouldn't be long now.

The Arabian desert train swooshed by with three dozen camels stepping in unison to the melodic chant of a herdsman. The scent of frankincense, cinnamon, myrrh, and aloes from the traders mixed with that of the jasmine growing nearby. Daphne leaned back against a cedar tree and bathed her senses in sheer delight.

Back on her feet, she reconsidered the wisdom of heading to the second pass. It was night, and there was no way that a tall, dark warrior would be haunting the hills. The caravan had come from that direction without being disturbed. Chasing a phantom would have to wait. She had a temple to clean.

Before she emerged from the darkness of the trees, the forest erupted around her. Dozens of horsemen walked their charges to the roadside and then mounted with swords drawn. "Now!" commanded a voice in Aramaic. "For the Magi and the King of kings!" At least twenty horses pounded down the road after the caravan. Heading home would not be such a wise decision after all.

Nabonidus made the decision to run moments after the cataphract disappeared into the arched building where the regent waited. The screams from the pit had ceased, and only the growls of lions feeding rose from his former prison. The test was over, but the result would not bring joy to the old man. The cataphracts would need time to sort through their rage.

He ran barefoot, but his heart relished the slap of sole against dirt, the strain of muscle against pain, the force of will against breathlessness. Where would he go? Adrina and Atossa had been chased away from their village. Daphne had disappeared. An image of the fire temple and the two women worshippers flashed into his mind. He took the fork to the left and increased his rhythm.

His thirst diverted his attention toward a stream he had seen in the area. A tranquil pool formed a heart shape by a small ravine. A small flock of Egyptian geese paddled away from him toward it. A few minutes cooling his feet, dumping water on his head, and washing down his body brought pleasure he had rarely experienced in the past weeks. He lay back on the grass a moment but sat up as horses' hooves echoed into the ravine. There was no question that the cataphracts were hunting him.

Without hesitation, he rolled down into the stream and submerged himself in the pool. He pulled himself across the bottom and emerged in a clump of papyrus he had noticed. Four of the soldiers stood halfway down the hill scanning the area. Satisfied, they remounted and headed off with the others on the road.

Outracing the soldiers to the fire temple wouldn't work. Attempting to avoid them in the barren countryside to the south was foolish. Trying for the hills without being seen by locals, who would report a big dark man on the run, was impossible. There was little option but to head back to the regent.

He stayed off the road and, along the way, dreamed of an idea so ludicrous it might work. He circumnavigated the compound and came in from the south. Two cataphracts stood guard outside his home with Sasina, and two others stood outside the arched home of the regent. Most of the horses were gone. He moved into the stables and found a sword and a dagger. Taking these, he made his move.

Crouching behind a hedge near the stables and then, out of eyesight, he scurried the best he could behind a large boulder. The lions' den lay a stone's throw away. The sun blistered its way across the sky until the two cataphracts moved toward the well. With their backs to him, he raced to the lions' den and jumped in.

The scene had been bizarre, she had to admit. Two camels running at breakneck speed had charged up the road with three horses hard on their tails. The shouts of the Arabs urging on their "desert ships" equaled those of the militia members commanding more out of their mounts.

Daphne had moved from the trees to the top of a hill at the first pass, to soak in the moonlight and to gain a higher perspective on which way she should go. The scene played out below her on the road. The camels split at the pass with one charging straight ahead and one turning into the cut through the hill. The three horses all followed the camel running into the pass. Moments later, the first camel rider pivoted and followed the others. The shouts echoed into the night sky.

From her perch, the strategy of the horsemen was clear. Catch and loot at least one of the traders. The response of the Arabs was also clear. Divide and surround them. The rider on the second camel pulled a bow and shot at the horsemen while they shot arrows at the camel rider lying flat on his camel in front of them. One of the arrows struck a horse and the animal tumbled, throwing its rider. The Arab sent another arrow into the fallen soldier and kept riding.

Seeing their colleague fall, the militia men split to either side of the road and faced the second charging camel. Arrows hit the camel in the neck and haunches. It lurched sideways, falling and taking its rider with it. The man rolled away as they neared the ground and scrambled to hide in a ditch. The first camel turned to join the fray. In minutes, the horsemen abandoned the fight and raced back down the road toward the others who had participated in the ambush.

The climb down the hill was easier because of the moonlight, but Daphne still took it cautiously, not knowing the attitude of the Arabs, who would be primed for the unexpected. The two riders stood around the fallen camel. It was dead by the hand of its owner, and the men were redistributing the load onto the lone standing beast.

She reached the road and approached them from the south. "Peace to you," she called.

Seeing a woman dressed in white and clearly pregnant, walking down a moonlit road alone in the middle of the night, must have been unnerving. The men took a defensive posture and chattered at her in Arabic before finally switching to Greek. "What spirit might you be?" one asked. "Whose life do you seek outside the desert?"

Daphne stood her ground. "I am not a spirit. Just a woman out for a walk."

The two conferred with each other and then tried again. "Why did you send the men to attack us? We are honest traders, sons of our father, a Bedu."

She held her hands out toward them. "I did not send the men. They are militia sent by the Magi to create trouble for the citizens of Susa."

The men approached her with something in their hands. "Perhaps, instead, you are the spirit who saved us." One of the Arabs extended a small pouch. "Here is frankincense as an offering of gratitude." She accepted it.

The other stepped forward with a small gem. "And here is a ruby to display in your shrine."

The two bowed, finished strapping down the load on the camel, and then climbed on board to walk toward Susa. One of them called as they passed, "A woman should not walk in the night like this. It is not safe."

Not long after they were out of sight, another set of hoofbeats pounded down the road.

V

THE PROSTRATE LIONS jerked up when Nabonidus landed among them. This time he had a lance and a sword. The helmeted head of the cataphract lay frozen in a death scream. A hand lay half buried in the shredded robes. A sandaled foot rested against the far side of the den. The shudder surprised him. He'd seen men die like this before. In the arena.

One lion, jaws still red with blood, lunged toward him, but he warded it off with the shaft of the lance. "Stay, beast, or you will be food for your brothers," he said. The lion snarled while another let out a deafening roar.

"Cataphract!" Nabonidus yelled. "Cataphract!"

Shortly, two warriors peered down on him. "By the crown of Bel, what are you doing here? The men are out looking for you."

"Tell the regent I'm still where he left me, but his cataphract didn't do so well with the lions. Hold the rope so I can come up, then take me to the regent."

The regent, lounging on his couch, perched on an elbow and shook his head. "Where did you find him?" he asked.

"He was in the den with the lions," one of the cataphracts replied. "He has powerful magic to shut the mouths of the beasts."

The elder pulled on his long white beard and swung his feet onto the floor. "Too many men have died. Where are the other warriors?"

"They are on the road looking for Nabonidus," the cataphract replied.

"Go, bring them back!" the regent commanded. "Send this troublemaker to his quarters and untie his consort to be with him. He deserves some form of reward before I destroy him for good."

Nabonidus bathed, dressed, and filled his belly before Sasina was escorted into the home. Her clothing was shredded, her hair matted, and her face covered in dirt. "Take this tramp and use her for your pleasure," snarled the warrior who escorted her. "We sure did."

Sasina sank to the floor. "You live!" she declared, laying with her head on her arm, convulsing in sobs.

Nabonidus touched her shoulder on his way past. "We both live," he said. Seven trips to the well filled the small marble washing pool in the corner. He laid out a modest robe to the side. "Wash, eat, and we will talk. I have a story to tell you. I'll be outside so you can regain your dignity."

The consort had curled up like a little girl when he reentered their living quarters. She hid her head under her arm like a dove. She had washed and dressed in the robe he had chosen for her. She was still and no longer sobbing.

"They will pay," he said. "I may not have claimed you as my own, but no man treats a woman under my care this way. Tell me who."

Hananel was as surprised to see Daphne as she was to see him. "Daphne!" He jumped off his horse before it had even come to a full stop. "What are you doing out here? Where have you been?"

Daphne stopped. "I think I know you, but my name is Humaya." She stepped back. "I'm a priestess of Zarathustra. Are you a worshipper at the fire temple?"

Hananel stopped. "What are you saying? I know who you are." He moved a step forward as she backed away. "You lived with my nieces Atossa and Adrina. They're hiding close to here. Come with me."

Daphne stepped off the road and backed toward the trees. "My name is Humaya. Vashti will be waiting for me to finish cleaning the fire temple. I need to go home now."

Hananel stopped at the edge of the road, still holding the reins of his horse. "Has someone bewitched you, woman? You lived with us, waiting for your husband, Nabonidus, a big, dark Persian who was a gladiator in Ephesus."

At the mention of the big, dark Persian, Daphne stopped her retreat. "That big, dark demon is my husband?" She sat in the grass and stared at the moon. "Life is so confusing."

"Yes, Nabonidus is the father of your child. You need to come with us so we can help you deliver and care for the little one."

"Bring the demon to me," Daphne demanded. "I will see by what means he claims to be the father. I will wait here."

Hananel held out his hands. "You can't wait here. It's dangerous in the middle of the night. There are bandits and highwayman who will take advantage of a woman on her own."

"And you appear to be one of those scoundrels," she said. "Now, bring me this man, and let him prove he is my husband."

Hananel sagged. "I can't bring your husband," he said. "The truth is, I've never met him. I only know about him from what you and my nieces have said. I don't even know where he is or even if he's still alive."

"I thought so!" she said. "Now leave me, or I will scream loud enough to wake the demons."

Hananel returned to his horse and mounted. "Listen. Why don't you hide in these trees until morning? I'll go home and return with Atossa and Adrina. They will convince you of what I'm saying."

Daphne stepped toward him. "Be careful. I've seen a caravan of Arabs and a band of militia from the Magi fighting near here. May Ahura Mazda guard you."

Hananel nodded. "I'm a follower of the Hebrew God, Adonai—the one true God. You are a follower of Yeshua, who is one with Him. Pray to Yeshua to restore your mind and your faith." He nudged the horse and galloped down the road.

Twelve of the cataphracts returned at noon the next day to find Nabonidus standing with Sasina by the well. The regent rested nearby on a carved ivory lounge chair. The warriors dismounted and bowed before the elder.

The old man hoisted himself to his feet using his cane and waved it over their heads. "Rise and report," he ordered.

The lead cataphract stepped forward, dipping his head. "We searched everywhere for this fugitive," he said, jutting his chin out at Nabonidus. "In the night, we camped by the road near Susa." He looked back at his colleagues. "We heard shouts and galloping and met the invaders. It was a caravan of Arabs being set upon by the Magi's militia. We entered the battle but no one knew who was fighting against whom." He folded his hands and stepped back. "Half of our men were killed in the battle. We returned as soon as possible to hear what we should do further about this Nabonidus."

The regent hobbled toward Nabonidus and glared. "Even when you're not killing my men with your own hands, they are dying because of you. Lions, militia, Arabs ... what next?" He turned toward the arched house. "Bring back the dead. Burn them with honors. What a curse it is to think that one could raise a Prince of Persia to be the King of kings."

"Where was he?" the lead cataphract asked one of the guards who had remained behind.

"In the pit with the lions."

"But I saw him flee," another interjected. "Why didn't the lions eat him?"

"They ate Arphaxad instead. This heathen gladiator stood by and watched them eat one of the best lancers we had. No one has survived the pit until now."

"Do you think he's angry?" Sasina whispered. She had a mischievous glint in her eye. "I think you and I should go for a walk and enjoy the snow on the mountains. It is getting cold around here for more than one reason."

Nabonidus took her hand and walked the perimeter of the fence.

It was dawn when Daphne reached the fire temple. She had tired of waiting, and fears had gripped her as the night wore on. Even the stars had closed in like wild eyes creeping through the darkness. The sounds in the forest around her didn't help—whether it was a leopard's scream, an owl's call, or the cry of a jackal on the prowl, she couldn't distinguish them and had backed up close to a tree.

She was sweeping the courtyard when Vashti slipped in through a side gate. She paused when Daphne noticed her and nodded. Pulling her veil tighter around her face, she crept through the doorway into the temple sleeping rooms. She would wash and worship as she did every day.

When she emerged, the first worshippers huddled around the glowing embers in the center of the fire temple. Daphne knew the routine by heart and no longer needed instruction. Vashti moved close to her apprentice and whispered. "So I see that nothing unusual happened during the night. Ahura Mazda has maintained his control over his world."

Daphne set aside her broom and offered a token amulet to a worshipper completing his rituals. "I see that love burns like fire even in a temple like this," she said. "I need to find the black demon we heard about in the marketplace. I think he may be the father of my child."

Vashti stoked the fire and poked the embers with a metal rod. "There is a lesson for us in this," she said. "Ahura Mazda insists that we tell the truth at all times—especially when we keep promises. You have promised to serve the true god here."

Daphne swept the stone pathway. "Who is this God, Adonai? And who is Yeshua? They sound so right to my ear."

Vashti jumped as if Daphne had snapped a whip to her feet. "Do not say those names in this sacred place," she hissed. "Never let the priest know you have been deceived by the infidels who stalk our marketplace. Remember, you should practice charity for all—especially those with little." She handed over a caged dove to a worshiper, who took it to a priest who wrung its neck and spilled its blood into the fire. "Show love for others, and practice moderation. These are the teachings of Zarathustra, and these are what we live by."

The day crawled by as the weight of the little one, the unanswered questions, and the lack of sleep combined to make her sag. "Who am I really?" she asked Vashti. "Where did I come from? I have no memory of my early years in this place."

Vashti set aside her broom and motioned toward a bench. When they were seated, she released a sigh and turned to her protégée. "The priest rescued you during a fire at the market." She tucked a loose strand of hair back under her head covering. "There was a boy trying to lift a post off of you, but another post fell on him and broke his back. He had been crying out 'Humaya.' That's how we knew your name."

"So I did not grow up as a priestess of Zarathustra?"

"Remember, we thought your name and your character marked you as someone from the north. We sent messages for a long time, and no one had heard of you. No one near here has reported you missing."

"Perhaps I have another name by which men might know me," Daphne said. "I met a man who called me Daphne and told me I was the wife of the black demon everyone is afraid of."

Vashti set her hand on Daphne's knee and patted it. "Such foolishness. Don't let your mind be captivated by those who would steal your soul." She stood up and retrieved her broom. "Come back to work. We don't want that little one to be marked by laziness."

It was the first time that Nabonidus had allowed Sasina to find comfort in his arms but after all that had happened, it seemed the right thing to do. She cuddled into him like a child as they lay on the couch in their quarters. "If only I had known you before the regent bought me for his slave," she said.

"I too was a slave," he said. "What is your story?"

She allowed the tears to flow and then shared her life account. "My family lived in Britannia when I was young. My father was the captain of a large ship. One day, he took my mother, my brothers, and me on a great cruise." She pulled at a section of his robe and wiped her tears. "We were off the coast of Alexandria when pirates raided the ship. The pirates snatched me and one of my brothers. I think they killed the others, because I saw my father's boat burning as we left."

"How did you get here?"

"A Roman galleon intercepted the pirates, and they fled to a strange port. They sold me to Arabs, who took me by camel to a marketplace. The regent bought me from them and kept me here."

"He never touched you?"

She moved away from him and walked to a washbasin where she bathed her face. "Let's not talk about that," she said. "I was trained to please a man. He said that one day I would be a queen and that he needed me to be ready for the coming King of kings. Now you are here, and I am as useless and unwanted as an old rag."

He went to her and took her in his arms. "Now, now!" He brushed her cheek with his hand. "You are neither useless nor unwanted. I think I need to tell you another story about the true King of kings who will always want you." He sat her on the couch and wrapped a blanket around her shoulders. "His name is Yeshua, and I fought in His name."

And through the night he shared a story so intriguing that she wanted to be a part of it. As the sun rose, she said, "Take me to Yeshua! All my life I have waited for someone like this. Come, let us run to Him and show the world that such love can exist."

Nabonidus peered through the window at the glistening snowcapped peaks. "He is not here," he said. "One day He will return to take His kingdom, but for now we wait."

Sasina threw off the blanket. "But where is He? Surely we can convince Him to come and take His rightful place. You can be His chief warrior, and I can be the one to wash His feet."

He took her head in his hands and pressed it against his chest. "Such a king would value a servant like you. But we can only wait until He decides the time. If we run, where can we run where the regent and his men would not catch us and enslave us even more cruelly?"

A knock at the door broke them of their sense of peace. "Warrior! The regent commands audience with you. Come now!"

Nabonidus stood in the center of the room and mocked. "And if I don't come, what will you do? Will you have me thrown to the lions again? Will you send me against the militia of the Magi?"

Several moments of silence made him wonder if the cataphract had gone. Finally, the soldier spoke up. "I am only the messenger. The regent desires to consult you on his war strategy. I will tell him that you will come when you are able."

Nabonidus ensured that Sasina was safely locked in the quarters and then followed the soldier to the regent. The regent sat in the arena on his throne. The sand had been carefully prepared. A Roman centurion in full battle array stood in the center. Nabonidus shivered. He was not ready to fight.

The priest's lectures no longer seemed of interest. Acting as if faith in Ahura Mazda was real, but living in a contrary state, only proved a person was truly aligned with Angra Mainyu. There was no escape from the darkness if you allowed the questions in your mind to surface. It all sounded the same. Make friends of your enemies, make the wicked righteous, and teach the ignorant. It was clear that she had been a project for Vashti, who worked to prove her own allegiance to the priest. Paradise was an elusive quest for someone like Daphne.

Daphne rose and knelt in the posture of a supplicant. When she was acknowledged with a touch of the priestly rod on her shoulder, she asked her question. "What happens with the seeker who perishes early on their journey?"

The priest intertwined his fingers in front of his chest and rocked back and forth. "The ultimate question, my child." He paced as he answered. "Zarathustra has answered all things including this. All humans are born with two essences, which divide at birth—a higher spirit which directs our soul through existence in our body to help us with the choices for good or evil. Three days after our final steps in this physical life our soul and body reunite and travel to the Chinvat Bridge, which spans the abyss between the living and the dead."

Daphne raised her head to search the face of her teacher. "What happens then?"

The priest stopped and pondered his response. "Two dogs meet us and welcome the justified soul but snarl at the condemned soul. After the dogs, there is the Holy Maiden, Daena, who is a picture of our conscience. If you are right with Ahura Mazda, she will appear as a beautiful maiden, and if you are not right, then she appears as an ugly hag. Thus you will know your state."

The priest gripped the sides of his robe and spread it wide. "Finally, she will walk you across the bridge, protecting you from the demonic hordes who wish to destroy you. At the far end, an angel will decide your final destination—whether you are ready for paradise or whether your deeds still need to be purified in a purgatory."

Daphne nodded. "And that's it? How can we know here if we have done enough?"

The furrows above the priest's eyes narrowed. "You can never know if you've done enough. There are still four levels of paradise after the bridge, if the angel does not first drop you over the edge into the House of Lies, where there are four more levels of darkness. You must always keep working if you are to have any hope."

Mornings and evenings flowed into times of meditation and menial labor. A week after Daphne's escapade on the road away from the fire temple, she visited the shrine at the far end of the compound. Vashti had sent her there to sweep. The shrine was called the Circle of Heaven, and it was indeed a place of peace. The white pillared marble sanctuary nestled in a grove of cedars. A large oval pool glistened in front of the eight stairs leading inside. Daphne stood meditating on all she had experienced. Across the ripple-free surface glided the image of a hawk. How wonderful it would be if she could fly free. But where would she go?

Thoughts of the man on the road who claimed to have two nieces spun like whirlpools in her mind. For a moment, his visage seemed to shine in the waters in the place where clouds had been. She looked up, but dissipating clouds alone greeted her.

Her feet itched to run to the road again. But how would she find the man? She finished sweeping up the pine needles and dirt and set aside the broom. If only whatever god there might be would guide her. Perhaps Vashti could give her another idea on how to seek wisdom and truth. Daphne needed someone to show her the way.

As she left the plaza of the Circle of Heaven, she chose to exit out a side gate and take a different path back to the fire temple. A hundred paces down that path, she saw a man on his knees by a bench with his hands clasped. Instincts took over, and she went to him, touching his shoulder. "May him who is true be your guide this day," she said.

The man jerked as if touched by a hot sword. It was the man. He clambered onto the bench, staring, mouth open.

"It is you," she said. "I wondered how to meet you again."

He patted the bench beside him, and she sat. He reached out and touched her hand. "It is you. You are real," he said. "I've been praying to

Adonai for a chance to meet you again. He brought me to this place. How did you find me?"

Daphne sat back. This was strange. Her meditation at the pool had focused on the man before her, and yet his God had sent him here even before. Was Ahura Mazda the one orchestrating things for this connection, or was there indeed another Almighty God who empowered the people of His world?

The man stood. "As I told you, I am Hananel, a follower of Adonai and Yeshua. He has sent me for you to come. I am here to show you the way."

That very phrase struck her deep. Her prayers had focused on the need for someone to show her the way. Now this Hananel had come, saying that he could show the way. "Where will you take me?" she asked.

He looked toward the road. "To Atossa and Adrina. They will tell you of your life in Ephesus and your life with Nabonidus. You will know from them more of who you are."

There was no hesitation in her first step, and she didn't look back when they left the temple grounds. "Tell me who you are and how you know me."

For the next two hours, as they walked, she heard stories which rang true. It was only a screech of joy that interrupted their discussion.

Atossa flung herself into the arms of Daphne and was soon joined by Adrina. "You've come back," the elder girl said. "We heard you were dead in the market fire. Have you truly been hiding out in the Temple of Fire all this time?"

The greetings felt genuine, and she allowed herself to catch the rhythm of the enthusiasm. "Take it slow," she said. "I have had others tell me who I am and what I must believe. My memories of the past are few. I only know I am with child and will soon deliver."

"Yes, yes, of course," Adrina said, taking one arm while Atossa took the other. "You must tell us your story, and we will tell you ours. We were chased from the village and have been in hiding ever since. It is a miracle of Yeshua that we found each other again."

"I am eager to meet this Nabonidus; your uncle tells me he is the father of my child. Take me to him."

Adrina and Atossa stopped in their tracks. They looked toward Hananel. He nodded. "Perhaps that part of the story can wait."

Nabonidus bowed before the regent and awaited the dreaded order. How would he say no? When the regent remained silent, Nabonidus looked up at the dais where the elder waited, stroking his long white beard.

"Have you ever taught someone else to fight?" the regent asked. He rose to his feet and pointed with his cane at the Roman. "Can you turn a warrior into a demon?"

Nabonidus examined the warrior—his stance proud and arrogant, the grasp on his sword loose, the focus of his eyes daring. "Whom will he fight?" he asked.

The regent smiled. "What if he were to fight you and another like you, back-to-back?"

Nabonidus knelt. "My lord, he would not last a minute with one true gladiator and certainly not with two." He spread out his arms. "Is this the best you can do? Send him against the Magi's militia for experience. His attitude alone will secure his death."

"Very well!" the regent said. "You have until the next full moon to prepare him. Your life will be tied to his. If he wins against two of my best cataphracts back-to-back, then you will pass your final test and enter training for the throne. If he dies, you will face a dozen of my warriors until you fall."

Nabonidus rose and interlocked his fingers behind his head. "Is it possible to face the lions again?"

The elder smiled. "You've already passed that test, my son. From now on, we look up, not down."

Nabonidus stepped down onto the sand and walked toward the warrior. He eyed the Roman, who stood his ground, hand on the hilt of his sword. He had no weapon, but as he neared the waiting soldier, he loosened the leather belt around his robe. He kicked off his sandals to the far side of the man, and as the warrior's eyes briefly followed the flight of the shoes, he snapped his belt and wrapped it around the wrist holding the sword. When the soldier pulled back, Nabonidus kicked a heel into the centurion's jaw and flattened him.

Picking himself off the sand, he retrieved his sandals and returned to the regent. "I will need two new moons," he said.

"You have one," the regent said. "I hope you didn't break his jaw, or you might as well prepare to die now." He tapped his cane three times, accepted the arm bridge of his bodyguards, and rode out of the arena.

Nabonidus watched the physicians attending to the warrior. When the warrior got to his knees, Nabonidus walked out and returned to Sasina.

The hovel hardly had space for the four of them. When all the reed mats lay side by side, no floor could be seen. Privacy was impossible. The icy winds off the hills made outside a nonnegotiable. Hananel agreed to move to a friend's place while Daphne built her relationship with Atossa and Adrina.

"Tell me again about Ephesus and Nabonidus," Daphne urged. "This man was the emperor's champion as a gladiator? He killed thirty other champions and then married me?" She rubbed her swollen abdomen. "I guess someone was responsible for this, and there's a good deal of fighting going on inside here."

Pictures in her dreams and waking moments fell into place as the days went by. Her thoughts reoriented, and the teachings of Zarathustra lost their grip. Her instincts to pick up a broom at every opportunity were harder to change.

Waking moments involved long strolls when the rains lifted as the women debriefed the teachings that had filled her time at the fire temple. "Zarathustra said that no soul would remain in the darkness forever," said Daphne, "because a Messiah would come, end time, and reunite us all with Ahura Mazda. All evil ones would be destroyed."

Adrina took the lead in responding. "A Messiah has come. He is Yeshua. Anyone who puts their trust in His work of life-giving will not perish but be saved to spend eternity with the true God." She laid a land on Daphne's arm and ran a finger over her calluses. "No amount of work can make us more acceptable. His work alone counts to cross the bridge of life." The teachings rang true to her soul, and she eagerly reframed her understanding of her own identity and belief system.

One afternoon as the three women sat absorbing the weakened sunshine, a young man dressed in the robes of nobility reined his horse to a halt and dismounted before them. "I know you," he said, pointing at Daphne. "Humaya, right? You sold me the amulet at the Temple of Fire for the healing of my son." He reached into his robe and produced a two-drachma gold coin. "My son is well, and I wish to make a sacrifice to the god for his goodness. Take half for the temple and half for yourself." He tossed the coin to Daphne.

She let it fall at her feet. "I cannot accept your generosity," she said. "I no longer work at the fire temple. I follow the true God."

His furrowed brow lightened, and he laughed. "A priestess of Zarathustra abandons her calling?" He pondered her extended belly for a moment and then nodded, having determined his own solution to the issue. "I see. Was it a priest or a guest who got a little too passionate in his worship with you? I know that no one leaves the temple without paying with their life. I'm glad they are giving you time off to have the little one."

Daphne struggled to her feet. "You misunderstand," she said. "No one took advantage of me. I didn't belong there, and I left of my own free choice."

The transformation to his face flowed as subtly as a mudslide in a spring rain. The sparkle in his eyes surged into flames of fire. The curled lips unveiled grinding teeth. Crimson cheeks and ears blended. He retrieved his coin and towered over her. "May the curses resting on my son now fall on you," he hissed. "The fire temple is essential if the reign of the Magi is to succeed." He mounted his horse and gripped the reins. "I truly hope you mock me with this jest. I shall offer my own sacrifices and declare my displeasure to the priest. The last thing you want is for the Magi to unleash their wrath on you and these sisters of yours."

The regent's banquet was as lavish as the first Nabonidus had tasted upon his arrival. This time, the regent welcomed twelve new recruits and four elite commandos who had offered themselves for service in opposition to the Magi. Each of the four commandos was given a consort of their own—none as beautiful as Sasina. Nevertheless, the soldiers clearly appreciated the women gyrating in front of them.

Nabonidus relaxed on a couch next to the powerful fighter from Gaul and another from Ethiopia. "Which one is yours, Persian?" the Ethiopian asked.

Sasina was nowhere to be found. Sitting up, Nabonidus scanned the room. Perhaps she didn't feel well.

"Where do we worship around here?" the Gaul asked. "These women intrigue my senses."

"Look up, look around, look in," the Ethiopian said. "Create what you want to empower you." He sipped his wine. "Or you could visit the Temple of Fire in Susa. I visited there on my way here and met an interesting young man who is allied with the Magi. He was ready to burn up some priestess with child who had mocked him in order to follow the true god. He actually pleaded with the priest to commission him to run the woman through with a lance."

The image of the two women bowing at the Temple weeks earlier flashed into Nabonidus's mind. The rapid thumping in his chest caught his attention. "What did this pregnant priestess look like?" he asked.

The Ethiopian laughed. "You have your own woman already, Persian. Or so I'm told." He joined Nabonidus as he stood. "Besides, I did not view the wench. She may be dead and buried by now for all I know."

Each of the four warriors proved themselves in the arena before the watching crowd, and there was significant applause as the four claimed their consorts and left for their new quarters. The regent rubbed his hands together and seemed to find a new energy in his step as he rallied his followers with condemnation of the Magi and with a long history of the Elamites and their failed truce with Rome to overthrow the Persian empire.

The absence of Sasina distracted Nabonidus from the speech, but when he heard his name being chanted to loud cheers, he faced the regent with a bow. "I serve at your command, my lord," he said. More cheers filled the arena.

"Hail your commander," the regent demanded, pointing his cane toward Nabonidus. "Hail your commander." The cheers increased.

VI

HANANEL DIDN'T HESITATE to move the women when Atossa and Adrina told him about the confrontation with the young nobleman. A donkey cart loaded with their possessions and food from the market slogged through the muddy trail and onto the road north. "We need to get away from this chaotic insanity," he said. "What did you do in that temple to rouse the hopes of men like this? All you did was sell him an amulet, right?"

Daphne rewrapped the sheepskin covering over her head to better keep the rain off. "I think it was because I told him that I left Zarathustra to follow the true God," she responded. "He seemed to think that anyone leaving the faith was meant to be killed by the priests. There seemed to be no option in his mind."

Adrina stepped closer to Daphne and whispered, "Do you think the priest would actually kill you for running away? You didn't even know who you were. You were being held there without understanding."

"He might try to hurt me if he thought Vashti wanted him to. He and Vashti had a relationship, and they left me to cover for them when they would disappear. They might not appreciate how awkward I've made things at the temple."

"How much longer?" Atossa asked. "I'm soaked to the skin, and this mud has crawled up to my knees. My robe feels as heavy as bricks. I can hardly walk through this muck."

Hananel held his hand against his forehead so he could peer through the rain. "We will be fortunate to find space at the next inn. If we could see the sun or a water clock, I might be able to tell you how many more farsangs we have left to travel. This mud is really slowing us down."

Adrina broke the mood, "Let's have Daphne sing us a song. Daphne, if you sing, perhaps it will help bring back your memory. We learned some great songs from the apostle John in Ephesus."

"I'm not sure I feel like singing," Daphne said. "Besides, I can't remember anything from before the Temple of Fire. You wouldn't want me singing those songs."

"I'll sing," Atossa said. "Then maybe something will come back to you. 'The Lord is my Shepherd. No lack of anything I have. He leads me beside the quiet waters and in green pastures makes me lie. He leads me in the right paths because He is true....'"

Daphne touched Atossa's elbow. "I don't think that last line is right. I remember the melody behind the song and the rhythm feels off. Sing it again."

And so, in song, small fragments flashed in Daphne's mind. A picture of a view from a hillside mansion. A quiet refuge in a garden. A powerful dark man dancing for joy as he emerged from water.

And still the rains came down.

"He what?" Nabonidus hurtled over the table and grabbed the Roman by the throat. "How did you hear this?"

The Roman drove his fists into the Persian's chest without effect. He stiffened himself and stopped breathing. A full minute went by before Nabonidus released him.

"How did you hear?" he demanded.

The Roman rubbed his throat, calmed his breathing, and stood a step back from Nabonidus. "You don't seem a worthy coach with this impulsive anger," he said. "In my country you would be dead in the arena in moments."

Nabonidus backed away. "You're right. The regent knows how to destroy me. He lifts me up and tears me down in the same moment."

"That's why he will lead us to install the next King of kings," the Roman said. "He knows the minds of men and how to twist them for his own ends. You live at his pleasure, and you die for the same."

"I have not even asked for your name," Nabonidus said. "Without a name you are simply a corpse waiting for a grave. Tell me your name."

"Tertius Silvanus Germanicus Vasilius of Rome."

Nabonidus rubbed the back of his head hard. "Vasilius will do," he said. "I see you only play the role of a warrior. Now, how did you hear that the regent sent Sasina away and where did he send her?"

Vasilius stepped across the room and picked up a gourd of water. He soothed his throat, waiting. "I was resting in the baths behind the arched house. My ears are very keen. I heard the regent instructing his new cataphracts that they were to take part in a test for their new commander."

"And what is the test?"

"Four of them were to wait until you joined the regent in the banquet hall. During the entertainment they were to take your consort and deliver her to the Temple of Fire in Susa. The priest would know what to do with her."

Nabonidus set his foot on a stool. "As your commander, I now have a test for you."

"Yes, my lord!" Vasilius answered.

"The moment the sun sets, take two horses and meet me at the first crossroads to the north. I trust your wit and will to do what must be done. Together, we will visit this Temple of Fire."

"The rains will make travel difficult tonight," Vasilius said.

"They will also make it difficult for others to track us."

The inn was full, but the owner kindly opened his barn for the group to rest in. Despite being soaked to the skin and layered in mud, Adrina had to giggle as the man of significant girth waddled ahead of them to show the way. "I bet all three of us could link arms and hardly encircle him," she said to Daphne.

Daphne covered her mouth and whispered back. "I thought you were going to tell me that he was the same size as me or maybe my husband. Right now, I don't care how big he is as long as he has a space for us to wash, dry, and sleep."

The owner's wife, only half his size, shuffled in as the group settled and handed Hananel a sheet. "For your privacy," she said. "I will send my daughter with a basin of water so you can wash and clean. You may refill it at the well, or you may set it outside and let it refill itself. Your choice."

"Where is the hostess?" a familiar voice yelled above the fray. "Where is my dinner? What kind of a place is this?"

Ice flowed through Daphne's veins. The voice of the young nobleman who had threatened her was unmistakable. The babe gave an especially hard kick. She motioned to Adrina. "Get your sister and hide. It's the nobleman."

The three of them lifted the sheet around them as the voice sounded nearby. "What are you doing out here with the pigs? Let these filthy peasants care for themselves. I paid you good money for a meal, and I expect one."

The voice of Hananel sounded. "Good sir! You look dry and warm. We will only be a moment, and then our kind hosts can serve you all they want."

The sound of a slap echoed off the walls. "How dare you!" the nobleman growled. "Hostess, I want this filthy ruffian thrown off the property. No one speaks to me like that and gets away with it. Now, my dinner." His departure relieved tensions all through the barn.

The women lowered the sheet and saw that Hananel's hand covered his cheek. The host stood helpless as the hostess waddled after the nobleman toward the inn itself. "If that is the same man who threatened you," Hananel said, "it is wise for us to find other accommodations."

"No," Atossa whined. "We've walked all day in the rain and mud. It is cold and dark out there. Can't we just clean up and hide until morning?"

The host patted his abdomen with both hands as he looked around. "The count is a distant relative of the former King of kings, and he hopes to take the throne when the time is right. He is courting the Magi and trying to demonstrate his authority among the people. I think it may be good to move you to the cabin if you can handle one short walk."

Daphne patted her abdomen. "I'm not sure how much farther I can go before this little one decides it wants to be born."

The cabin was a three-room brick and tile enclosure several hundred paces into the forest. It involved wading through a swelling creek and pushing through undergrowth that had meshed together. The daughter of the host and hostess barged ahead and welcomed them into the dark enclosure. She lit a single clay lamp and bid them good night. The blankets they had carried were now damp. Fortunately, kindling and dry wood lay in a fireplace, and Hananel was able to use the flame from the lamp to start a warming fire.

Adrina took charge. "Let's set aside this room at the front for washing and cleaning ourselves one at a time. We women will sleep together in the room to the right, and, Uncle, you can sleep in the other room, keeping guard. Please try to keep the fire going, as it feels like an ice box in here."

"I don't trust that nobleman," Daphne said. "After his meal he'll probably force the hostess to tell him where they put us. He'll come looking."

Hananel looked out the window. "I'll be watching for him. You girls get changed. I'll keep the fire going until it warms up. At least we have a place to sleep."

A howl sounded from the forest outside. Daphne joined Hananel at the window. "I'm not sure any of us will be sleeping tonight."

Dawn trickled over the horizon as the two horsemen trotted into the outskirts of Susa. The Temple of Fire still had its gates closed but the acrid odor of smoke hung in the air. The rain had turned the roads into rushing rivers through the night. "The snows will be coming soon," Vasilius said. "What do you think the regent will do when he finds we are missing?"

Nabonidus turned in his saddle. "I suspect he knew already that I would do what I'm doing. He probably has a surprise waiting for us here. Before he surprises us, we need to think of how we will overcome this test."

The two men hid their horses in a wooded ravine a short distance away and circumnavigated the property until they could see a way in. Nabonidus led the way through a hedge near a white-pillared shrine with a large oval pool in front. The eight steps led up to closed doors. The stone pathway helped hide their footprints as they rushed toward the square structure where the fire burned.

Nabonidus paused and pointed toward a squat stone building. "I've seen the women going into that place. They either sleep there or are trained there. I saw a woman who looked like my wife here once, and I'm sure this is where they would keep Sasina."

Vasilius crouched behind a hedge and then moved to stand behind an oak tree. He motioned toward the firepit. Sure enough, a woman with a broom swept, added wood to the fire, and arranged a small table with amulets. The rain had dwindle to a sprinkle.

Another woman arrived with the priest and opened the gate wide for worshippers to enter. She waved toward a hut. A shifting shadow inside was the only response. There was the surprise. If he rode into the front entrance, there would likely be an arrow to take him down. He motioned Vasilius to move around the women's building, out of sight.

Twenty paces behind the building, as they hid behind a hedge, the woman with the priest sauntered by. The priest was right behind her. "Vashti," he called, "why do we have to keep that woman here, and how long will these men stay around?"

"Don't worry! It should be over soon." The woman stood close to the priest. "The regent says that the Persian will seek his consort in here, but I have her in the Circle of Heaven. All the women are safe. Only warriors wait here, hidden inside."

The priest wrung his hands. "The path of Ahura Mazda has been defiled by this act. We will have to work all day to purify this place. I hope there isn't too much blood."

The woman laid her hand against the priest's cheek. "Don't you worry. We lost that pregnant Ephesian who asked too many questions, but we will keep this one for our own profit. The men you hope for will find new reasons to sacrifice here."

A pregnant Ephesian? Could it have been Daphne he had seen after all during his last visit? Where could she be? Could he rescue Sasina and Daphne at the same time?

When the priest and his helper had disappeared, Nabonidus motioned for Vasilius to follow. He retraced their steps to the white house by the oval pool and hid behind it. Sure enough, there were muffled voices inside; this must be the Circle of Heaven.

They backed away into the trees. "Strip down to your undertunic," Nabonidus said. "Pretend to be a gardener cleaning up the front stairs. Get someone's attention, and I will find another way in to take the women." He moved away and then turned back. "Listen for the owl, and meet me outside the hedge."

Vasilius shed his hooded riding cape, his breastplate, his sandals, and his armored girdle with its sword attached. In his undergarment, his physique was enough to draw the eyes of any woman. With no hesitation, he stepped out of the trees and walked to the front of the building. He fished a branch out of the pool and moved slowly toward the front stairs. Soggy leaves spotted the entranceway. He began to whistle as he worked, picking them up.

A door opened. "What do you think you're doing?" a woman's voice asked.

Vasilius answered. "Don't worry. I'm here pretending to be a gardener to protect the women in case there is unexpected trouble."

"But how do you know the women are here and not in their quarters?"

"Oh, Vashti told me. She is quite concerned that the regent's plan may not be thought through enough. The priest assured her, but she sent me anyway."

"Well, if Vashti sent you, then we are lucky women." It was clear the speaker had moved outside onto the porch. "It's not too often we see men in such fine shape as yourself moving freely about our property in such a state of dress," she said. "Are you not worried that such temptation may be too much for a woman like myself?"

A splash echoed. "Join me in the pool, and we will see who falls for the greater temptation," Vasilius said.

"I can't join you, but I can watch," the woman replied. Other voices sounded. "Back inside," the woman said. "You can drool through the window."

Nabonidus crept to the back part of the house and noticed the shutters of one window ajar. There was no light inside, so he hoisted himself up and squeezed through the small space. The women had gathered at the front of the house and lewd comments and suggestions were met with tittering and gasps. As he moved to the doorway of the room, he heard a faint movement behind him. He pivoted and set his back against a wall. He allowed his eyes to adjust. A reed mat was on the floor and a figure rested on it.

The figure sat up and before anything could be said Nabonidus jumped and clamped his hand around the mouth of the person. It was a woman. He knew from the scent of jasmine that it was Sasina. He had found one. Could he find Daphne?

He whispered. "It's me, Sasina. I've come to rescue you. I will take my hand away, but don't scream."

"Thank you," she said.

He helped her up from the bed, and she covered herself with a robe. "I've come to find another as well," he said. "An Ephesian woman who is very pregnant."

Sasina waited and then shook her head. "There is no one like that among the women, but I did hear Vashti talking about someone named Humaya who had run away."

"No, her name is Daphne."

"I've only been here a day," Sasina whispered. "Please don't leave me with the regent's men again. They are foul. I don't want to be left here either."

"Come!" he said. "Out the window. We will escape together."

He lowered her to the ground and tossed a pair of sandals after her. Squeezing through the small space was harder on the way out but he managed. Picking up Vasilius's discarded gear, he sounded the call of the owl.

A short time later, a dripping Vasilius sauntered by. "I see you found your treasure," he said. "I think I'd like to come back here another time when we can stay a little longer."

A shout from within the house preceded a series of screams. Sasina's disappearance had been discovered.

The little one was restless, and the forest sounds heightened as the rain stopped. A leopard's snarl mingled with a horse's neigh, a dog's bark, and a drunkard's belligerent rebuke at another telling him to be quiet. Daphne sat up and watched Adrina tossing in her sleep.

"Are you awake?" It was Atossa. "I can't sleep thinking about that nobleman coming for us. Ever since we were chased from the village, I haven't felt safe. Something in our world is changing, and I don't like it."

"I feel it too," Daphne whispered. "I haven't been here that long, but it's almost like some sinister force is trying to destroy us all. Perhaps it was this way in Ephesus as well. I just wish I could meet Nabonidus and rebuild more of my memories."

"What are you two talking about?" Adrina propped up on one elbow. "It's the middle of the night. Maybe you can talk in the morning."

A pounding on the front door stopped all their talking. Hananel looked into the room. "Shhhh!" he whispered. "Lie low."

"Open the door!" It was the innkeeper's daughter. "Open the door."

Hananel opened the door. "Hurry! You need to run deeper into the forest," the girl urged. "The nobleman found out from my father that you are still on the property, and he is looking for his sword to come after you. I hid it, but it won't be long."

Daphne pulled on her robe and walked out of the room to where the girl stood with Hananel. "How am I supposed to run like this?" she said, patting her abdomen. "Can't you distract him or direct him to go in another direction?"

Hananel stood in the doorway. "Let me go," he said. "I'll lead him away from here, or if he catches me, I'll beg his mercy. All he needs is for someone to make him feel strong and powerful."

"Stay here!" the daughter said to Daphne. "We'll try to keep him busy and distracted."

Hananel looked back. "Pray for me. If I'm not back before dawn, then find some horses and head north. I'll try to catch you when I can."

Nabonidus, Vasilius, and Sasina circled back to the horses in the ravine and waited. Cataphracts and archers galloped along the roadways, and chaotic voices rose from the temple grounds as searchers gathered and then crashed through the undergrowth outside the walls.

"Someone will know this refuge," Nabonidus said. "Take Sasina on foot and move toward the river. I'll take the horses and lead them away from here. If you can find another horse, take it and move quickly." He grabbed the reins. "Whatever happens, do not let them take the girl." With a nod at Sasina he turned to go.

Vasilius grabbed Nabonidus by the shoulder. "She's your woman. You should take her. I'll go with the horses. If they catch me, they won't know who I am, and I can lead them astray."

Nabonidus paused a moment, then nodded. He released the reins, grabbed hold of Sasina by the hand and pulled her along the stream away from the Temple of Fire.

Vasilius pulled the horses up the bank, waited for a break in the patrols, then mounted his ride and galloped at full speed toward town. A moment later, a shout from the temple alerted the sentries, and five horsemen chased down the road after the fugitive. Shouts from within the compound alerted the forest searchers, who returned to their base.

Nabonidus held on to Sasina and walked fast. Apart from a brief break to gulp a handful of water, the two kept moving. "When we get to the Tigris River, we'll find a boat and get away from here," he said.

"Where will we go?" she asked.

"Somewhere safer," he said. "You need to be in a place where the regent can't use you to manipulate me anymore."

She laid her head on his shoulder for a moment as they walked and squeezed his hand. "It's been special being your queen, even if you don't want to make me feel like a whole woman," she said. "Sometimes it feels enough to be your friend. Your wife is a very lucky woman to have you as her own."

"You need a man who is free and able to treat you like a woman," he said. "Perhaps Vasilius might prove himself worthy one day."

She laughed. "He does have the looks any woman would admire. Sometimes, that type of men are too good to be true. Besides, after all the others have done with me, I'm not sure he would want me."

"More walking, less talking," he said as they crossed a trail. "Hurry! Someone's coming."

It was true. A mad crashing in the bushes forced them to their bellies behind a large tree. A wild boar hurtled past, followed by a rider with a lance. Fortunately, the cataphract was so focused on the wild pig that he didn't notice them. Not too far down the trail, the soldier bagged his trophy. A shout of triumph reverberated through the forest.

Nabonidus motioned for Sasina to follow and slid under the bushes away from the stream. "We are fortunate that boar came by," he whispered. "We need to find a longer route to the river."

A stone's throw in front of them, more hoofbeats pounded. The trail circled around them to merge with the trail where the boar hunter waited. "They can't have gone too far past this," shouted the first of two riders as they trotted by. "That maniac and his boar might have scared them off. Our tracker is still walking along the stream but this trail looks like the shortest route to the river if he's going there."

The horses stopped and began to walk. "Do you think the Persian snatched the woman, or do you think that Egyptian has her?" the second rider asked.

"The regent said they'd be cunning," replied the first. "Perhaps they have others helping them. All I know is it is us or them."

Dawn had come and gone without any sign of Hananel. Adrina wanted to sneak through the forest and find out what might have happened, but Daphne and Atossa convinced her to follow her uncle's plan and head north. There hadn't been any horses available, but they did find a willing donkey cart driver. They'd been on the road for an hour when the first caravan appeared. The Arab on the first camel stopped them.

"Peace on you," he said. "Do you intend to go far on this road? It is dangerous for women. Bandits attacked us last evening."

Daphne stepped down from the cart. "Peace to you as well," she said. "You can see that I'm in no condition for a long journey. How far does this road stretch?"

The Arab chuckled. "This Royal Road stretches all the way through Babylon, from Nineveh even to Sardis if you wish," he said. "Or you could take the other branch and join the Silk Road along the Great Khurasan

Road to the east. Or if you are wise you will turn around and head south to Susa and Persepolis."

"Going back is not an option," Daphne said. "How long do we need to walk? Our cart driver needs to return home from here."

"If you are a royal messenger for the king, you can cross it with an edict in nine days. For you it would take three or four full moons—time you clearly don't have."

"How far until the next village?" she asked.

He smiled. "By camel it is not far. We have come through Anatolia one full moon ago. We left the last village when the rains slowed last night." He looked toward the hills. "The snows have hindered us, and we wish to get back to the desert heat again. If you delay much longer, the snows will fall on you as well." He motioned to one of the others, who brought his camel close. "Throw these women some blankets," he instructed. "We are indebted to King Darius for creating this road, and the least we can do is care for some of this country's citizens."

Three woven blankets were tossed down, and the women gratefully wrapped themselves in the unexpected gifts. "Guard yourself against the Magi's militiamen," Daphne warned. "They are close and trying to prove themselves."

The Arab saluted the women and moved on. A short time later, a Royal horseman galloped by at full tilt. "Turn and flee! Bandits!" he called into the rising wind.

Adrina turned immediately. "Come!" she called. "I saw a trail back a short distance, and we can shelter there until the bandits pass."

The three slipped into the forest enclave and found a rocky overhang with a dry space underneath. "The provision of Adonai," Atossa said. "We would have been better to have hidden here last night."

The flash of color through the trees combined with the soft thudding of hooves on damp ground proved the bandits had arrived and passed. The Arabs would have to fight once again to preserve their wealth.

The sun reflecting off the surface of the Tigris River affirmed the illusion of a peaceful day. The fisherman who had agreed to take Nabonidus and

Sasina downriver "for a price" reset his sail and maintained his sentry position at the helm. "I see none of these rebels," he announced in Greek. "You should be free to come out now. Despite the sun, let me warn you that this winter wind is cool."

Nabonidus and Sasina emerged from under the extra sail bundled in the bottom of the vessel. "Thank you for taking us," Nabonidus said. "We were afraid for our lives." They wrapped themselves in the woolen blankets the sailor pointed to.

"It looks like you are quite capable of taking care of yourself," the fisherman said with a smile, "and I think your woman would be a good incentive to do that." He waved at a passing boat and set his face toward the sun. "The price you were willing to pay makes me think I might be in the wrong business with fishing. Remember, if you are captured by the Magi's militia, I have never seen you before."

Sasina ran her fingers through her hair. Turning to Nabonidus at the ship's rail, she whispered, "I have never been so filthy in my life. My hair is a mess. My clothes are ready for the rag pile." She leaned on the rail next to Nabonidus. "Tell me a story about your life before Ephesus. I know you are more than a gladiator. Tell me about the man I should know."

Leaning on his forearms, the wind whipping into his face, he rubbed the stubble on his chin. "I too need to be cleaned up. Perhaps a story would distract us both. I wish I had more stories about Yeshua to teach you."

She pushed closer, standing shoulder to shoulder so he could block her from the wind. "I don't want to make you uncomfortable, but I want to know the man whom Yeshua has molded for Himself. I want to know you outside your form as a warrior."

"I'm not sure where to start," he said. "As you know, I was taken around here by bandits and shipped to Armenia as a houseboy. Then I was sent to Damascus, where I was purchased as a laborer to load and unload produce for a warehouse." He shifted and wrapped half of his blanket around Sasina. "On a trip to Caesarea, I somehow displeased my master, and he sold me to a Jew who was a cross maker. He was kind, but a Roman centurion wanted him to build more crosses and so sent his men to hold me for ransom to secure his demands. For some reason, I ended up rowing in a Roman galley." He stood up straight, letting his part of the blanket fall away. "Twice I was sure we were sinking after encounters with pirates who rammed us. Finally, I was sold to a gladiator school in Ephesus, where I learned to fight. When I was done fighting, I bought a house, started a church, and married Daphne. That is my life in a grapeseed."

"Do you ever miss your family?" she asked.

Resting his elbow along the rail, he drank in her blue eyes, petite nose, and full lips. Right now, she was as much family as anyone he knew. "That's a hard question to answer," he said. "It's been so long that I've had to make my own family."

Sasina wrapped the blanket around his broad shoulders and stood silent. "I guess I should tell you my story," she said. "Do you really want to hear it?"

Nabonidus nudged up close, shoulder to shoulder. "Tell me what you can, like a sister to a brother."

"Oh!" she said. "So we're family now. I guess it's better than friends." She waved at a woman washing clothes along the bank of the river and then at two young boys jumping up and down beside a dog, yelling their greetings. "I think I was born twenty years ago to a farmer and a seamstress who lived in Britannia. The years are a blur to me." She twirled the ringlets of her hair with a finger. "The Romans marched onto our farm one morning, and my father decided he didn't want to give up his home. I saw his body on a pole when I came in from town with my mother. I cannot tell you what they did to my mother, but they put me in a cage on an oxcart."

"That must have been hard for you," Nabonidus said. "No girl should have to endure such a thing."

"You went through the same thing," she said. "I was left in a school and trained to please men before being shipped to Alexandria. I spent some time there serving in a temple to Diana, getting further training before I was taken to Caesarea and then caravanned through Damascus, Nineveh, and Babylon. The regent bought me from someone and brought me to his camp, where I made the men happy until he gave me to you."

"You do make me happy," Nabonidus said.

"You know what I mean," she said. "Listening to stories is not what satisfies most people. At least, in the training I was given. —So what do you think of me now?"

Nabonidus grasped her hand and held it. "You and I were children manipulated by adults who were in turn manipulated by the evil one. Yeshua loves us despite what we have experienced, and He can give us a fresh start to a life with no regrets." He raised her hand and kissed the back of it.

"I wish I could believe that," she said.

"Hey!" the fisherman yelled. "Are you expecting anyone to be chasing you?"

Nabonidus looked behind. Sure enough, two sailing ships, larger than the fisher's, were closing quickly. Three cataphracts stood on the bow of the first, lances in hand.

"Is there any place we can sail where they can't?" Nabonidus asked.

"Not this far up the river," the fisher replied. "If you think it might help, I can go closer to the shore near those willow trees and you can slip off the side. I'll keep going to draw them away from you."

"Perfect!" Nabonidus said. "The water is freezing, but it's a better choice than facing those lances. I'll give you extra if you can persuade them to look elsewhere."

The fisherman looked at the coins Nabonidus laid before him. "For that, they'll have to feed me to the lions before they track you down."

"You'll have to get us to the willows first," Nabonidus said.

VII

THE GREEK INNKEEPER was the perfect host as Daphne, Atossa, and Adrina devoured the plate of cheeses, flatbreads, oranges, dates, cucumbers, and generous slices of lamb. The watered wine quenched their thirst and he kept their cups refilled. Lamps hanging from the ceiling filled the room with the pleasant scent of olive oil and frankincense. The laughter of traders and pilgrims flowed like a gentle stream along the halls covered in Persian rugs.

They had bathed in warm water brought by servants, accepted warm changes of clothing, and settled into a spacious room with feathered pillows and quilted beds resting on wooden frames off the floor. A warm fire heated the room and left them drowsy.

Daphne moved a clay lamp from a counter to the table where she sat with Adrina. She wrung her hands and then pulled at her earlobes. "What do you think has happened to Hananel?" she asked, anxiously. "That nobleman could have destroyed him just for sport. Maybe we should have stayed together."

Atossa called from the washtub on the other side of a hanging blanket. "I need someone to scrub my back and my hair. It feels like I'm infested with lice."

Adrina replied, "Do it yourself. We've all had to clean up on our own."

"Seriously, I think I have lice. I need you to come and look."

"With the places we've been staying, she's probably right," Daphne said. "I can go if you don't want to."

Adrina rose. "She's my sister. I'll look after her—if I don't pull her hair out first."

The squabbling over the next hour, as lice were being hunted and destroyed, evoked a strong sense of family for Daphne. Images had filtered into her dreams during the past nights, and she caught the dread of not pleasing men. The haunting sexualized portraits dancing across the walls of the pillared worship center bounced in and out of her mind's eyes. Her neck and shoulders were so tight she curled up by the fire wrapped up in blankets.

Sometime in the night she lashed out as someone grabbed her by the shoulder, shaking her. "Daphne! Daphne!"

Eyes wide open in the darkened room, she took in the embers and a single flickering lamp across the room. "What's the matter?" she asked.

"You're having a nightmare," Adrina said. "You said, 'Selsus, don't.'" She rubbed Daphne's back. "You can sleep now. There's no Selsus anywhere around here."

Atossa arrived with another lamp, newly lit. "Who's Selsus?" she asked.

"Shhh! We want her to sleep," Adrina rebuked.

"Well, we're all awake now," Atossa said. "I guess we might as well find out who Selsus is. It looks like your memories are coming back."

Daphne rubbed her temples with her thumbs while soothing her forehead with her fingers. "In my mind, Selsus was a gladiator. I saw him standing over a big dark man with a dagger ready to take out the heart of the warrior wounded on the ground."

"The dark man is your husband, Nabonidus," Adrina said. "Selsus must be that German giant he defeated when we had to run for our lives." She patted Daphne's shoulder. "Don't worry, the lions ate Selsus. Your husband is alive. Perhaps this is a message from Yeshua that Nabonidus is in danger and that we need to pray."

Daphne got on her knees and clasped her hands in front of her face. "Yes, we need to pray."

As the three knelt together, a ram's horn blasted into the night.

Nabonidus's feet touched the river bottom first and he reached back and pulled Sasina under the hanging branches of the willow. Sasina's teeth chattered between her gasps for air. They had dived under water, and the bulky clothing nearly kept them there.

The fisher did as he had promised and sailed down the river. The two vessels following were closing on him fast. The three cataphracts standing on the bow of the first ship with their lances urged the boatman to go faster. The second boat held two cataphracts and two archers, and a third figure was standing on the far side.

Nabonidus was about to turn away when the figure in the back of the second boat turned and walked to the near rail. It was the Roman pretending to be an Egyptian, Vasilius. He'd been betrayed.

By the time the pursuers came within calling distance of the fisherman's vessel, Nabonidus had pulled Sasina from the water. No one appeared near them on the shore. They stepped across a roadway into a clump of bushes. Decency would have to wait as they shed their outer clothing and wrung water from it the best they could. "I'm assuming that if I haven't tempted you by now, then you'll be able to handle this," Sasina said.

"Don't assume anything," Nabonidus said. "Fortunately, right now, there's ice in my veins." They laid out their tunics on top of the bushes and hugged themselves, patting their arms for warmth.

"You know they won't quit hunting us until they find us," Sasina said. "Why don't you leave me somewhere and get away? You've put yourself in enough danger for me."

Nabonidus kept focused on the boats now locked together downstream. "Hush! Hush! I told you we're family now. I couldn't leave you even if I wanted to."

"Where will we go?" she asked.

"It seems that we have lost our allies," he replied. "We can return to face the regent, we can live like fugitives, or we can see if the Magi are looking for support for their cause."

She lifted her tunic and shook it. "I'm too cold. We need to find shelter." She pulled the damp clothing on over her head. "The regent won't be happy until we're on the throne or we're dead. The Magi will not forget what you've done to their militia. We can run and hide, but how will you find your wife if we do that?'

Nabonidus pulled on his own outer tunic and shivered in the cool breeze. "Let's find shelter and then see if we can think up something else for ourselves."

The three women remained on their knees as the ram's horn sounded again. Agitated voices swirled like an eddy around their shelter at the inn. "Respect my guests," the Greek innkeeper spoke up to someone. "No! I don't have room for the Magi. Try the next inn."

Additional shouts mixed with the neighing of horses and the clatter of hooves on the stones outside. "This place!" shouted a commanding voice. "I want this place for the Magi. Clear the guests, and we will make it worth your while. Refuse us, and you will regret it."

A solid knock rattled the door. "Friends, I need to talk with you."

Adrina threw on her robe while Daphne and Atossa scrambled to stand in the adjoining space wrapped in blankets. "We paid you for our stay. We have nowhere else to go," she called out through the door.

The innkeeper cleared his throat and then spoke again. "I apologize for the inconvenience. You may stay in my home. The accommodations are even better than this."

"We will be coming in soon, so hurry!" the commanding voice shouted.

The three women gathered their belongings, cinched their robes tighter, and sauntered outside. A golden coach drawn by eight coal black horses pulled up to the edge of the road. Four men wearing glittering headpieces and ornate robes descended and followed a nobleman into their quarters. Servants from the inn scrambled after them with platters of food and flagons of wine. In moments, the door was shut, and the innkeeper's wife motioned them to follow inside her chambers.

"The Magi like to stay here," the innkeeper's wife proclaimed. "It is not a good thing to ignore their desires. Thank you for making adjustments to keep the peace." She moved around the room straightening pillows, adjusted the bed quilts, and laid out a bowl of grapes. "They sometimes travel with a future queen whom they guard, waiting for the King of kings to claim her. She is of royal blood from some unknown family."

The room in the inn was indeed luxurious, with a golden bowl for washing, sumptuous quilts, plush carpets, and a roaring fireplace. "Where will you sleep?" Daphne asked.

The innkeeper's wife chuckled. "There is no time for sleep now. The roosters will be crowing soon, and the Magi are already crowing. If I wanted to sleep, I should have found a better line of work for myself." She stepped around items strewn on the floor until she reached the door. "I'll send over a food platter to calm your stomachs," she said, bowing on her way out.

Daphne, through a window, watched the innkeeper's wife march across the paving stones toward the kitchen area. "Poor woman. Hasn't found her voice and probably never will in this business."

Atossa joined her. "It's men like those Magi who keep all of us silent. They used to have a proud heritage when Daniel led them hundreds of years ago. You know that one of them, Balaam, first predicted the coming of the Messiah to Judah, and it was the previous generation of this very group who traveled to Bethlehem to honor Yeshua."

"Where did things go wrong?" Daphne asked. "Why are conditions so brutal now?"

Atossa turned to Adrina. "Your turn. What did Abba tell you?"

Adrina reached into a bowl of grapes and popped one into her mouth. She chewed slowly before speaking. "That first caravan went to Judah with such hope and faith. They came back confident they had found the new King of kings. They built up the hopes and expectations of people here, but others took the throne, and the Romans had their way in Judah." She reached for a cloth and wiped out a dish. "The young generation stopped believing and decided to find their own King of kings."

"Should Nabonidus have stayed in Ephesus?"

Atossa moved a stool closer to the fire and sat on it. "Your husband was a fighter, and things had gone bad. We had no choice but to run. Whether he should have come here or not, I can't say." She stirred the embers and added two more small logs. The flames leaped to life. "Our father was the one who put the thought of royal blood into his head. He wanted to find his roots by coming here. I don't think he truly expected that things would turn out this way."

Adrina extended her hands over the fire to warm them. "Didn't your husband say that he had a sister who was snatched at the same time he was?"

Daphne wrinkled her brow. "That sounds familiar, but I can't remember for sure. What do you remember about her?"

"I don't remember anything about her except that she existed," Adrina said. "Only when the innkeeper's wife mentioned the existence of some royal woman guarded by the Magi did I begin to wonder if she might be more real than we realized."

Daphne pivoted. "Are you saying you think my husband's sister might be here, guarded by the Magi?" She reached for a grape. "If she's going to be the queen, then there's no way that Nabonidus could be the King of kings."

"Unless they married," Atossa said.

"That can't happen," Daphne said. "I'm married to him."

"Only if you stay alive and the Magi don't find you first," Atossa said.

"What happens if the Magi find me first?" Daphne said as she slumped onto the bed holding her abdomen. The grim faces did not need explanation. "No matter what happens, this little one has got to be born. If I can't raise it, then you two must."

Wrapped in blankets by the fireplace in the inn, Nabonidus and Sasina warmed their feet and draped clothing over stools. The steam drifted up from the tunics. "Do you think the fisherman will tell them where to find us?" Sasina asked as she wrapped her hair in a towel.

Nabonidus picked up a piece of kindling and adjusted the fire so that it blazed again. "I paid him enough to keep quiet. Once a man sells his soul for money, it isn't that hard for him to sell it again if someone offers him more."

"So you think they might find us here?"

Nabonidus went to the window and looked through the curtains, which had been drawn. "I think if they believe we were on that boat, that they'll imagine we left it earlier upstream." He picked at the plate of cheese, flatbread, and cucumber, rolling a treat for himself. "Once these clothes are dry, we need to get some sleep, then move on as soon as we can."

"I wish you didn't look so tempting," Sasina said, running her hand along his arm.

Memories of his gladiator conquests with adoring women flooded his mind, and he shook his head. "True strength is often more than physical," he said.

"There's only one bed," Sasina noted. "I won't mind if you want to keep me warm."

Nabonidus knelt by the bed and pulled back the blankets. "No! I'm too vulnerable right now. You take the bed, and I'll keep watch." He returned to the platter and rolled up more bite-sized edibles. "I'm hungry, and I need to stay hungry for the right things." He turned his back. Her blanket fell against the back of his bare legs as she moved toward the bed.

"You're a strange man, Nabonidus Maimonides," she said. "You're bringing me to believe that I might exist for more than a man's pleasure. Normally, I would use all my training to persist in satisfying your senses, but today I will try to still my mind and sleep."

Nabonidus waited until the room quieted to her easy breathing and then turned. Sasina lay on her side, her golden head resting on her arm. He picked up the blanket and laid it gently on top of her. "Sleep, angel!" he said. "May God give me grace to stand strong with you."

When his tunic dried enough, Nabonidus tugged it on and headed outside. Dusk had come and there was no sign of the regent's soldiers. He draped himself in a dark headscarf and slipped out toward the market. Most of the vendors would be closed, and the few who remained might have some special deals for a late arrival. They might also have news of the day.

A fruit vendor, gnarled and bent, carefully laid the last of his produce in a reed basket but looked up when Nabonidus approached. "Peace to you, my friend," Nabonidus said. "What can you offer a man who is late to feed his family?"

The man pointed toward a donkey cart half-filled with baskets. "How much do you need, and what can you offer?"

A silver drachma was enough to purchase an entire basket of various fruits. As Nabonidus selected his food, the vendor gladly stood aside. "I haven't seen you in these parts," he said. "What is the news of the day?"

Nabonidus finished selecting what he wanted. "I am passing through. A traveler trying to understand the land of the Magi."

"The Magi, is it?" the man said. "You had best be careful in these villages if you want to talk about the Magi. The Magi have secured a queen from noble blood, and now they are looking to find their king while eliminating all pretenders. I remember my father telling me that the empire under the old order of Magi used to be much different."

Nabonidus set the basket on his shoulder. "How was the old order of Magi different than this order?"

The old man raised his hands to his temples. "How are they different? If only you had enough time to hear the ways." He adjusted a basket in his cart and untied his donkey. "These young ones are brash, forceful, impulsive, self-focused. The older ones gave us hope that peace would come again. I can't say any more."

"Thank you for your help," Nabonidus said. He lowered his basket to carry it in front of himself.

"Next time you're through here," the old vendor whispered, "try to avoid bringing the regent's men with you. There's one waiting outside the main gate for you. There's another hiding behind the potter's stall. They're clearly interested in you."

"Which is the best way of escape?" Nabonidus asked. He set his basket down.

The old man moved to the front of the cart. "I will dump my cart. If you get down on your knees, as if you are helping me, then crawl through the hedge and run down the path, you will give yourself time to get away."

When the cart dumped and the produce scattered, Nabonidus made much of his desire to help. "Wait! Old man," he said, "I will help you. Stay where you are." He squeezed through the hole in the hedge, trying not to hurry enough to shake the bush and give himself away.

The old man played his part well. "Don't trouble yourself," he said. "The fruit is old and ruined. No, No, don't clean it all."

An old olive tree provided a shelter to stand behind. The man outside the main gate slipped into the row of canopied stalls and motioned to the man by the potter's table. They ducked low and moved toward the upturned cart. Nabonidus ran.

The cramping passed, and Daphne rested while Adrina mopped her brow with a cool, damp cloth. Dawn wrapped its wings around the inn like a mother hen with her chicks. The songbirds twittered, and the voices of servants chattered from the courtyard.

"We should find a midwife," Atossa said from her place at the window. "The Magi are waiting for something out there. Two of them have been standing on the edge of the road since first light."

"Do you think they've called for reinforcements?" Daphne asked, still struggling to steady her breathing. "I can't imagine they think we're that dangerous."

"Maybe they forced Hananel to confess terrible things about us," Atossa said. She backed away from the window and knelt to stir up the fire. "What are we women expected to do on our own?"

"Shhh! Calm down," Adrina urged. "Adonai gave us minds just as He gave minds to men. Yeshua has promised never to leave us or abandon us. Before we think of running, we need to pray."

And they did pray. For Hananel, for Nabonidus, for the believers all over the world who this night needed Adonai to protect and provide. When all was done, they rose to their feet and consumed the rest of the platter delivered by the innkeeper's wife.

"I feel better now," Atossa said. "Wait, there's a caravan approaching, and all the Magi are out there now."

The two sisters stood by the window, waiting, while Daphne lay on the floor, hugging a pillow. An ornate carriage covered in black leather and silver inlays arrived pulled by four black Friesian stallions. When the door was opened, a tall dark woman descended to the ground. Her incandescent blue dress sparkled in the morning sunlight. Her elegant posture and confident stride set her apart as one at peace with herself. And yet, there was something incomplete about the smile she offered to those who bowed in her direction.

"It's the queen!" Atossa said.

"It's Nabonidus's sister!" Daphne added, struggling to get up. "I've got to go and talk with her to see if she knows where her brother is."

"No!" Adrina commanded. "This woman is with the Magi. Your husband was taken by the rebels. They are on opposite sides." She turned to pace the center of the room, rubbing her jaw. "If these Magi find you're the wife of a competitor for the throne, we are all dead. Somehow, we've got to find Nabonidus and tell him about his sister."

"How are we going to do that when we don't know where he is?" Daphne asked.

"There's only one place I know where we can find out," Adrina answered. "First, we have to find a way to get there."

The tingle up Nabonidus's spine stopped him in his tracks. The door was open. The moonlight provided enough shadow to deepen the darkness at the room's opening. Sasina might still be sleeping but he had closed the door when he left. The presence of the rebels at the market earlier spiked his adrenaline here.

Nabonidus circled the inn but there was no movement visible within the room. His eyes continued to adjust. The clench in his gut was too strong to ignore. He turned his head toward a dog bark in the distance. Something was out there.

Rushing through the open door, he raced toward the bed. The blankets were in disarray off to the side. He rolled toward the wall waiting for an attack. Nothing.

"Sasina!" he called. "Sasina, where are you?" The dog barked again, and he raced out the door toward it. The clatter of hooves on the roadway echoed, and the muffled cry of a woman drifted on the breeze.

The road was empty both ways when he emerged through the bushes.

The black leather carriage rumbled around the corner and the four horses brushed past Daphne as she stood, bent over, on the side of the road.

She sank to her knees and waved wildly. Four outriders streaked past as a woman extended her neck out the window.

A moment later, the carriage slowed and then stopped. The riders assembled around the queen, and then two of them rode back as Daphne stumbled to her feet. "Were you hurt?" one of the riders called out in Aramaic, then Greek, then Persian."

"I'm ready to have my baby," Daphne said. "I need to get to Susa."

The rider reined his horse around and trotted to the carriage. After a brief discussion he returned. "The carriage will turn and pick you up," he said. "The queen desires to take you to your destination. Show your respect or we will leave you on the side of the road again."

Daphne bowed and waited as the carriage slowly wheeled around in the middle of the road. "I humbly accept your help," she said.

Two soldiers hoisted her up into the carriage, and she lowered herself onto a bench opposite the queen. Between gasps, she gulped out, "Thank you, your majesty."

The woman nodded. "A strange thing for a woman in your condition to be on the road alone. Who else might we expect?"

"Your wisdom is only exceeded by your beauty," Daphne responded. "I had two women who are close friends staying with me at the inn. They wait behind."

The queen hesitated. "They will have to find their own transport." She scanned the forest and then waved at her coachman. "Drive on to Susa," she commanded. Turning, she asked, "Who are you?"

"In this land I am known as Humaya, but my true name is Daphne."

"A goddess?"

"A woman caught up in life bigger than myself."

The washboard surface of the roadway irritated Daphne's spine as she bounced along, but this was no time to be disagreeable, so she tried not to grimace. Her riding companion watched the passing landscape and then spoke. "I am under no illusion that you chose me to carry you to Susa by chance. Speak truthfully before my men discard you on the roadway and trample you with their horses. Believe me, it was suggested."

Daphne swallowed. "I would never want to presume upon your grace, your majesty."

The queen smiled. "Let's both forget this nonsense. I am queen only in the imagination of the Magi who use me as bait to draw out the true heir to the throne. I am a slave in a gilded cage at the mercy of those who prop me up for their own purposes."

The strong kick in Daphne's abdomen elicited a small yelp. She gritted her teeth. "This little one is active before you," she said. "I only hope to discern whether you are the one I think you are."

"And who might that be?"

Daphne patted her swollen belly. "Please allow me to tell you a story that may give us both guidance," she said. A nod gave her courage. "My memory is poor due to an accident, but this much I know. As a young girl I was taken from my family to serve in the temple of Artemis in Ephesus. It was in that city I chanced upon a gladiator who would become the emperor's champion." She waited, watching the face of her traveling companion. "We married, and this child is his."

"What is that to me?" the woman asked.

"That man was a Persian who told me a story of how his family had been ambushed near here. He was taken as a five-year-old boy and sold into slavery. He claimed to have a sister who he returned to find."

The wild eyes of the queen drew her in as the woman clutched hard onto the edge of her cushioned bench. "Where is this one who claims such a story?"

Daphne hung her head. "I don't know," she said. "When we arrived, he went to find his uncle. He never returned. We heard he was taken by the rebel soldiers of the regent south of Susa."

"Who is this uncle?" the queen asked.

"He is Ardeshir of the family Maimonides," she answered.

The queen leaned forward and grabbed Daphne's wrist. "You lie!" she said. "Swear before the gods that you don't."

The pain in her wrist was as intense as the pain below. "I swear before the true Creator of all men, and before His anointed Son, Yeshua, that I speak only the truth." She gasped as another cramp seized her. "My husband's name is Nabonidus, and you are his sister."

The woman lurched back into her seat. "He lives?"

"As do you, my queen."

"My name is Laleh of the family Maimonides." She leaned forward and spoke slowly. "We need to find my brother and release him. We also need to hide you for now. If my men hear you are connected to him, then they will kill you."

The shudder down her back had nothing to do with the bumpy ride. "I trust that you will keep this between us," Daphne said.

As if on cue, a rider approached the queen's window. "Your majesty, we need to take evasive action. The rebels have set up an ambush ahead. It may be good to leave your guest here."

Laleh pierced Daphne with her gaze. "This had better not be because of you."

"I know nothing about this," Daphne answered.

"Leave us both," the queen said. "Leave us a guard, and use the coach as a decoy to draw the rebels away."

Another rider approached. "The rebels have circled around. We need to make a run for it."

Nabonidus should have stolen a quicker horse. The old mare seemed to sag under his weight, and Nabonidus knew the rebels had outdistanced him. At least, he knew where they were headed. It was only a matter of time before he faced them again.

It might have been easier to walk away and ignore Sasina, but the regent knew his weakness. Even if he hadn't taken advantage of the seductive consort given to him, his heart had been twisted and claimed. There was no turning back now.

He dismounted the moment he saw the increased number of homes along the main road. Releasing the weary horse into a meadow, he crept along a pathway circling the settlement. Twice at outlying farms he looked for horses without success. At a third farm, a dozen young men practiced their archery. He dove under an arrow released in his direction. The group shouted and raced toward him.

He lost the pursuers in the forest trails as he forged higher into the foothills of the Zagros Mountains. He realized that whatever fate Sasina faced was beyond him now. By an outcropping overlooking a valley, he sat on a fallen log and prayed. "Yeshua, true Shepherd of Your people, we are lost without You in this land. Open up my eyes to see the way You have ordained for me."

A passing hawk caught his attention as it drifted on a thermal. In the distance, the white peaks of the Zagros gave the illusion that all was well. The Tigris River snaked through a lush valley where numerous peoples lived unaware of the battle for the soul of the nation. Susa huddled under a cloud of smoke in the distance. He followed the path of the meandering waterway until it reached near the regent's camp. Despite how hopeless the gambit, his next steps were clear.

The drizzling rain added discomfort to the quartet barging through the bush. "Widen the path," Laleh ordered the two militiamen slashing at the brush with their swords. "This mother has enough trouble without fighting through branches."

"I'm ... okay," Daphne stuttered between breaths. "No, I'm not. Rest. Cramps are bad."

"I am not delivering your baby in the middle of a forest," Laleh said. "And I'm sure you don't want these cutthroats handling your newborn."

"I should have waited for Adrina and Atossa," Daphne moaned.

Laleh halted, looking back. "These men are trained to fight, but the rebels have been destroying them with these ambushes. Reinforcements will be here tomorrow from the north, but that won't help them now. The regent is trying to destroy me to avoid competitors to his selection." She hurried after the militiamen. "Let's hope they give up after they find an empty carriage. The last thing we need is them charging through the forest after us."

"Why would you put yourself in danger like this, if you know the rebels are out to get you?" Daphne asked.

"One of the regent's representatives sent an ambassador requesting dialogue, and I agreed to meet. This ambush proves that deception and manipulation are still the language the regent lives by. I can't believe that old man is still alive."

A frantic motion by one of the militiamen cut the conversation short. He rushed back toward them. "Horsemen ahead, my queen. We will leave the trail and move toward that outcropping on the hill. If we need to make a stand, we need a place where we can protect you."

Laleh laid her hand on Daphne's shoulder. "Are you okay?" she asked.

"It looks like I have to be," Daphne paused. "I leave this little one ... in the hands of Yeshua."

It was late evening by the time he reached the river. The raft he found under a pile of branches suited his purposes and he launched it after securing a long pole to steer it. The current was turbulent and although he preferred to stand, he balanced on one knee and dug into the bottom near the shore to keep himself moving. The rebels would be back at camp with Sasina by now.

The unexpected rapids under the moonless, cloudy skies nearly dislodged him. He toppled over the edge of the raft and floundered, clutching the sides of the raft. He'd lost the pole and was at the mercy of the river now. The raft spun in and out of eddies as the night wore on. Fires along the shoreline reflected religious ceremonies, family gatherings, and pilgrims sheltering for the night. Music, chants, and voices hovered over the waters. No one seemed to notice his passing.

The idyllic scenes brought back memories of the small church in Ephesus where the apostle led the times of reflection over the bread and the juice. The decision to flee to Persia had been impulsive but Nabonidus's drive to understand his roots had been relentless. Daphne had been willing as long as he stayed by her side. Discovering who he was had only brought trouble, and it upset him that Daphne was all alone.

When he passed the wharf of a major settlement the chill overcame his resistance and perseverance. Sharp tingles, stronger than thorn pricks, settled in his feet and legs. A throbbing ache squeezed his calf muscle—enough to make him massage the area roughly. He slipped off the raft and swam toward a shoreline which never seemed to get closer. The lights in the settlement passed and still the current dragged him downstream. Strength was fading. "Yeshua, help!" he called.

"Who's there?" a voice called nearby.

"Help me!" Nabonidus called. "I can't make it to shore. Help me!"

A torch lit up on the prow of a fishing vessel. The fisherman looked across the water. "Where are you?"

Nabonidus raised his hand, waving. "Here! I'm past you now, caught in the current."

The fisherman launched off from the shore, paddling hard. "Keep calling," he said.

"Here!" Nabonidus called. "A stone's throw downstream. Hurry."

A few more hard strokes, and the vessel nearly ran him down. He pushed back hard and grabbed the oar as it dug into the water.

"Whoa!" the fisherman yelled. "I've got a big one." The boat spun in the water, and the fisherman reached over the side to give his hand to Nabonidus. "This is not the time of year to be swimming," he said. "What are you doing out here?"

Nabonidus dragged himself up over the edge of the gunwale and fell onto a pile of netting. He gasped in the chilly air as the fisherman stood over him. "I fell off my raft and couldn't get to shore."

"Sounds like a senseless thing to do," the man said. "Let me get this bucket straightened and back to shore. The gods have been merciful to you, unless you were meant to be an offering to them. We need to get you warmed up before you die of exposure."

VIII

THE TWO MILITIA men had done their work in leading the rebels astray closer to the roadway. The distant shouts of the warriors reflected confusion and frustration. The Magi's men had paid with their lives to protect their queen. Now, Laleh and Daphne had lost their last guardians.

"What do we do?" Daphne asked.

"I've never had to think about that until now," Laleh responded. "I've always had men surrounding me telling me what to do next. What do you suggest?"

Daphne stood and peered over the ridge of rock they sheltered behind. "I know a village on the other side of Susa where someone may help us. I don't know if I can make it there before the child comes, but it's our best hope. I think that if Yeshua is gracious, we could be there by nightfall—if no one finds us first."

Laleh joined Daphne on the ledge. "I don't know this Yeshua god you keep speaking of, but if He can get us through this trouble, then you'll have to tell me more. I hope He's not a Roman god."

Daphne put out her hand and took Laleh's arm. "Yeshua is not the God of one nation, and yet He is the God over all nations. One day we will talk. Your brother would be happy to hear that you might know Him."

"Lead the way, and tell me more of this supposed brother of mine," Laleh said. "I had given him up for dead long ago."

"Maybe later," Daphne said, groaning. "I'm not going to make it … ahhh … much farther." The sound of galloping horses had them hunkering down. Daphne tried to moan softly.

"Those are men we don't want to find us," Laleh said. "It's fun to disappear and realize that no one knows where you are. It may not be so much fun if they realize who I am and decide not to support me."

"This isn't so much fun for me... ahhh ... no matter who finds me," Daphne said between gritted teeth. "Tell me your story," Daphne urged. "A woman doesn't get to be queen on her own."

"You're right, there," Laleh said, pushing a branch out of the way so Daphne could pass. "When my parents were killed and I was snatched by the bandits, they took me to a marketplace." She hopped a puddle and reached out to help Daphne waddle around the outside of it. "Someone who knew my family recognized me and paid the price to take me with them. Their family was connected to the Magi, and they knew our family story." She stopped as a hunter holding two quail by the tail stepped out onto the trail in front of them.

The hunter's brow furrowed as he cocked his head and examined the women. He held up the quail. "You wouldn't be here flushing out a poor man's last game for dinner, would you now?" he said. "Where's your menfolk?"

"You know they aren't far off now, don't you?" Laleh said. "Have you seen them?"

The man stuffed the quail into a reed basket he carried on his back. "Can't say that I have, although a woman dressed as you are is likely to be able to help me remember what I might have forgotten."

Laleh turned and pulled a change purse out from between her breasts. She handed two drachma coins over. The examined coins disappeared into the folds of the hunter's tunic.

"Three days back, I saw a big, dark man with a woman heading to the river. She had hair like ripened wheat." The hunter checked over his shoulder down the path. "He was holding onto her hand like they needed to get somewhere fast." He nodded toward Laleh. "He was dark like you but big as a mountain. Don't suppose that's who you're trying to find?"

The twist in her gut stopped Daphne short. Was this Nabonidus? Had he abandoned her for another woman? Surely there weren't too many men who could fit the hunter's description. "Have you seen anyone else of interest?" she asked.

He held his hand out toward Laleh and smiled as another drachma dropped into his palm. "Keeping my eyes open is better than hunting these days." He set the reed basket of birds down on the ground and took some time to think. "I've seen more rebel soldiers and more of the Magi's militiamen riding around. Figure they might have to do with that dark man being a fugitive or something like that." He was watching their facial expressions closely. "I was at an inn on the outskirts of Susa last night and saw the priest from the Temple of Fire bringing in some woman. They didn't leave too quick either." He waited without success. "Can you tell me who you might be looking for? There's a lot of rumors going around."

"What kind of rumors?" Daphne asked.

"It seems that the King of kings may have been found. It's not clear who found him, though. We're expecting some bloodshed while the Magi's militia and the rebels sort this out. That's why I'm out here getting some supplies before it gets too dangerous."

"How big is your family?" Laleh asked.

The hunter smiled broadly. "Me, my wife, and six sons," he said. "We got one coming we're sure is a girl."

Laleh flipped him another coin. "For the daughter," she said. "Save it for your daughter."

Shouts from a distant road they had left behind alerted them both. Someone seemed to have picked up their trail.

"Is that trouble coming for you?" the man asked. "You're looking mighty troubled if it's not."

Laleh looked past the hunter. "Where can we go to hide for a while?" she asked. "This woman is about to give birth."

"Follow me!" the hunter said. "But first, let me prepare a distraction for whoever that is."

A towel wrapped around Nabonidus's waist after the fisherman's robe proved far too small. It seemed like half the night passed before Nabonidus felt warm enough, and yet there were times when the flames from the fireplace seemed to surge onto his own skin and deep into his veins. The pain in his toes tingled as he soaked his feet in a basin of warm water.

Blisters popped up on the shin, calf and thigh area. The scars on his bare chest and back screamed their presence.

"There's a cream for that," the fisherman said, pointing at the blisters. "My wife once cured a gash in my leg when my fish knife slipped. I think she told me that it had lint, turmeric, boar grease, and honey."

The blister patch expanded. "I once had a healer mend my wound with a poultice of purple cabbage," Nabonidus said.

"I've seen that too," the man responded. "But this isn't summer and there's no purple cabbage close by." The fisher's eyes focused a little too long on his chest where the scars were prominent. "Looks like you've seen your share of combat."

Nabonidus shifted his feet in the bowl away from the hearth of the fireplace. He nodded toward the bubbles forming. "These are blisters, not gashes. Is your wife some kind of sorceress?"

"Not at all!" The fisherman walked to the door. "Stay here, she's visiting a friend down the road. I'll bring her back."

The prod to his senses was as strong as a hornet's sting. Whose wife visited a friend in the middle of the night? Was there no safe place to hide?

He'd lost his sandals in the river so he had no choice but to run barefoot. He hobbled to the bed area and grabbed a blanket. There was no way to disguise himself but at least during the remaining short time before dawn he could try to find a hiding place. He grabbed an extra blanket and headed back to the river.

A large grove of date palms was the key marker for his directions, and his bare feet testified along with his eyes that he had found the tree plantation. His gurgling stomach rebuked him for not taking the small woven basket of fresh dates on the table in the fisher's room. The man had offered the fruit as part of his hospitality.

The fisherman's boat had been hauled ashore and overturned to drain the water. Nabonidus navigated by starlight toward the river and eventually found what he was looking for. He righted the boat, located an oar, and pushed it into the water. As he climbed into the boat, a shout erupted from the wharf nearby.

Nabonidus ignored the wharf's occupant and pushed off. In moments, he was paddling back out into the strong current. The river would carry him away faster than anything else.

※

The cramping gripped Daphne with a pain like no other she'd experienced before. She writhed on the reed mat as Laleh stood nearby. "Something's wrong," Daphne moaned. "It hurts so bad!"

The hunter's wife gathered boiling water, cloths, and blankets. "Here, wipe her face with this cloth," the woman instructed Laleh. "You look like you haven't seen a birth before. Hold her hand, sit with her. I've had six and this is not the easiest part about being a woman."

Laleh winced as Daphne gripped her hand and groaned.

"I've never been an aunt before," Laleh said. "Can you tell if it's a boy or girl?" She rubbed Daphne's forehead with a cooler cloth. "The way you're hurting, I'm imagining this has got to be a boy as big as my brother. Does your Yeshua have a ritual or prayer He orders for times like this?"

Daphne breathed in and out quickly. "*Have mercy!* is one." She rolled onto her side. "Rub my back. Oh, this hurts."

Laleh rubbed Daphne's back and tried to make conversation with the hunter's wife. "Do you think your husband managed to fool whoever was following us?" She sat rigid as Daphne breathed in and out quickly through her mouth. "Are you okay?"

"No! I'm not okay," Daphne snapped. "I'm being torn apart from the inside out. Keep talking about that stupid hunter. For all I know, the rebels have this place surrounded."

The hunter's wife set up a three-legged birthing stool. "Okay, you've been lying around long enough. Time for some real work." She adjusted the wooden stool closer. "In the old days we used to sit on the lap of a birthing assistant so the muscles could do their work in helping the baby be born. Your friend here looks like she wouldn't be up to the task, so I'm going to get her to massage and pamper you while we do the work. Now, ease yourself up onto this stool, and we'll get this baby out."

※

The stolen tunic hardly closed around Nabonidus but it helped with the chilly wind. Without a drachma to his name, without proper fitting clothing, and without sandals, Nabonidus's plight elevated his discomfort. Drifting snowflakes started to settle on shrubs and grass along the roadway. The boat had carried him far enough downstream to give him a direct path toward the regent's camp.

Traffic on its way to the harbors at the gulf steadily continued despite the weather conditions, so he plodded along the animal trails paralleling the human conduit. His size and the condition of his dress would alert those who trafficked in spreading news about the unusual. And this was the regent's territory.

Nabonidus rested briefly at the entrance to a small cave he noticed along the path. When a bear arrived unannounced, he backed away and returned to traipsing along the road. The dim moonlight on the fresh snow helped light his way. It was noon on his second day before he spotted the arched building where the regent lived. Snow continued to fall. A dozen cataphracts stood alert near the entrances.

He was tired and broken, but he was also proud and determined. He slipped around to the back of the property. A break in the hedge near the stable provided his way in. The horses nickered and stomped as they moved to keep warm. A broken cart rested against the back wall under an opening near the top of the barn. He hoisted himself up and through the opening. A large bed of hay provided a soft landing.

"I could smell you coming," a voice said. It was Vasilius. "You're too late. The regent commanded that the moment you step onto this land is the moment we feed Sasina to the lions. You should have stayed away."

Nabonidus lay where he had landed in the loft. The horses continued to move below.

"I could have made her happy," Vasilius continued. "Finding her in that bed where you left her alone makes me believe you don't know how to make a woman happy. Maybe I shouldn't have brought her back here. I just hope the regent decides to give the lions another chance with you as well."

Nabonidus rolled and peered over the edge of the loft. Vasilius stood facing him, holding a lance and a sword. "Betrayal is not the mark of a true warrior," Nabonidus said. "What price are you willing to pay to serve an old man who can hardly last through this winter?"

The Roman-turned-Egyptian chuckled. "I have no illusion that he would promote me to be King of kings, as he would do for you," he said. "To command a fighting force of men who may one day confront Rome itself. Now, that would be glory enough for me."

Nabonidus lowered himself slowly to the floor and faced the warrior. "You and I could have done what you desire," he coaxed. "I know the regent. He has a hold over you. How has he enslaved you to his service?"

Vasilius raised his weapons, setting his stance. "I serve of my own desire. Of course, he thinks that because he holds my two daughters as collateral that he can bend my heart any way he would choose."

"And what would you desire for your daughters?"

"Only that they be free."

"You and I can free them," Nabonidus said. "Where are they?"

"It's too late," Vasilius said. "I've already had to make my choice. I had to choose to offer Sasina or my two daughters to the lions upon your arrival. I cannot offer my own flesh and blood."

Fire burned in Nabonidus's gut. The same fire that raged when he had fought as the emperor's champion in the Ephesian arena. Why had his arrogance and pride driven him to come back one more time? He should have fled and focused on finding Daphne. Revenge was now his undoing. The regent had known his weakness even as he fought off the temptation right before him. Life was cheap and meaningless to a man who only sought power.

Vasilius backed toward the door. "You can come peacefully on your own, or you can face those who are here ready for you. You can give yourself time to discern what other options there might be, or you can end your struggle here and now. The regent is waiting."

Nabonidus knelt and bowed his head. "Yeshua, into Your hands I commit my life."

The cataphracts rushed in and pummeled Nabonidus to the floor, where they secured his hands behind his back with a leather strand. He was stripped of his robe, dragged to his feet, and force-marched toward the arched building. The regent sat on his throne with the golden-robed Sasina beside him. While others in the room examined him unabashedly, she lowered her eyes.

"It seems we have to start our relationship over again," the regent said. "It is clear that neither your consort, your students, nor my own cataphracts have been able to humble you so that you are ready for the throne. It is time to change that. We have waited long enough." He pointed at a warrior and beckoned him over. Taking the cataphract's lance, the regent resumed his monologue. "Persia could take Rome as easily as I took this lance. We could do it more easily if you sided with us. You no doubt know the humiliation of the Roman army when one thousand of our cataphracts and nine thousand of our horse archers destroyed seven legions." He handed the lance back to the warrior. "Twenty thousand of their elite warriors executed in battle with our bows, ten thousand captured as prisoners, and ten thousand fleeing for their lives. We brought Rome to her knees, and she has never dared to march this far again. Sometimes those who are arrogant need to be humbled."

Two of the warriors formed their armchair for the regent and he sat in it like a king. He nodded toward two archers who escorted Sasina behind him. The cataphracts marched Nabonidus next in line. The onlookers followed.

When the pit of lions came into view, the next steps in the drama were clear. Sasina turned toward him, "Why did you leave me? I honored you with my respect. I listened to your stories about Yeshua."

One of the archer's escorting her slapped her. "Shut your mouth. Save your voice for what is ahead."

Nabonidus wrestled with the cataphracts holding him and almost gained his freedom before he was clubbed from behind. Dazed, he marched groggily toward the feast of the beasts. Vasilius stood at the edge of the pit. The growling lions were clearly hungry.

The group dispersed around the perimeter of the pit. The regent raised his rod like a scepter. "To rule an empire like ours, there must be mercy, and there must be justice. But most of all, there must be submission to authority. Without obedience there can be no will strong enough to guide such a diverse peoples." He glanced around at each of his subjects, piercing them with his gaze. "It takes a strong hand to mold the hearts and minds of rebellious people. There are too many contenders for the weak to survive."

He nodded toward an archer who raised his hand in signal. The crowd parted and two young girls were escorted to stand near Vasilius. They were not yet ten. "The lions are hungry," the regent said. "It is time to feed them again. I have given the honor of deciding their next meal to our Egyptian friend. He knows his choices."

The crowd melted away from the warrior as he gently placed his hands on the shoulders of his two girls. He pulled them back from the edge of the pit. Slowly, he moved toward Nabonidus. "You had better be who I think you are," he said. He turned and walked toward Sasina. When he stopped in front of her, terror filled her eyes.

The regent nodded, and the archers dragged Sasina to the pit. "Save the robe," the regent ordered. The men stripped it off of her. "Now!" the regent ordered, and Sasina was hurled to the waiting jaws.

Her final scream was "Yeshua!"

The scream seemed to unleash an unseen wave that hurled the archers, the Egyptian, and the crowd back. Even those who held the regent fumbled and he tumbled to the ground.

Nabonidus crumpled to his knees and roared, "Nooooo!"

The first two nights with a new son meant little sleep. Daphne did her best to nurse, rest, and care for herself, but the house was a busy place. Laleh was disquieted, pacing around the home, looking out windows, muttering to herself. The hunter dropped in regularly to boast about his latest endeavor to mislead those searching the woods. The six boys dropped in to see the little one and to complain about the baby crying in the night.

On the third day, Laleh sat cross-legged on the floor near Daphne and reached out for the little one. "He's the perfect shade of brown between you and my brother. I haven't seen anything more beautiful in all my life." She patted his curly hair. "I know you wanted your husband to help with naming his son, but I'm about the closest thing you have to family. We have to give this boy a name. How about Ardeshir, after his great-uncle?"

Daphne propped herself up on an elbow. "That sounds like a good option. Why don't we put it on the list to consider?" The little one's lips were sucking away during his sleep. She smiled. "This one even dreams of eating. He'll be as big as his father."

Laleh rocked the baby. "Why don't you go wash yourself, and I'll take care of the crown prince?"

The hunter's wife boiled some water and set up the wash area. Daphne shuffled across the room. She exalted in the luxurious warmth and the sense of cleansing. Scattered portions of the hymns and songs sung by the church in Ephesus came to her, and she hummed what she'd forgotten. The sense of missed fellowship washed over her and robbed her of the joy that had filled her earlier. She dried, dressed in a clean robe, and stepped carefully back to the bed. Laleh wasn't there.

Looking into the main living area, she saw one of the younger sons playing with a collection of rocks and pine cones. "Son, have you seen Laleh and the baby?"

The boy looked up from his play. "They went for a walk with Momma."

An uneasy feeling squeezed up from her gut. She stepped quickly to the outside doorway. No one was visible. Around the corner of the house two boys could be heard arguing loudly. She moved in that direction. The two wrestled over a fox skin their father had likely trapped.

"Boys! Boys!" she called. "Be kind. What is happening?"

The younger one released his hold on the fox tail. "I had it first. He's always taking things that father gives me. Make him give it back."

Daphne moved toward the older boy with her hand outstretched. "Why don't you give your brother back his fox skin?" She waited, but the older boy refused to move.

"We don't have to listen to you," the boy said. "You and your black baby need to go back where you came from. My momma says there are getting to be too many of your kind around here."

She'd developed a hard shell against the verbal barbs of prejudiced adults, but the arrows from a child took her breath away. She set her hands on her hips and stared him down. He dropped the fox pelt in the mud and walked away. Turning to the other boy she asked, "Have you seen Laleh and my baby?"

"They went with the soldier," the boy answered nonchalantly. "Momma complained that he didn't give her enough money. She's gone to find father."

Her mind spun, confused. "What do you mean, they went with the soldier? Where did they go?"

"I don't know. He had a horse for her to ride."

"Did she fight with him?"

"No."

"Did he hurt the baby?"

"No."

"Which way did your mother go?"

"I don't know. I think that way." He pointed north.

"Which way did the soldier go with my baby?"

"They went that way." He pointed west.

She ran to the path, and there was no question that horses had been there moments before. Fresh hoofprints and steaming dung gave evidence. Had she been set up by Laleh to steal her baby? Had the hunter and his wife betrayed them for money? It was too much to take in.

The cataphracts left Nabonidus for a week on his bed in the old room. A haunting loneliness reverberated off the walls without Sasina in the space. What good had his morals done her now? How did his stand for purity and right make a difference? The regent had still had his way. The shutters he'd smashed only served to let the cold air in. The broken marble washbasin only left him dirty and miserable.

The ripping growls of the pride tearing into Sasina's flesh left him with nightmares. Her cry, "Yeshua!" echoed like an empty prayer in the chambers of his soul. What good had it done to tell her the stories of a God who loved her? A God who valued her as a daughter and a princess? Why hadn't he ripped through the cataracts and archers and fed them all to the lions. Why hadn't he twisted the head of the ugly little regent off and thrown it in as well?

A knock each day accompanied the food being delivered. He hadn't touched it all week. His tongue stuck to the roof of his mouth. Weariness filled his body, mind, and spirit. Numerous times a day he envisioned himself jumping into the lion's den so they could have their way. And yet, in the back of his mind, an image of a baby kept forming. This was the time when Daphne would be delivering. If only he knew where she was.

On the seventh day, Vasilius pounded on his door. "Nabonidus. You have paid your penance. I had to choose between my daughters, Sasina, and you."

Nabonidus stayed quiet.

"Listen, you washed-up gladiator," Vasilius persisted, "the regent is setting up a combat drill for all the new cataphracts. You and I against them all. If anyone understands the importance of putting the past behind, it has to be a champion gladiator like you."

Nabonidus remained still.

"Fine!" Vasilius yelled. "I'll leave you to be chopped up for lion food. I thought we could do this together. You guard my back, and I guard yours." Apart from a horse neighing the outside went silent.

When they came for him, he was ready. He let them kick his door down but he was on his feet and facing them. Snow had piled up over the grounds, and the footsteps of the Egyptian could be seen. The tracks of the six cataphracts at his door could also be seen. So could the tracks of another who had circled the building. Nabonidus stood in his doorway waiting. One of the cataphracts briefly looked up, and Nabonidus knew. An ambush.

"I forgot something," Nabonidus said to the cataphract. "Wait here." He propped his door over the opening and slipped toward the back window. Sure enough, the footsteps ended under his window. The sun was shining toward the front of his house and no shadows betrayed the presence of someone close. He carefully removed the broken shutters and pulled himself out. Using the window ledge, he hoisted himself up and climbed onto the roof. Someone had been here recently.

Crawling on hands and knees, he reached the peak of the house and peered over. The new recruit crouched, ready to drive a lance into his back when he emerged. The other cataphracts chattered below, urging him to hurry out. He slipped over the top and crept down. One quick twist of the neck and the recruit lay dead. He hadn't made a noise.

Taking the lance with him, he slipped back off the roof and created footsteps toward a hedge. He retraced his steps and waited outside the house. The taunts continued until the door was kicked over. Surprised shouts erupted. A cataphract arrived at the window and the lance in Nabonidus's hands ended his vigil quickly. Another shouted a warning, and the group rushed out.

As they circled the house, Nabonidus slipped back inside and waited. One of the men saw the footprints heading for the hedge, and the group barged off after the fugitive. They were so focused on their pursuit they didn't see Nabonidus follow their previous tracks back to the regent's arched home. Nabonidus was inside before his ruse had been solved. He moved toward the throne room and huddled behind a thick curtain.

Vasilius was talking with the regent in the throne room. All the regular cataphracts crowded into the space. "My desire has never been to take your place or the place of Nabonidus," he said. "I didn't dare to kill Nabonidus because he was your anointed, and I would never undermine your plans. Besides, he is no fool. Even now he is probably feeding those recruits to the lions."

"He's weak and confused," one of the cataphracts said. "He hasn't eaten all week. The ambush will get him. Even a trained gladiator can't beat seven armed men when he has no weapons."

"His mind is quick," Vasilius said. "I know you want to set the two of us against each other. The two of us together are better than a dozen of your best warriors."

The regent stood to his feet. "If he somehow survives, then you'll have your wish. First, you'll face the recruits."

Vasilius bowed. "I don't understand why you work hard to decimate your own forces," he said. "You know better than I."

"Saving your own daughters showed me you are too vulnerable to trust," the regent said. "Four of you—go and see if Nabonidus still lives."

"I should go with them," Vasilius said.

"Silence!" the regent ordered. "You would find some excuse to turn an innocent walk here into a slaughter so that you and the gladiator can escape. There is no place out there for the two of you. I'm the only one who understands the mysteries, magic, and methods of the Magi."

A messenger marched in and waited. "Speak!" the regent ordered.

"He's gone!" the cataphract announced. "Two of the new recruits are dead. He vanished like smoke right before their eyes. His footprints end without reason."

"Nabonidus!" the regent called. "I know you're here. Step out. I promise you no harm."

Daphne was on her knees in the mud sobbing when the hunter found her. The youngest son stood nearby hunching his shoulders. "What fool thing are you doing out here in the cold?" he said. "Here, I'm doing my best to keep you hidden, and you're announcing your presence to the world."

Daphne struggled to her feet. "Where have they gone?" she asked.

"Who?"

"Laleh and my baby! Where have they gone?"

The hunter looked around. "How should I know? They were here with you when I left." He turned to his son. "Do you know anything about this?"

The boy shrugged until his father shook him by the shoulders. "Spit it out," he said. "What happened to the baby?"

"A man came looking for the lady, and Momma sold her to him. She took the baby with her."

The hunter got down on one knee, looking his son in the eye. "What man? When was he here?"

The boy broke into tears until the hunter slapped him. "Stop it!" he commanded. "What man? When was he here? Where did he go?"

The boy sobered up. "I don't know what man. He was a soldier with a sword and lance. He said that Persis told him that a strange black lady was in our house."

"Persis? That no good son. Which way did the soldier go?" the hunter persisted.

The boy pointed down the trail he had shown Daphne. "He rode his horse that way. He had another horse for the lady."

"Did he hurt her?" Daphne asked.

The boy shrugged. "She just got on the horse and left," he said.

"Where's your mother?" the hunter broke in.

"She went to town," he said. "She said she was sick of living like a peasant."

The hunter ran for his shed. "I'm going after the soldier. No soldier breaks into my house and takes what is mine to protect." He raised his bow for emphasis.

"Be careful," Daphne called as the man mounted his horse.

"He's the one that had better be careful," the hunter snarled.

"All of you, out!" the regent shouted as Nabonidus stood defiantly before him. "You two, stay!" he ordered, pointing at Nabonidus and Vasilius. The cataphracts, clearly dismayed, shuffled out of the room. The hunched old man stroked his white beard with one hand and clenched his other fist. "How many more have to die before you learn your place?" he said. "There will be one more test. If you survive it, I expect you to take your stand with us and lead us to the throne of this empire."

Nabonidus stood quietly, back straight, head up. He would not cower before a bent-over, wizened figure—not now, not ever.

The regent shifted his eagle-eyed gaze to Vasilius. "Your life is now tied to his. You stand or fall together. The test begins at dawn." He sat down on his throne. "You will leave from here at first light. The cataphracts will surround this place. All you have to do to gain the throne is to reach the Temple of Fire in Susa." He lifted his hand in dismissal. "Now, go and prepare yourselves."

"He had a sword, what could I do?" the hunter's wife said. The donkey cart filled with food and new purchases stood beside her on the trail. The falling snow filled in the track left by the cart wheels.

"He gave you money!" Daphne said. "How could you take his money for my baby?"

The woman retreated to stand on the other side of the donkey. "It wasn't for the baby," she said. "He gave me the money to say thank you for looking after his queen. I thank the gods for his generosity at my hospitality."

"Why did your son Persis go and find the soldier?" Daphne asked. "How did he know where to go and who to talk to?"

"It's not like you two don't talk out loud," the woman said. "We can all hear you talking. We didn't have to be one of the Magi to understand that there was a reason they were looking for you. You don't understand how hard it is to care for six sons with winter coming." She grabbed the donkey's halter and pulled it toward the shed. "You can talk to my husband when he returns. I'm not going to be able to keep you in this house anymore."

Daphne retreated to her room, knelt down and put her forehead and palms flat on the floor. "Yeshua, You who see the orphan in the darkest shadows, You who brought the worlds into being, You who understand the broken heart of a servant girl like me: place Your hand on my son, Ardeshir. Wrap Your hand around my husband, Nabonidus. Stand with us in this place where we have only You to fight for us."

When the hunter's horse arrived riderless that evening, the hunter's wife howled as loudly as Daphne had done. The two oldest boys hopped on the horse and set out down the trail their father had taken. "We'll bring him home," they said. The hunter's wife howled louder.

By morning, with no sign of the boys, Daphne wrapped herself up in an extra robe and blankets and set out on foot. Three shekels had been given for her loss. She'd never find her baby sitting in the middle of a forest with a woman howling like a wolf.

IX

THE FIRE AT the temple shrine felt good as Nabonidus and Vasilius warmed their hands. "I counted six dead and four wounded," the Roman said. "I don't think they knew what they were up against." He unbuckled his bronze breastplate and set aside his helmet.

"It is best not to boast in the sufferings of others," Nabonidus said. He laid his weapons on the hearth. "The regent sent those poor boys like sheep to the slaughter. We could have killed at least a dozen more if they dared to stand. I think half of his men were dispersed to cover other roads we might have taken."

"What do you think he's trying to do through all this farce?" Vasilius asked. "I think he's either using us to get his warriors in shape, or he's trying to convince us that we are invincible enough to fight against the Magi's militia."

Nabonidus tapped his boots against the stone wall and shook the snow and mud free. "The warriors he sent against us were inexperienced, overconfident, ill equipped. Clearly, he wanted us back at this place where we rescued Sasina. There is something about this temple he considers part of his plan."

Vasilius turned his back to the flames. "It would be like that old man to set up an ambush to destroy us at the moment we think we triumphed." He rebuckled his breastplate and retrieved his helmet. "I thought I had enough calluses for one day. How do you want to go about this? He'll probably send someone who looks innocent to draw us into the trap."

Nabonidus picked up his trident and sword. "Look toward the women's quarters. It's that Vashti woman we saw with the priest. Sending a woman would be a perfect way to disarm us."

Vashti made no pretense about her destination. She ignored the three dead cataphracts lying prone at the entrance to the temple grounds. "So you two dare to return after desecrating this sacred space?" She glanced over her shoulder and straightened her robe. "I have a message from the Magi for you and that weasel of a regent." When neither Vasilius nor Nabonidus responded with surprise, she continued. "The Magi have your sister and your son. If you will deliver the head of the regent and return where you came from in Ephesus, then we guarantee their lives."

Nabonidus noticed shifting shadows behind the hedges. He focused on the woman who stood patiently in front of him. "You deceive no one with this ambush," he said. "Enough men have died already today. What evidence do you have that the Magi have my sister and my son?"

Vashti moved closer to the fire and opened her palms over the flames. The fire roared into an inferno of ravenous heat shooting out arrows of glowing embers. Nabonidus and Vasilius stepped back, but the woman stood immobile as her robe burned around her. "I give myself to the god of the fires to show my word is true," she said. The shawl and hair of the priestess ignited like a lamp, yet she stood reaching up to the heavens. Her knees buckled and she fell in a heap as the flames consumed her like a hungry dragon.

"To the women's quarters," Nabonidus said. "The ambush is set behind all the hedges. There are horses moving toward the front entrance. They will charge us to drive us into the lances of those who wait."

The two sprinted to the building and burst through the door. An arrow bounced off the shoulder of Vasilius's breastplate and clattered against the doorframe. The large open room they rolled into erupted in screams as half-dressed women dashed down a hall toward other rooms. "They'll try to burn us out of here," Vasilius said. "We'll cut up through the roof and then jump over the hedge. This time, they brought archers."

Nabonidus crouched in the center of the room facing the open door—sword in one hand, trident in the other. "What if we dressed like women and then rushed out with the others?"

"They'll expect something like that," Vasilius replied. "Besides, who are we going to fool as two giants running among dwarfs?"

"The regent probably has his veterans here," Nabonidus said. "How are we going to use the training we've given these men against them?"

Frostbite nipped at her toes as Daphne stumbled into the first village at the end of the snow-covered wagon trail. No signs of the soldier, the hunter, the queen, or the baby were evident along the way. She stamped her feet on a cobblestone path to rid her goatskin boots of the snow and mud. The hunter's wife had graciously gifted her the worn footwear.

Townspeople bundled in long robes and furs huddled around fires or hustled through the snow toward homes or places of business. Daphne scanned the residents. A bricklayer was beating a donkey stubbornly refusing to pull its load. A butcher standing outside his shop held two geese upside down by the feet. A trio of ragged young men poked at a fire with long sticks. A priest strolled down the middle of the road with five young boys listening to his pontification. Families, bands of bearded elders, a cluster of women haggling with vendors over fruits and vegetables—it all appeared innocent enough.

She stepped into the street and crossed over to check out any hiding places her shelter had kept her from seeing. Two soldiers, holding the reins of their mounts, huddled under trees at the far end of the street. Neither of them had swords or lances. Daphne stepped in behind a group of women emerging from a clothing shop and followed them down the street. Halfway along, she saw the perfect witness.

An old woman sat roasting corn on a grill over a small fire. A passerby bartered for the treats as she added fresh corn to the flames. The distinctive aroma of the charred husks drew her in. "That sure looks good," Daphne said. "How much would it cost a poor pilgrim to have one of your treats?"

"Six for a shekel," she said. "Name's Bita. I don't sell to strangers."

Daphne rubbed her hands together and then tucked them into her armpits. "Name's Humaya. Staying with the hunter's wife in the forest. Trying to find a woman friend who came into town a few days ago."

"If you want to talk, the corn will cost you three for a shekel," Bita said without blinking. "The hunter's wife had quite a few coins to spread around yesterday," she said.

Daphne laid a shekel into the palm of the corn roaster. "My friend had a baby and came on horseback with a soldier," Daphne said. The shekel disappeared.

The woman turned the roasting corn and poured water on the coals. Smoke hissed up into Daphne's face. She stepped away. The woman rubbed both cheeks with her fingers and closed her eyes. "Yes!" she said. "I saw the black woman with a bundle. It could have been a baby. She followed the soldier willingly and got into a black leather coach pulled by four black horses."

Daphne looked around. "Where? Where did they go?" she asked.

The woman rolled a cob off the grill into a wooden bowl. "This is an expensive time of year for corn," she said. "A woman like me has to work hard to provide for so many little ones. Gifts are always appreciated."

Daphne placed a second shekel in the woman's palm. It too disappeared. One left. "The baby is mine. It was stolen. I need to get back my son."

The woman sat back, folded her hands, and closed her eyes. "Yes! I see the queen with your son. She is not yet where she hopes to be, but she is beyond your ability to reach her."

Daphne snatched a cob of corn and rolled it between her hands. "I have nothing else I can give you," she said. "The hunter's wife has sent me away. I have no one of my own and no place to stay."

Bita nodded. "For one shekel you can get a ride to Susa and stay at the Temple of Fire. They have a home where they take in women who have nothing and who are willing to give themselves to make the worshippers happy. They will feed you and clothe you if you do your work well."

The ram's horn shattered the stillness as Nabonidus and Vasilius lay on the roof of the women's quarters. They'd already sent the women out two by two to delay the ambush while they dug a hole in the roof. The blast came from near the Circle of Heaven pool at the far end of the property. A dozen pigeons launched off the edge of the roof nearby. The few cataphracts, crouched behind hedges as they prepared for ambush, hesitated and looked toward the blast.

A young servant scrambled into the opening near the pile of ashes where Vashti had given her life. "It's the Magi's militia," he shouted. "Run! Run!"

Dozens of camouflaged soldiers threw off the branches and coverings they had been hiding under and sprinted toward the entrance. "Assemble at the crossroads," yelled one of the warriors as he led the sprint away from the compound.

Vasilius rolled toward Nabonidus. "It's a good thing we didn't have to fight. I don't think we would have seen half of those men before they surprised us. Do we run?"

"Where would we go?" Nabonidus replied. "Lie still and see what happens. They'll be coming from the other side, and we can see them over the roof. As long as these pigeons don't give us away."

Moments later, a dozen riders trotted into the plaza where the women were sweeping Vashti's ashes into a basket. "Where have the regent's men gone?" the leader called down to the quaking women.

"That way," pointed one of the women, showing the way.

"It's amazing how one trumpet can win a battle," the leader said, laughing. "Go and get the queen. We'll house her and that baby overnight. Someone should have gone back and gotten rid of the mother."

"Now that we have the heir to the throne, do we need the queen anymore?"

"Hush! She's insurance for us in case something happens."

The riders dismounted and several searched through the premises where Nabonidus and Vasilius hid. One of the searchers asked a priestess, "Where is the best place to keep the queen?"

"The monument near the Circle of Heaven has the best facilities," she answered. Nabonidus was certain she had noticed him lying flat on the roof.

"What are you looking at?" the militiaman asked.

"Pigeons," she said. "I don't want the pigeons to be disturbed."

"Fine! The men will stay here, and the queen can stay at the monument."

When the caravan leader stopped to let her off in Susa, Daphne shuddered. The wind swooping down off the white peaks of the Zagros was one reason, but the thought of being at the mercy of Vashti and the priest was another. The last time she worked at the Temple of Fire, her concussion and amnesia kept her from knowing who she was or what she believed. Now what would she say? Her breasts were aching from the need to feed her boy.

If only Hananel, Adrina, and Atossa were here. They'd help her find her son and they'd help her survive this nightmare. But no, she needed to face reality. Perhaps Vashti would let her sweep without having to satisfy the worshippers.

Four of the Magi's militiamen stood at the front gate. Others were inside making advances at the ladies sweeping around the main shrine for the Temple of Fire. What was going on? Daphne covered her lower face against the howling wind and circled around to a hedge where a woman dressed as a priestess stood throwing seed for the pigeons huddled together on the roof of the women's quarters. "What's happening?" she asked.

The priestess pulled her headscarf across her mouth and spoke softly. "The militiamen are here with their queen. You must go."

"I have nowhere else to go," Daphne said. "The queen has my baby. I need to speak with Vashti."

"The queen found a wet nurse for the baby," the woman said. "Vashti has gone the way of all."

"Where has she gone?"

"She has given herself to the fire god in penance for her waywardness."

"You mean, she's dead? How am I going to get my baby back?" Daphne said.

The priestess pointed up, but as she did two of the militiamen stepped out of the building and yelled. "What are you two doing?" One of the two grabbed the priestess and dragged her inside the building. The other reached across the hedge to grab Daphne, but she backed away. "Run, scum!" he said. "Unless you are ready to serve as a priestess here and make us happy, then go."

Daphne headed for the closest trail and hid herself among the trees.

Nabonidus and Vasilius lay flat listening to the exchange below. The newcomer sounded like Daphne, except she was speaking in Persian. He'd only heard her in Greek or Latin. The howling winds whistled across the rooftop and swept away the conversation. Words like *baby*, *Vashti*, and *penance* whisked by on the wind, but nothing made sense. The words of the militiaman dismissing the woman were clear enough. She was not a priestess here.

Nabonidus cupped his hand over his mouth and whispered toward Vasilius. "That woman sounded like my wife. Did you get a look at her?"

Vasilius smiled. "I've had days like that. No, I've had my head down the same as you. She's probably some village girl making a delivery."

As night fell, the two men slipped off the roof, rolled over the hedge, and skirted the perimeter toward the Circle of Heaven. The wind had died down, but the chill wrapped its fingers around everything and everyone. "Don't expect me to jump in that pool again to create a diversion," Vasilius said. "The queen has a lot more protection than the last woman you had to rescue."

Flickering light from the main window of the pool's monument highlighted the four militiamen standing on the stairs. A single torch anchored into a stand in the garden added its own light. The black leather carriage rested near the pool. The horses were nowhere to be seen.

"That window in the back is still the best way in if they haven't fixed it," Nabonidus said. "Get rid of the torch, and push the carriage into the pool. That should provide enough distraction for me to get in and out."

Vasilius peered over the hedge. "You do realize these guards have lances and swords?"

Nabonidus gripped his forearm. "You do realize I have to squeeze through a small hole, extract a queen under guard, plus take out a wailing baby, all without getting killed?"

"Good point!" The Roman-Egyptian sprinted away into the dark.

Nabonidus circled through the trees until he reached the bush closest to the broken window. The night was so dark he couldn't distinguish the window from the wall. He crept up and ran his hand along the stone surface until he reached the shuttered window. With the distraction of shouts echoing into the night around him, he pried off the first slat.

When the last slat was freed, he hoisted himself up and into the room. The fall was not graceful, and he was still on his knees when a sharp edge dug into his neck. "Don't move an eyelid," the woman's voice warned. A hand rested firmly on his head. "If you had anything to do with my carriage getting wet, then kiss your life goodbye."

Nabonidus froze. "Laleh?" he said.

The hand on his head lifted. "Who are you?" she asked.

"Don't bring a light yet," he answered.

"Tell me who you are, or this dagger goes straight through your neck."

"It's Nabonidus."

"Stay!" the woman commanded. Her footsteps blended into the din of soldiers yelling in front of the monument. A torch appeared and filled the room with light. A door shut. Nabonidus blinked as his eyes adjusted. "You're not my brother," she said. "You're some oversized rebel warrior here to molest me. How did you know my name?"

Nabonidus sat back against the wall with his hand shading his eyes. "We were on the road to Susa from the farm when the bandits came. They killed our parents and snatched me. I was five and you were seven."

"What did you do with my carriage?" she asked. "How did you find me? And why did you sneak in here like this?"

"One question at a time," he said. "I didn't know you were going to be here. I came to Susa from Ephesus to find Uncle Ardeshir, but the regent captured me. My wife was staying near here." He waved the torch away, and she moved it to the side. "I heard the militiamen say that since they had my son, they didn't need you anymore. I came to rescue you."

Laleh stood with the torch and dagger and turned toward the door. "No! This is too bizarre." She walked to the door, opened it, and stepped out before Nabonidus moved. "In here!" she yelled.

Nabonidus was halfway out the window when hands grabbed his legs and pulled him back into the room. A fragment of broken shutter dug into his side and ripped a deep gash. Fists pummeled him before he hit the floor. He tried to cover his head, but his arms were pinned. Someone grabbed his forehead and tried to hammer the marble floor with the back of his skull. He stiffened his neck and held on.

"Stop! That's enough," Laleh commanded. Two more punches still landed.

"Where's the other one?" a militiaman yelled in his face. "Or are there more?"

Nabonidus sat quiet.

"Tie him up and take him to the fortress in Der," Laleh said. "I'll come later with the baby."

"We can take the baby," the militiaman said. It was the same voice Nabonidus had heard earlier saying that they didn't need the queen any longer.

Laleh glared. "The baby and the wet nurse stay with me. Now go!"

Daphne huddled in the hedge near the Circle of Heaven pool as the chaos continued. She was hurting badly from not being able to feed the little one. Half a dozen men had retrieved horses to pull the black leather carriage out of the water. She had been in this exact place on the ground when the broad-chested Roman in dark had crept into the plaza, doused the torch, and pushed the wheeled carriage into the pool.

He had brushed past her on the run, knocking her over. A tree provided the perfect refuge as she scaled higher in the branches. She waited as torches lit and men scoured the grounds. Two of the men tracked the fugitive past her and onto the trail leading into the forest. A baby's demanding cry split the night air before being silenced.

Whoever had caused the mischief, it seemed he wasn't the only one. A large dark man, with a blanket over his head, was marched out of the monument's main door and down the stairs. A trail of red smeared across the white marble plaza. "Throw him in the pool," a soldier ordered.

Two militiamen dragged the dark man to the edge of the pool and jumped in with him, attempting to hold him under with the blanket still over his head. As they found their feet on the bottom it was as if Neptune himself boiled up from the depths. The men arched into the air and then disappeared under the surface, kicking and struggling.

An archer pulled his bow and three cataphracts poised their lances, but they couldn't distinguish friend from foe in the dark recesses of the pool. As the drama unfolded, a certainty grew within Daphne. It was Nabonidus. She slipped down a branch and then stopped. It would do him no good if she exposed herself now. She had to find the baby.

Every soldier and spectator stood around the pool, waiting for the combatants to surface. Daphne crept down the tree, branch by branch, until she reached the ground. The plan was fuzzy but taking form in her mind. She skirted behind the hedge until she found the gap leading to the side of the monument.

"Weapons down!" commanded the queen. "Take him alive. No matter what."

Daphne kept to the darkness and approached the building as Nabonidus rose out of the water with a roar. The soldiers seemed to surface and float facedown. One soldier launched his lance, but Nabonidus sidestepped and caught it by the shaft. "Who else will die?" he roared.

She'd never seen her husband like this. As all focused on Nabonidus, she moved up the steps and into the open door. A baby could be heard crying in a back room. Her baby. She slipped into the room and lifted him from the cushion on the floor. She gave her breast, and the little one latched on and whimpered into contented sucking.

Now what? Was there another way out? She scurried down the hallway looking into each of the six rooms. In the last room was an open shutter where the breeze flooded in. As she stepped inside, a large shadow separated from the darkness. Her scream was stifled as the warrior put a hand over her mouth and pulled her from the door.

"Give me the child," he said.

"No! It's my son," she said.

"Daphne?" It was the Roman-Egyptian who had pushed the carriage into the pool.

"Who are you?" she asked.

"I'm with your husband, here to rescue the baby."

"How can we get out?"

"The window!" The man pulled her toward the opening. "I'll let you down, hand you the baby, then show you where to run. Quickly, your husband is sacrificing himself for you."

It took six of the cataphracts holding Nabonidus down in the pool before he finally surrendered. Vasilius had let him down again. Nabonidus endured the beating as the militiamen dragged him out of the water and bound him hand and foot. A woman had been called to repair the wound in his side, and he lay silently as she worked amid the mocking of the soldiers.

During the fighting, he had seen Laleh watching. She didn't want him dead. That meant she was giving him time to prove his identity. If only he could find a way to get free and grab his son. If that was going to happen, Vasilius would have to intervene soon.

He was on his knees, waiting on the final wrapping of his abdomen, when Laleh raced out of the monument's main door. "The baby!" she called. "Who took the baby?"

The clench in his gut rivaled the pain in his side. His son was gone. He'd come so close. If he found whatever soldier harmed his baby, there would be no mercy. He wrestled against the ropes but only served to tighten their hold around him.

"Yeshua!" he called. "My son."

A sentry standing nearby smacked him on the back of the head with the shaft of his lance. "Stay still, you oversized dung-beetle before we drown you for good."

As he lay on the marble plaza like a beached walrus, four men holding down his limbs, the four black horses were hitched up to the carriage. Towels were used to dry down the leather interior before blankets were laid out. The two dead soldiers were laid out on the plaza beside him, their unseeing eyes fixed in a death stare. He turned away and focused on the horses.

Once the queen disappeared with half a dozen others in search of the baby, the remaining men took extra liberties with their feet and fists as they walked by him. The wound in his side reopened as numerous kicks were planted in his abdomen.

Sometime in the night, he was bundled up and tossed into the back of the carriage. A bag was put over his head and tightened around his neck. He struggled to breathe as the endless ride over washboard roads began.

It was dawn by the time Vasilius permitted Daphne to stop moving. Her feet were numb with the feel of frostbite. Their breath condensed in a heavy vapor in the morning fog. Her stomach grumbled; she had not eaten in two days. A small empty shack, likely set up by a hunter, provided shelter from the wind and cold. The baby had suckled on the way and slept peacefully in her arms as she sat cross-legged on a reed mat covered with a sheepskin. She rubbed her feet, trying to restore the circulation. They tingled with needle-like pains.

"You know your husband keeps looking for you?" Vasilius said. "He's been through a lot staying faithful to you and trying to escape from the regent. They want to make him the King of kings, but that means marrying his sister and getting rid of you. I would win a great favor if I brought the heads of you and your son to the rebel leader."

Daphne stroked the head of her son. His hair was soft and curly. "I'm sure you would have done that by now if you were going to. Why don't you tell me who you are and why you're fighting so far from home with my husband?"

Vasilius pulled out a stool closer and sat on it, watching her feed the baby. "My wife used to feed my daughters just like that," he said. "They'd be crying away, and she'd take them and let them suckle, and before I knew it, they'd be out."

"How old are your girls?" Daphne asked.

"Six and nine," he answered without hesitation. "My name is Vasilius, by the way."

"Roman!" she said. "This country is sworn enemies of Rome. No wonder you pass yourself off as an Egyptian. What brings you so far from home?"

Vasilius stretched his arms overhead and let out a great sigh. "Revenge, mostly." He rooted through the cupboards and kicked at a rat running across the floor. He stood over Daphne. "Lucky boy. At least he's got something to eat." He held up his dagger and stepped out the door.

A short time later he was back with handfuls of greens. "Dinner!" he said, holding up his collection.

"What did you find out there?" Daphne asked. "I hope you know enough not to poison us."

Vasilius found a flint in a corner of the room and struck it against a rock face to set up a spark. He fired up some dry tinder he had shaved into a pile. Soon the blaze brought heat to the room, and Daphne shifted her reed mat in front of the hearth. She wiggled her toes. "I'm not sure I'm ever going to walk again. My feet feel frozen."

The Roman-Egyptian chopped the greens into a small metal bucket. "Haven't seen one of these things before," he said. "Wonder how an old hunter can afford one? I'll boil up some water, cook the greens, and see what else we can find to add to this." He scavenged around without success. He headed toward the door again. "Maybe I can find some roots to add to it or maybe even a hare. If the gods look with favor on me, I'll find a deer." He looked down on Daphne rubbing her feet. "Don't you go running off without me. You know they'll have their trackers after us soon, and you won't last without me."

Vasilius had hardly left when the door to the shed flung open. Daphne cradled her son from the gust of chill air. Before she could speak the door slammed shut. There standing with her back against the door was a small waif—perhaps eight or nine but little more than skin and bones.

Frizzled hair sprouted in all directions like a wind-blown sheaf of wheat. Dirt smeared from chin to forehead. "Ahura Mazda, forgive my darkened ways," the child whispered. With that, she cracked open an egg on a knuckle and slurped out the contents. Dropping the shell on the floor, she turned toward the fire. That's when she saw Daphne. "Mother of Bel!" she exclaimed. "What are you doing in here?"

Daphne attempted a smile. "If this is your home, my son and I were cold." She pulled the blanket away from Ardeshir's face so the girl could see. "There's a man with us who went out to find something to eat. He'll be back soon."

The girl's eyes went wild. "I thought it was the hunter leaving," she said. "I stole an egg from the farm close by and thought I could come in and get warm. Don't tell him it was me."

"Where's your mom and dad?" Daphne asked.

"Gone, they are!" she said. "Left me and my brother when I was six and he was four. I got so tired of my brother complaining he was hungry

I went out to find food. When I came home, he was gone." She eyed the fire. "I think someone snatched him. I've been running from the snatchers ever since. You're not one of them, are you?"

Daphne shook her head. "No, little one. I'm not one of them. Neither is the man who is with me." She tucked Ardeshir under the blanket again. "We've got to keep him warm. Here, you come by the fire and get warm."

The waif gingerly stepped closer to the fire with her muddy goatskin slippers. "The hunter comes and goes, you know?" she said. "When he goes, he doesn't come back until he catches something. I try to wait for him to throw out the bones. Sometimes there's bits of meat on them." She rotated slowly in a circle. "I could share the bone with the baby when I'm done."

Daphne nodded. "You can have the bones. He's a little too young for bones. Maybe the man with me will find us a hare or a boar, and we'll have ourselves a real feast."

The girl sat down and put her head on Daphne's shoulder. "I miss my mom," she said. "She used to call me Yasamin, but my dad called me Yas. I don't know which one I am, but if you want to call me Yasamin or Yas, I will probably answer. Some days I forget I had a brother, and on other days I forget I had a mom and dad." She slipped her feet out of the goatskin slippers. They were as dirty as if she hadn't been wearing the footwear.

"Did you have a name your mom or dad used to call you different than the ones your friends used to call you? It's probably a pretty name?" She snuggled under Daphne's arm. "What did you call the baby? I bet he's got a nice name too? Does his dad know his name? Do most moms and dads forget their children? I keep thinking that one day I'll see them again." In an instant her eyes and then her lips closed, and she went limp as a sack of oat flour.

A thumping on the door startled the girl. She wriggled out of Daphne's grasp and backed into a corner—eyes wide with terror. "Don't let him get me," she said.

Daphne rose and opened the door. It was Vasilius, arms loaded down with roots, berries, and a hare. "Tonight, we feast!" he said. The girl tried to squeeze by him, but he blocked her with his hip. "And who is this?" he growled.

Daphne glared at him and shook her head slightly. "This is my friend, Yas," she said. "We just met and were trying to warm up together by the nice fire you made. We're both very hungry, and we'd be happy to help make something to eat."

Vasilius moved away and dumped the harvest on the hearth by the fire. "I'll skin the hare, and you boil up the rest. We'll roast him and have ourselves a fine stew." He crouched down before Yas. "I've got two girls just about your age, and I'm missing them a lot. I guess we'll be happy to have you eat what Ra has provided."

"You mean Ahura Mazda," Yas said.

"No, he means Yeshua," Daphne said.

"Who's Yeshua?" Yas asked.

Daphne set Ardeshir down on a blanket and started sorting through the roots, berries, and greens. "I'm not sure how much I remember about Yeshua, but I'll tell you what I can. I bumped my head, and sometimes I forget the way things used to be."

"Do you remember your mom and dad?" Yas asked.

Daphne wrinkled her brow and rubbed her cheeks. "No, I don't remember my mom and dad. I don't remember any of my family."

Yas wrapped a tiny arm around Daphne's waist. "I know how you feel," she said. "It's like a big empty space where your heart should be." She leaned in hard and tears trickled down her cheeks.

It took most of the day to rumble along the roads to Der. The torrential rains had worn small trenches across the main routes, and the carriage wheels bounced along as fast as the horses could pull. Nabonidus lay in the mud-filled storage area of the carriage, tied up but not tied down. He was tossed like a ball from side to side and vainly tried to protect his head along the way. The ride was worse than a beating.

When the clip-clop, clip-clop of the hooves stopped, he released himself like putty to mold to the muddy floor. Four militiamen opened the back of the carriage, grabbed him by the feet, and pulled him out onto the ground. The fall winded him. As he gasped for breath, a dozen daggers dangled above him.

"Doesn't look like a King of kings or even a prince of Persia to me," one of the men said. He was dressed differently than the others. Tight leopard-skin leggings with leather boots fitted under a loose-fitting vest that hung to the knees. A crimson cape flowing over shoulders and down to the knees matched the snug cap perched on his head. His long gray beard spoke of age and wisdom. "We Magi can't allow pretenders to rise in the empire."

"The queen told us to hold him here," one of the militiamen responded. "She will no doubt want to consult with you and the others."

"So this is the rumored brother," the Magus said. He crouched and ran his hand along Nabonidus's jaw line. "Even covered in mud, they do look alike. Maimonides always do."

"There was a child with another woman," the militiaman said. "We had it for a short time, but someone snatched it from us."

The Magus stood and motioned to the militiamen who wrestled Nabonidus to his feet. "If we had the heir, we could have disposed of the queen and her brother. For now, this is who we have for the throne. Send out the hunters to find that child. Dispose of the mother."

"What about the rebels?"

"You mean that old toad who calls himself the regent?" The Magi smiled. "While he held this black demon, we had to tread carefully. Who knows what magic he may have used to manipulate this beast? It's hard to believe the emperor's champion could be reduced to this quivering specimen of humanity." He turned and walked away, calling over his shoulder, "Prepare him for the queen."

X

FOR TWO DAYS, Daphne, Vasilius, Ardeshir, and Yasamin sheltered in the hunter's shed, taking up the entire floor space when they slept at night. Daphne and Vasilius alternated sleeping times to watch for unwanted visitors. Apart from a curious bear scratching at the door, there was only the peace of birdsong by day and crickets by night. With the increasing chill in the air, Vasilius kept the fire going constantly.

The third morning, while he scoured the forest for another hare or deer to supplement the greens they chewed on, Yas jerked upright from her place playing with Ardeshir. "He's here!" she whispered to Daphne.

The muscles in her neck and shoulders tightened. "Who's here?" Daphne whispered back.

"The hunter," Yas said as she backed into a corner behind the door.

Daphne snatched up Ardeshir and faced the door. A moment later the hunter burst through the door with his dagger drawn. "Who are you, and what are you doing here?" he snarled.

"I got lost in the forest and needed a place to shelter from the cold," Daphne blurted. "My baby is too young to be out there for long."

The hunter pivoted and fixed his eyes on Yas. "And this little monster again! Is this one yours as well? She owes me a lot." The man grabbed for Yas who rolled under his reach and scrambled to hide behind Daphne. "All summer you've been harder to catch than a wise old jaguar. This time, you're not going anywhere. You'll be sold to the rebels to pay off your debt."

Daphne fumbled in her tunic and withdrew her last shekel. "Sir, for your hospitality. This is all I have." She tossed it to him.

The hunter caught it, examined it, bit it, and then shoved it into his pouch. "I'll take this for the baby," he said. "You and your daughter are still going to have to pay your way. Get your things; I'm marching you to the market to see what you might be worth."

The three slaves who stripped Nabonidus and doused him with buckets of water scrambled out of the way as the former gladiator kicked out from his position on the floor. "Enough!" he shouted. "Untie me and let me finish washing. I need to relieve myself." He struggled to his knees and held out his hands to one of the slaves who was little more than a boy. "You! Free me. Now!"

The slave looked toward the five cataphracts laughing and mocking Nabonidus nearby. Their lances rested against a wall near the entrance some twenty paces away. His hands and knees were shaking.

One of the men jutted out his chin in permission. "You go ahead and free that dog. Cut him deep so there's no more kids to chase after. Show him that even a little boy like you can take him down."

"Don't hurt me," the slave whispered to Nabonidus.

Nabonidus braced himself. He was naked but unafraid. "Free me, and I won't hurt you," he said. "I shall be your defender."

The slave stepped up to a cataphract and held out his hand. The soldier offered his dagger, and the boy took it. For a moment, he looked deep into Nabonidus's eye and then gave a slight nod. With a quick stroke he severed most of the rope tying Nabonidus and turned away. Then, with a yell, he drove the dagger into the side of the cataphract.

Nabonidus snapped the remainder of the rope and stepped toward the chaos. The boy eluded the grasp of another militiaman and raced with the dagger toward Nabonidus. He dropped it and kept running. Nabonidus snatched it up and faced the two soldiers who had mocked him. Two others attended their fallen comrade.

"Get out of our way!" the leader yelled. "No one gets away with assaulting the Magi's guardians."

Nabonidus stood firm. One guardian looked toward the lances across the room. He withdrew his own dagger and set himself for attack. His partner did the same. The daggers slashed at the air an arm's length from Nabonidus.

Nabonidus circled and outflanked the two as they attempted to manipulate him into an indefensible position. He noted that both brandished weapons in their right hand. The warriors were experienced and refused to get within striking distance.

As Nabonidus neared a cupboard, he could see the eagerness on the warriors' faces to trap him against the barrier. He feinted right, leaped toward the cupboard, and jumped left, slashing the arm of the soldier closest to him. The return dagger traced a red slash across his thigh. He rolled and bounced back to his feet—energy rushing through his veins. The man's dagger dropped as he reached for the wound.

The second combatant glanced briefly at the injured comrade and then charged. A sidestep and a thrust to the belly stopped him.

Nabonidus saw one of the two remaining healthy militiamen running for his lance. He pivoted, snatched up the cape of the first militiaman and followed the slave boy out the door. Halfway down a set of stairs, he came face to face with Laleh.

"You didn't have to tie us up like animals," Daphne said as she struggled to cuddle Ardeshir and to keep from tripping over Yas, who yanked on the restraints.

The hunter herded his captives along the soggy trail, prodding Daphne with his bow when she lost her tug-of-war with the girl. "Keep moving!" he ordered. "I should get a healthy price for such feisty slaves."

"We are not your slaves," Daphne declared.

A crashing sound off to the right made them all stop. The hunter nocked an arrow and focused. "Probably a boar," he said.

"Maybe you should go shoot it for dinner," Yas taunted.

The hunter shrugged. "I'll get it on my way home after dumping you into the market."

A chopping ahead to the left made the hunter stop and listen. "Someone getting wood for their fire," he said. "Hurry! We don't want to be late." He turned to Yas. "I can't wait to see you tied up there on that platform, naked as a newborn rat, crying about how cold it is while those Arabs poke you and check your teeth and teach you not to lip off against your elders."

"That's no way to speak to a little girl," Daphne said.

The hunter chuckled. "Good news for you, woman. They don't have favorites at the market. They treat young and old alike."

Yas dug her feet in like a stubborn mule, throwing Daphne off the trail and forcing her to clutch Ardeshir hard. The boy began to scream.

"Shut that thing up, or I'll feed him to the wolves," the hunter demanded. He lifted his bow to strike Yas, but instead sank to his knees. His eyes grew big. His mouth opened but no sound came out. He reached for his chest, clutched it, and fell face first into the ground. A large dagger protruded from where his heart would be.

Daphne covered her mouth and backed off the road.

Yas slid in beside her. "What is it, Momma?" she whined. "Is it the wolf? Don't let it get me."

"Stay still, child," Daphne said. "It's not a wolf."

As they huddled, looking back down the road, someone spoke from behind them. "Didn't expect me, now, did you?"

Yas screamed and then hugged Daphne's leg, crying.

"Vasilius!" Daphne said. "Look what you've done to this little girl."

Vasilius knelt down beside the fallen hunter and yanked out his dagger. "Help me get him off the road. The last thing we need is some road sentry coming after us." He rifled through the man's clothes and pouch, collecting several coins, a small carving knife, and a chunk of dried fruit.

Daphne handed Ardeshir to Yas and helped Vasilius pull the hunter into the bush. "Another short time and we would have been sold at the slave market," Daphne said.

"He could never have passed you off as the mother of that girl," Vasilius said. "You're dark as dusk, and she's light as dawn. Don't get too attached."

"Sometimes the heart does things the mind doesn't understand," she replied.

Vasilius handed the dried fruit to Yas. "I've been tracking you from the house. This stubborn little girl gave us all a chance to catch up." He rubbed the top of the girl's head. "Now, where do we leave this waif?"

Yas clung to Daphne and looked into her face. "Can't you keep me? I'll be good, and I can help look after Ardeshir. I'm a good big sister."

Daphne sank to her knees. "What if your mom and dad come looking for you?"

Yas hung her head. "They won't be coming for me," she said. "They died in the fire set by the militiamen." Tears started, and then sobs racked the little one's body.

Daphne hugged the little girl while Vasilius stood silently. "Of course you can be my little girl," she said.

Laleh stared down the lance at the militiaman threatening to skewer the man who claimed to be her brother. "Stop right there!" she commanded. "Who let this man loose?"

The warrior lowered his lance, glaring at the fugitive daring to stand near the queen. "We were preparing him to greet you, and he escaped."

"Naked?"

"We were washing him down. He was dirty from the journey."

"Dress him properly, then take him to meet me in the throne room."

"But he killed two of your guardians."

"And what were you doing to him while he was tied and helpless?"

The warrior bowed and turned back to his comrades.

Two slaves directed Nabonidus to follow them while four more militiamen with lances followed close. "Give me time to recover from the journey before you bring him," Laleh called. "He looks as tired as I feel."

Money crosses many boundaries, and the hunter's coins provided two rooms at an inn for Vasilius and Daphne, who shared hers with Yas and Ardeshir. She was sure Vasilius got the better rest. He managed to visit the market early and brought food for two days. The rest soothed her soul as much as her body. The warm wash reached right to her spirit. Thinking of reasons to explain a second child was not getting any easier. Where was Yeshua in all this?

Yas had pressed her from the first hour in the room. "I don't want to get in that wash bucket. I'm not dirty. I'm hungry. I'm not going to sleep in this place where someone will find us and trap us again."

She coaxed the little girl down beside her as Ardeshir suckled. "Yasamin, rest with me a while. If you're going to be my daughter, I need to get to know you."

"Yasamin is what my momma called me, so you can only call me that if you're for sure going to be my momma."

"I will be your momma."

"Why did that man say you couldn't be my momma because you're dark as dusk and I'm light as dawn?"

Moments passed as Yas examined her potential mother's face. Daphne wrinkled her brow, pursed her lips, and set her jaw. Words eventually arrived. "Put your arm next to mine," she said gently. "See the difference."

Yas suspended her arm next to Daphne's until she tired of the effort. "We both have hands, elbows, and shoulders. I don't see the difference."

"Then I guess there's no reason I can't be your momma," Daphne said. "If anyone says anything strange like that again, then you tell them what you just told me."

"Okay!" Yas said. "I think I'm tired now. It's easier to sleep in the day because there's no wolves running around."

"At least wash your feet," Daphne declared.

"Why?" Yas asked. "When they're dirty, they look more like yours. No one will wonder if I'm your daughter if our feet look the same."

"You're so smart," Daphne responded. "But no one sees your feet in bed, and it will make it easier to wash the bed if you save the dirt for outside."

Yas formed a little pout, walked to the washtub, and stepped in. "Hey, this is warm," she said. "Can Ardeshir come in if I'm careful with him?"

The throne room where Nabonidus's sister sat was far from the ghoulish glitter flaunted by a Roman senator or the rebel regent, but it declared a clear claim to royal privilege. Gold glittered in the reflection of light from hundreds of golden lampstands along the edges of the room. The walls and floors boasted the finest of Persian weave in seamless carpeting. Teakwood tables with ebony inlays bore foods from orient and occident. Sheer silk curtains draped behind the throne and the chairs on both sides. Musicians featuring stringed and percussion instruments blended their offerings in gentle rhythms of international melodies. A hundred warriors, backs as straight as the lances in their hands, lined the walls.

Laleh watched him survey the room and then rest his eyes on her. She wore an Indian sari, purple with inlaid diamonds. Her hair was woven into a fountain of curls; her dazzling tiara captured every lamp in the room. She popped a grape into her mouth and chewed it slowly as the giant scarred warrior, claiming to be her lost brother, approached and stood before her. She sat cross-legged and barefoot. "What do you think of my little kingdom?" she asked.

"This is not the way I last saw you as a child," he said. He wore white pantaloons and sported a royal blue shirt with balloon sleeves and a tight collar. Leather sandals adorned his feet.

"And how did you last see me?" She picked up another grape and poised it near her full lips.

"Screaming! Being taken by bandits." He eyed plates of cheese squares and flatbreads but made no move to help himself. Rich wine filled silver goblets lined along the table center.

"You were young," she said. "What could you remember?"

"A boy who sees men kill his parents and then take the only one he loves does not forget."

"Sit with me! Eat something!" she said, waving her hand at the bountifully laid table. "I especially like the dates."

"And the apricots," he added.

"Tell me of your life. Leave nothing hidden. How did those barbaric Romans treat you?"

"When I defeated the champion from another country, they treated me like a king."

"And when you lost?" Laleh leaned forward, waiting.

"I never lost." Nabonidus straightened his shoulders and set his legs.

"Why are you here?" She leaned back, fingers fishing on the plate for another date.

"Your men brought me."

"And you consider this winning?" she asked. She chewed the date slowly, eyeing him. "Why have you come to this country if you were so exalted in Ephesus?"

"An old man told me that he knew of our family story and that I might be the lost prince of Persia. I came to find if I might be more than a Roman toy to pleasure the mobs. Could I be of royal blood?"

"And what have you discovered?"

"I have discovered that our uncle prophesied my coming. I have discovered that I have a sister. And I have discovered that I wish I had stayed quietly with my wife in some place where there was no hunger for a lost prince."

"Do you know what I have discovered?" she asked.

"No."

"I have discovered that in all my memories there has only been me in my family. I have grown up believing that I am the only one to share my family's tragedy. And now here you are, claiming to be not only the lost prince but also the lost brother."

Nabonidus took a step toward her but stopped as the lances of two cataphracts flashed inches from his chest. He gathered himself and stepped back. "Sometimes, in our search for identity and meaning, we discover things about ourselves and others we wish we never knew."

"Tell me the rest of your story."

Daphne stood beside Vasilius on the bank of the Karkeh River as Yas played with Ardeshir on a blanket nearby. Despite the weather, the river traffic of fishing vessels and small freighters was heavy. A passenger ferry, more like a raised raft, nudged into the wharf nearby. "Here's the question," Vasilius said. "Do we cross this river and run so that your children will be safe, or do we head back toward the Ulai River and search for your husband before he gets himself killed?"

Daphne pulled her cape tighter against the biting wind. "Yeshua knows how to care for Nabonidus, but I'm not sure he knows how to stay out of trouble. I would appreciate it if you could leave us in a safe space and then go look for him. The Magi's militia probably captured him and took him back to be with his sister." She shivered. "They will want him to marry her, but he won't, and that will put his life in danger. You must try and rescue him."

Vasilius waved a no signal to the ferry master who was motioning for them to board. "Do you think you can hide in Susa?" he asked Daphne. "You spoke of Hananel, Adrina, and Atossa. Do you think you can find them while I'm away? I know you're independent, strong, and intelligent, but I don't like leaving you on your own."

Daphne scooped up Ardeshir and snugged the blanket around him. She took Yas by the hand and nodded. "To Susa it is. I will search for the three, and you will search for the one. I like my chances better than yours."

Nabonidus had sketched out his life with the cross maker Caleb, his life as a rower on a Roman warship, and his life as a gladiator. It all seemed a distant blur as he sampled the feast before him. The presence of his sister so close was dizzying.

"Those are nice stories," Laleh said, "but anyone who knows anything could make themselves out to be a suffering hero. The scars on your body tell me that you've suffered a lot, but how do I know that you're not a pawn of the regent trying to make a power grab at the throne?"

Nabonidus stayed quiet, propped up on his elbow on the dining couch, munching on a dried apricot.

Laleh continued her verbal interrogation. "I know what you did to the Magi's militia—killing a whole cohort. Why do you think these men will allow you to live, never mind gain the throne as their King of kings? You were naive to step into the hornet's nest of the Magi."

"I think you want to first establish whether I truly am your brother before thinking about my aspirations for any throne," Nabonidus said. "It is true that I was captured by the regent and forced to fight. I thought he had my wife, and I wanted to rescue her. What do you think of Daphne and our baby?"

Laleh sat upright on her couch. "First, the mother of the baby is named Humaya. This lets me know that either you are not the father, you are not my brother, or the little one is not the heir to the throne we are searching for." She stood and rubbed her chin thoughtfully. "The Magi would like to torture the truth out of you. Do you think that is necessary, or do you have another story you wish to tell?"

He stood up and towered over her. Three of the militiamen stepped forward with their daggers drawn. "I have one clear memory of you when you were young," he said. "When you lied to mom, your left eye would twitch. We always knew when you weren't telling us the truth. Your left eye is twitching."

Her hand moved to cover her left eye. "No one could know that," she said.

"And yet I do." He smiled. "So what is the truth you should be telling me?"

She motioned for him to sit, and they both sat facing each other. "I met your wife and I've held your baby. His name is Ardeshir."

"So where are they?"

Laleh hung her head. "I left your wife at a hunter's cabin in order to protect her. Someone took your son from the monument at the Temple of Fire where we found you. I can only hope that they're both alive." She looked around at the army of militiamen standing erect around the room. "I am as much their prisoner as I am their queen," she said. "Without the Magi's permission I can't go anywhere or do anything."

"What can I do?" he asked.

"You are now their prisoner too," she said. "The Magi are trying to secure the Parthian empire while the regent is trying to restore the former Elamite dynasty. If you are to be King of kings, you must know the history of our peoples."

Conversation halted as the wine steward refilled their glasses and hovered close by for further instructions. Laleh raised her head slightly to signal Nabonidus about the newcomer.

"All I know is that we and the Romans have been at war for as long as anyone can remember." He picked up an orange and bit into it, letting the juice run down the stubble on his chin before wiping it away with his forearm. "Susa alone has a story bigger than I can remember."

Laleh nodded. "The world's first great war was fought on these lands when the king of Kish invaded," she said. "A thousand years later, Hammurabi conquered Susa and took away the city gods. Ashurbanipal of Assyria wreaked his revenge on us. Cyrus the Great and Darius the Great beat us down and built us up." She too picked up an orange but peeled it. "Those of you out west know Ecbatana and Persepolis as important cities because of Alexander the Great, but Susa is the queen city here."

"Why do you stay here in Der if Susa is so important?"

"The Magi are building up a library here," Laleh said. "The tablets and scrolls fill a building as big as a palace. They collect knowledge from all over the world. We have the histories of the Achaemenids, Seleucids, Egyptians, Romans, Greeks, and Armenians to the west, and the Qin and the Han dynasties to the east."

"Do you have anything on the Hebrews?"

"Of course, but they are such an insignificant people that their wisdom will pass away in the dust of time," she said. "Apart from the caravan of Magi, many years ago, who searched for a candidate out there to be the King of kings, there is no reason to pursue what that land has to offer. They will soon be crushed under the boot of Rome."

"I know the One for whom those Magi searched, and He will not pass away in the dust of time," Nabonidus said. "His name is Yeshua, and He is the true King of kings."

Laleh set her orange aside on a table. "Your wife said something very much the same," she said. "One day you will have to tell me more about this competitor to our throne."

"There is no competition," Nabonidus said. "I need you to help me find my wife and son. How can we do that together?"

Laleh turned her back on the servant who hovered close, taking in all their conversation. "Get me some better grapes," she ordered. "These are too sour."

When the steward left, she spoke quickly. "The Magi will make us marry to secure the empire. They will also try to kill your wife and son." She looked over her shoulder to see the steward returning. "Tonight, the guard will change when the light is least. You must be ready to get away and go find them. Your wife mentioned a town near Susa—start looking there."

Vasilius continued to stand at the edge of the forest grove watching as Daphne, Ardeshir, and Yas pulled away in the donkey cart. They would take the cart to the next crossroads and then join a caravan of chariots and carriages. A light rain sprinkled on them, and Daphne pulled a sheepskin tarp over their heads. With the leather side out and the wool side in, it provided protection from the rain and warmth for the passengers.

As they neared the crossroads, the driver called out to her, "Militiamen have set up a checkpoint ahead. I hope you are not carrying anything that will get me in trouble."

Daphne pulled Yas and Ardeshir close. The baby was sleeping, and she tucked him under a spare sheepskin. Yas stood up to see the soldiers as Daphne held her around the waist. "Yeshua, we are Your children," Daphne prayed. "Spare Your children."

The militiamen were busy searching dozens of carts ahead of them as the rain continued to drizzle. Finally, one of the soldiers approached the driver. "So what are you carrying today?"

"A woman and her children," the driver said.

"Let me see!" the soldier commanded.

Daphne and Yas stood up with the sheepskin overtop of them. "A girl?" the man proclaimed. "No, we're not looking for girls. Move on. Hurry! We have a lot of traffic we have to clear."

As they moved on past the knot of carts and carriages being inspected, the driver turned. "I don't know who this Yeshua is that you prayed to, but I've never been cleared so quickly. The stop for the caravans is just ahead. May whatever gods you call on protect you on your journey."

By the time the caravan pulled up with a covered carriage able to carry a dozen passengers, Daphne and the two children were wet to the skin. Ardeshir whimpered and then cried to be fed. Four passengers alighted from the carriage at the crossroads and made room for Daphne. One bald-headed man frowned at the howling baby across from him. Once they were settled, the child nursed and the scowl disappeared as the passenger nodded off to the rocking of the carriage.

At the next stop manned by militiamen, there was little more than a brief conversation between the driver and the two soldiers on the ground. They were waved through. It was clear that Yas had become Yeshua's gift to get Daphne through the maze of those looking for her.

At the next crossroads Daphne got off with the children and waited for another carriage heading to Susa. They'd already been on the road most of the day, and it would be evening before they could find shelter. The discomfort from being wet made them all edgy.

The next security check proved they had crossed into rebel territory. The rebel archers in their white pantaloons, baggy blue shirts, and long flowing hair held back by leather headbands carried leather capes to shield themselves against the elements. They boarded the carriage and questioned each passenger. When one young man approached Daphne near the rear of the carriage, he chose to question Yas instead. "Where are you and your mother going?" he asked.

"She knows," Yas said. "Is that your very own horse?" she asked, pointing out at the black Friesian warhorses with the powerful, sloping shoulders. "He looks strong. I like his tail."

The young man glanced back at the trio of horses grazing at the side of the road. "Mine's the one closest to us. Right now, I'm only borrowing him until I serve for three years. After that, I get to keep him."

"Wow! I wish I could get a horse like that," Yas said. "Do girls get to be soldiers?" she asked.

"Not in this army," he said. Noticing his commander waving, he smiled. "You all have a good journey. If you see any big dark man, let one of our soldiers know. He's a dangerous killer, and you need to be careful."

All the passengers got off at Susa by the temple of Inshushinak, the patron deity of Susa. Little carved statues depicting him as an old man were everywhere. Daphne ignored those stopping to make offerings by the graves and the altar to the god of darkness. Copper axes and ceramic vessels filled with spices were popular gifts. She headed for the nearest inn. That one proved to be full. As she followed the suggestion of the owner toward the next location, she noticed the man following.

Nabonidus approached Susa from the south. At Laleh's insistence, he'd been kept in a lightly guarded section of the palace. He had feigned sleep and during the change of guards, he had stuffed pillows under the blankets and stepped into the shadows near the entrance to his room. When the new guard had raised his lamp to look in through the barred opening, Nabonidus had knocked away the lamp, grabbed the soldier around the neck, and taken the keys to release himself. The tied-up guard would be found by morning.

A horse provided quick transportation to the river, where he caught a fishing vessel south of Susa. A large ziggurat consecrated to Inshushinak towered beside a temple complex devoted to the snakelike Napirisha—the great god of Elam. Millions of bricks, made locally by slaves, supported the inner core with a layer as thick as Nabonidus was tall.

A young boy, noticing his hesitancy, stepped up beside Nabonidus and pointed out the various attractions. "Of course, this isn't as exciting as Susa," he said. "We Parthians made Susa the main capital of the empire because the Romans kept raiding Ctesiphon. You're not Roman, are you?"

He walked confidently along until he noticed a fish symbol carved onto a post. "Do you see that fish symbol? It's a sign of the dreaded Christ sect. The Romans have tried to wipe them out, but they are flourishing like flies in this area." He took out a small carving tool and tried to erase the symbol. "I hope you're not a Christ follower," he said. "The merchants and the priests from the other religions are on the lookout because they've destroyed so many businesses that sell amulets, charms, and figurines."

Nabonidus stepped up beside the boy to look at the site of the erased carving. "Why do these Christ followers carve fish symbols?"

The boy stood back. "Do you know nothing? If you spell out the word fish in Greek, the letters stand for Yeshua, Christ, God's Son, Savior. These people think that the Christ is the One True God." He scraped the symbol one last time and walked away.

"Wait!" Nabonidus said. "I know what it stands for, but why do they carve them here?"

"Oh! They think they are smart by using the fish symbol to direct people to their meetings. If a follower sees the symbol, they look to see which way the fish's head is pointing, and they walk that way until they find another symbol. At the end of the trail someone will meet them to take them to the meeting." The boy kept walking until he came to another fish symbol. Again, he took out his carving knife.

Nabonidus grabbed his wrist. "Why are you carving out the symbols? Do you hate these people that much?"

The boy shook his head. "Not at all. The meeting from these fish is over, and they pay me to erase the old fish. There will be new fish for followers to find in another week."

"So! Are you the one telling the authorities how to get rid of these people?"

"Why would I do that?" the boy said as he carved away the fish. "They pay me so I can help feed my mother. Without a father we need the money, and these people take care of the orphans and widows like no one else does. By erasing their fish, I help them stay hidden."

The trip to Susa was a pensive one as Nabonidus rode cross-country on a horse he had hired from one of the boy's contacts. Yeshua's message had reached across geographic, social, ethnic, and faith barriers to transform people. It spread like a virus on the tongues and souls of traders, pilgrims, travelers, and the curious. While the Magi and rebels fought to set up a political kingdom for their King of kings in one nation, the true King of kings was building His kingdom in the hearts of men, women, and children through all nations.

XI

THE SNOW FELL lightly as the innkeeper welcomed Daphne into the entrance and allowed her to escape out the back door. The man following her had hesitated outside. His blue cape and white pantaloons made him too easy to spot in a crowd with the brown and black attire of common folk filling the streets.

Despite the successful escape, it was difficult to hide with two children. They were all exhausted. When Yas stood her ground and refused to budge, Daphne almost lost her grip on Ardeshir. The baby, jolted, let out a piercing cry. "Shhhhh!" Daphne said to the baby as Yas broke away. "Come back here!" she said sternly to the girl. Yas turned her back and kept walking. She held her mouth open with her tongue out to catch the snowflakes.

As Yas passed an alley by the bakery, the blue-caped man stepped out and grabbed her. Yas struggled, yelling, "Let me go! Let me go!" The man held his ground, holding Yas by her wrists as she tried to kick and squirm.

The crowd slowed to a halt as people watched them. "Whose girl is this?" the man shouted.

"She's mine!" Daphne said, hurrying forward. "Let her go! She's mine."

The man stood behind Yas, holding her wrists tightly. "You! Dark as dusk and she light as dawn! Who are you trying to fool?"

An old Persian in the crowd hobbled forward with his cane. "By the life of Inshushinak himself! What purpose do you have for bringing your rebel ways into the life of this family?"

The blue-caped man backed away as Daphne and the old man got closer. "This woman thinks she has borne the next heir to our throne. She hides her husband from the regent and Magi alike. Now she steals an orphan to disguise her true identity."

"What are you jabbering about?" the old man said. "She's a poor, tired mother looking for a place to rest her children. Leave her alone."

The crowd closed in. The snow continued to fall.

"Wait!" Daphne said. "I'll go with him." She turned to the old man. "Thank you for protecting the weak and vulnerable. Your mother raised you to be a hero."

Yas stopped struggling. "Momma! Don't let him take me."

Daphne walked up to the blue-caped intruder. "Show me where you want me to go."

The man let go of Yas and walked away. Daphne grabbed hold of Yas's cape and tugged her after the man.

"Momma, I'm tired!" Yas objected. "Where are we going?"

Nabonidus spotted the blue-caped rebel warrior loitering outside the front of the inn in Susa. The snow wasn't thick enough to leave footprints yet. An alcove near a weaver's shop provided the perfect refuge. He had planned to rest in the inn but waited until the man scooted down an alley. A young girl could be heard screaming, "Let me go! Let me go!" For whatever reason, the soldier was accosting a little girl. There was no way he would risk his mission when he was so close.

The girl quieted down and Nabonidus slipped into the inn through the front door. "Quite the noise out there," he said to the innkeeper.

"Yes, some woman and her two children. Probably trying to run away from the master of the house."

After the lost sleep from the past two nights and the long journey, dawn came far too early. Nabonidus enjoyed a breakfast of cheeses, fruit, and wild pheasant, then set out on foot to explore the nearby towns. The place where he had dropped off Daphne to find Adrina and Atossa seemed an obvious first stop. To find her after months apart seemed a vain hope.

The people on the west side of Susa were amazingly friendly and welcoming as he exchanged greetings along the way. By noon, news of his passing would have been shared from tongue to tongue all through the district. He would have to move quickly. As he rounded the corner to the place he'd last seen Daphne, he could see a lone figure at the entrance to the settlement.

The sitting watchman, hunched over on a rock like a vulture, hardly lifted his head as Nabonidus approached. His stiff arms braced on his knees alone kept him upright.

"Remember me?" Nabonidus asked. "I asked you about two women named Adrina and Atossa on the day your son died in that fire."

"If you're here to torment me, then get in line," the watchman said. "I've died a thousand deaths cursing the gods over that day."

"May the true God restore your joy in His time," Nabonidus said. "I am still looking for those two women, their uncle Hananel, and the woman you called Humaya."

"Cursed cultists!" he said. "Allowing them to live in this village is probably why I was cursed. If I saw them again, I'd kill all four myself."

Nabonidus held out a gold shekel his sister had given him. "Old man, I know you hear things—things maybe others hope you will forget. Where have you heard that cultists like this might go?"

The old man eyed the coin like a hungry dog eying a beef bone just out of reach. His lips quivered, and his hands trembled. "Follow the fish!" He reached out and snatched the coin with remarkable dexterity. Then, like an old tortoise, he curled into himself and went still.

Despite weariness and high anxiety, Daphne kept pace with the blue-caped warrior. Twice the man doubled back on his track in and out of alleys, checking over his shoulder, stopping to loiter in alcoves or the doorways of inns. He muttered to himself and wrung his hands, ensuring she was close.

"How much farther?" Daphne asked as they neared the edge of Susa.

"Fish!" the man said. "We have to find the fish."

"There was a fishmonger on the last street," Daphne said. "I can wait here with the children while you get what you need. We've been traveling a long way already and need to rest."

"Not real fish," he snapped. "Look for pictures of fish—on the trees, posts, buildings. Our contact was supposed to leave us a fish."

Daphne pulled Yas to a stop. "I have to feed this baby and this girl. There's a market near here. I'll go get what we need to eat, and you find what you need to find, then meet us." She turned and marched toward the plaza of canopied stalls with vendors hawking their wares. Yas happily skipped along beside her.

"Momma, who was that man?" Yas asked.

"I don't know," Daphne answered. "All I know is that he said the same thing to me that Vasilius said, and he seems to be trying to help us without knowing us."

"He's dressed funny," Yas said. "What did he say to you?"

"He's dressed like a part of the rebel army that captured Ardeshir's daddy. He may know something. He said that I was dark as dusk, and you were light as dawn."

"Oh!" Yas pulled Daphne toward a fruit stall. "Can I have an orange?"

The vendors happily supplied them with fruit, bread, cheese, meat, and a variety of vegetables. Yas chewed her orange, peel and all. The juice raced down her chin and dripped onto her clothing. Ardeshir hungrily nursed as Daphne sat on a stone bench watching the crowds pass by. No one seemed overly interested in a mother with her two children sitting in a market.

Near the potter's table, a woman chattered buoyantly. Daphne recognized her as someone from the village where Adrina and Atossa had sheltered her. She pulled the shawl across her face and watched. Twice the woman looked in her direction but quickly glanced away. A tingling like ants racing up and down her spine preceded a shiver throughout her body.

"What's wrong, Momma?" Yas asked.

"We're supposed to wait here for the man," Daphne answered, "but he's taking too long. We may need to find another place to wait. Aren't you getting cold?"

Yas shivered. "I saw a fish," she said.

"What do you mean, you saw a fish?" She stood and looked around. The fishmonger's stall was several streets away. "Where did you see a fish?"

"It was a carving, like the man said."

"A carving? Where?"

Yas pointed toward a small shrine they had passed coming into the market. "It's there, on a rock."

"Show me!" Daphne urged, wrapping Ardeshir more snugly in his blanket. She followed Yas to the rock. The fish was clearly etched for all to see. "What do we do now?" she said out loud.

"You follow the direction the head is pointing you toward." It was the chattering woman from the market. "Look for the next fish and the next until you find the shelter you need." The woman walked on as if she had other business to finish.

The fishmonger in Susa played dumb when Nabonidus asked about the watchman's reference to fish. "Surely, others have asked you about fish," he said. "What do you tell people who ask you about fish?"

The vendor reached into a sawdust-covered bucket of ice and pulled out a bass. "I tell them that we have beluga and binni, we have minnow and eel, we have barbel, loach, and sturgeon." He looked around. "If you have a discerning palate, you can even get catfish, clams, and cod." He set the bass back in the bucket. "Some of our customers ask for herring, octopus, lobster, crayfish, or perch. You give us a few days, and we can get you what you want."

Nabonidus stared him down; then he turned and walked away. Someone had to know something about fish. It was too much of a coincidence that the boy who carved away the fish had linked them to the Christ followers in the area. Where could he go, and who could he talk with? The blur of the blue cape fading back into an alcove caught his attention. The rebel warrior was a little too obvious. It was time to strangle the truth out of the miscreant.

Strolling casually down the main street of Susa, he stopped at the bakery to purchase a sweet bread roll. Munching it, he meandered down the alley next to the shop and waited around the corner. A few minutes later, the blue cape stepped out in front of him. He grabbed the man by the throat and threw him up against the wall. "Why are you following me?" he growled.

The man's face turned red, his eyes got big, and he gestured wildly with his hands. Nabonidus released his neck and let the man gasp for air. "Why are you following me?" Nabonidus hissed. "If you're here to take me back to the regent, I'm not coming."

The man shook his head as he bent over, breathing deeper now. "No! I'm not with the rebels. I only dress like this so that people don't question me."

"Who do you work for, and why are you here?"

The man straightened up and looked around. "I help Christ followers," he said. "I know you're one of them. I was helping a woman with her two children after a man named Vasilius gave me a shekel to take them to an assembly for their safety. While I was looking for a fish, they disappeared."

"A fish?" Nabonidus grabbed his shoulder and pulled him closer. "You were looking for a fish?"

"Yes."

"And Vasilius told you to look for a fish?"

"He only hired me to find a safe place for the woman and her children. I knew that the Christ followers would be the safest place. They use the fish to show how to find them."

"Where is Vasilius?"

"I think he went looking for you."

"What did he do with my wife?"

"I know nothing about your wife. I was only told to find the woman who was dark as dusk with the girl who was light as dawn."

"What does that mean?" Nabonidus asked. "As dark as dusk and as light as dawn?"

"I think it has to do with skin coloring," the man said. "She's dark, and the girl is light."

The snow provided a muffled echo for the horse's hooves as a dozen archers galloped around the corner of the market plaza. Nabonidus pushed the man away and raced down the alley toward the bakery. The horses squeezed into the alley, one at a time, right behind him. Outracing the Friesian war horses on foot was not how he had planned this day.

The carpenter shaping the sign under the apple tree shook the snow off his shoulders and patted the cedar plank tenderly. He stopped his work as Daphne approached with the two children. It was clear they were examining trees and rocks and even the side of a bench. "Looking for something?" he asked.

"A fish?" Yas blurted out as Daphne vainly put her hand over the child's mouth.

The man smiled kindly. "You're a long way from where the fish are swimming," he said.

Daphne looked around. "We need shelter," she said. "Someone told us to come this way, and we might find some."

"It looks like you've been looking at trees and rocks and benches. I'm not sure you'll find very good shelter in those places," the man said. "Who sent you this way, and what did they tell you to look for?"

Ardeshir's cry determined her answer. "A blue-caped man told us about fish, and a talkative lady at the market told us to follow some carvings."

"Ah!" the man said. He removed a scarf that was hanging over his sign. Underneath was a small carving of a fish. "Does it look anything like this one?" he asked.

"Yes!" Yas said, jumping up and down. "Yes! We're cold and hungry and tired, and we need to find the place where the fish go to school."

The carpenter's confused look prompted Daphne to chuckle. "I told her that we would have to find a school of fish before we rested," she said. "She is right that we're cold, hungry, and tired. We've traveled a long way over the past few days."

"What does this fish tell you?" the man asked Yas.

"Go that way," Yas said, pointing in the direction the fish head directed.

"Yes!" the man said. "My wife is waiting at the end of the path. Follow her, and she'll show you where to rest."

The gold shekel he'd thrown to the innkeeper proved its worth to Nabonidus. The large-bellied man with a beard like a tumbleweed smiled through it with his large teeth. A black patch over his left eye gave him the look of a pirate. "Business is good today," he said with a wink from his good eye.

The horses halted outside, and shouts surrounded the building. The innkeeper directed Nabonidus to an attic opening, which he squeezed through seconds before the doors burst open below him. The rebel warriors streamed through the rooms—creating chaos and screams of terror from those invaded. Nabonidus lay still and waited.

One of the soldiers discovered a trapdoor to an underground storage area, and the flurry and din of activity increased as that area was searched. "Nothing!" a soldier called up the stairs. "He's got to be here somewhere."

"Are you sure you have the right building?" the innkeeper asked. "Who told you he stayed in here? Why don't you have your men wait outside, and I will make sure everyone clears the space for your thorough search."

"We saw him come in here," the rebel leader yelled. "If we find him, then you'll be the next meal for the lions right after him. Or should I say two meals?" Footsteps faded, and a voice echoed from outside. "Search every building in the area. Do not let this fugitive get away again."

When the noise lessened, the innkeeper walked right below the opening to the attic. "If someone had another gold shekel," he whispered, "there might be an easy way to get out through the storage cellar tunnel."

Nabonidus dug into his change purse and dropped a coin into the open palm.

"I'll keep everyone busy outside for a moment," the innkeeper said. "Look in the storage for a shelf with tins of spices on it. Pull it gently away from the wall. Behind is a passageway." He hesitated. "I saw it when I was a boy. Pull the shelf closed behind you when you get into the tunnel. Take a lamp to light your way, and follow it until you can emerge."

The large man shuffled toward the rooms. "Everyone out in the street for a moment," he said. "Sorry to trouble you, my special friends, but these soldiers are a pain. This will only take a moment."

When the rooms below were silent, Nabonidus lowered himself from the ceiling and scrambled down the stairs into the cellar. A flickering clay lamp rested on the floor at the edge of the opening, and he snatched it up. The spice rack sat in the darkest corner of the underground space, and he tugged it firmly. It almost toppled from his effort. He reached lower on the shelf and pulled it gently. It creaked away from the wall, pulling a section of the wood with it. The overlapping panel provided a clever disguise, making it appear flush with the back wall.

Inside the tunnel, he set down the lamp and pulled the wall unit back into place. Rats scurried away from the light as he batted away a virtual wall of spiderwebs linked across the entire opening. Ten paces in and he still had to clear away the webs. The place was icy and damp along the side walls but fairly dry underfoot. The musty air, mixed with the freshly disturbed dust from his steps, made breathing difficult. He slowed his pace to let everything settle. The noise overhead grew loud again, and dust danced in the dim lamplight.

"Thank You, Yeshua!" he murmured. Nothing had gone the way he hoped or planned since his arrival in Persia, but every detail had somehow worked together. If only he could find Daphne and his newborn child. If only his sister could get away from the clutches of the Magi. If only the regent could be eliminated from this deadly game he had no desire to play.

He took another swipe at the wall of webs, covered his mouth and nose with a scarf, and stepped over a half-eaten dead rat toward the darkness.

Ardeshir's cry broke into Daphne's dream of sharing communion with the believers in Ephesus. Yas squeezed Daphne's shoulder, shaking her, urging her to wake up. She moaned and turned toward the baby's cry. "Momma's here," she said, rubbing her eyes.

"Momma, I thought you were dead," Yas said.

Daphne flung back the blankets and reached across the bed for the little one. His fists were balled up tight, tears were flowing, and his lungs were getting a workout. She hugged him to her shoulder and gently patted his back. When she took him in the crook of her arm, the little one latched aggressively.

"What time is it?" Daphne asked.

"It's tomorrow," Yas responded. "The lady Elizabet stopped by to see if we wanted something to eat. That was a long time ago."

The night before, she and Yas had hardly been able to sit through the welcome and dinner shared by Elizabet and her husband Samuel—the carpenter.

The quick wash in warm water and the snuggling into clean beds was a touch of heaven. Getting up was a shock to the system, and every muscle in her body ached. She continued to let the little one feed as she lay down to rest.

Once again, it was Yas who shook her into consciousness. "Momma! Momma! Wake up, we need to eat," she said. "The lady came twice with food for us." She was chewing on an apple, pleasure suffusing her face.

The next time Elizabet arrived, she was ready. Brushed hair, fresh clothes, a warm wash. It made a world of difference. And to be welcomed by followers of Christ in Persia. This was what they had dreamed of. If only Nabonidus was close.

Nabonidus sat in an enclosed garden listening to Samuel speak on the finer art of carving figurines. For complete strangers, they shared like friends.

He'd met the carpenter the evening before, a few feet from where he emerged out of the tunnel. The man had been carving a fish on a small plaque he hung on a tree limb. "Shalom!" he said as he towered over the hedge two strides away.

The man was visibly shaken. A large dark man, covered in cobwebs and dirt and smelling like rat dung, had appeared from nowhere as the sun slipped behind the mountains. The carpenter had been speechless, shaking even, as the intruder crashed through the hedge and lifted the plaque out of his hand. "Where did you get this?" the man had asked.

Nabonidus had led him to a bench and then stepped back to give the man space. In time, the man shook his head, wiped his jaw with the back of his hand, and looked at the plaque. "You caught me by surprise," he said. "Shalom." He waited as Nabonidus handed him back the plaque. "I carved it for some friends," he said.

"I was told that the fish was the sign of cultists," Nabonidus said. "Are you a cultist?"

The carpenter squeezed his forehead between his thumb and forefinger, eyebrows furrowing. "I'm not sure where you heard that," he said, "but I can assure you that my friends are no cultists."

"I'm looking for followers of Yeshua who use that fish to identify their group," Nabonidus said. "I was told to find and follow the fish. Here I am."

The carpenter nodded. "I'm Samuel, and I'm the one you're looking for. How you found me is a mystery. I've carved away all the signs from our meeting yesterday." He held up the plaque. "Except this last one which I keep each week. There is no way you could have found us if the Almighty had not led you."

"Would you have a room, a wash, some food, a chance to stay safe for a while?" He held out his last gold shekel. "I am a follower, and I can pay."

"Keep your money," the man said. "Yeshua has sent us a full house now. We have a man with his two nieces plus a woman and her two children. My wife, Elizabet, and I never imagined meeting so many believers here when we left Damascus." He pointed toward the house nearby. "We purchased this home just after the last full moon and promised Yeshua we would use it to start a community of believers if He would only bring us some."

Nabonidus devoured every morsel of food they offered; he used every drop of the warm water to wash himself down; he burrowed down into the blankets and relished the peace of not having to run anymore. He was beyond the reach of Magi and regent alike. "Praise You, Yeshua," he said as he drifted off.

The rooster roused him into stretching and facing the dawn. He loved the first tendrils of morning light and drank in all the new energy that came with it. Elizabet and Samuel were already up and preparing for the day. He'd happily fetched a bucket of water from the well for them and watched as Samuel chopped the wood for the morning fire.

As the fire kindled inside, warming up the oven for fresh baked bread, the two men settled onto a bench in the garden. Nabonidus had his back to the home, so he missed the arrival of the third man. "Good morning, Samuel," he said. "And whom have we here?"

Nabonidus turned to acknowledge the man. "Nabonidus!" he said.

The man's eyes grew large. "It's you!" he said. "I've got to tell the others." He turned to go, but Nabonidus caught him by the arm.

"I don't know who you think I am," he said, "but if you think you're reporting me to the regent, the Magi, or anyone else, then I can't let you leave this place."

The man smiled. "You truly do have the grip of a gladiator. We haven't met, but I'm the younger brother of Anoshiruvan. I'm the uncle of Adrina and Atossa." He slipped his arm out of Nabonidus's grip. "They're here with me. It was them I was going to tell. They haven't seen you since Ephesus." He rubbed the back of his head and then shook it. "We were sure you were dead by now." He hobbled with his crutch back into the house.

"We're glad you were able to get a good rest," Elizabet said as she laid the food tray down on the table in Daphne's room. Yas pawed through the fruit, cheese, and flat bread, filling her hands with all she could carry.

"Yas!" Daphne said. "There will be enough for all of us. Wait until we give the blessing to Yeshua for all He has provided."

"We are pleased to know you are followers of Yeshua," Elizabet said. "Samuel and I have been praying that Yeshua would send us His people so we can start a community in this part of His world. He has faithfully filled up every room in our home."

"Who else is here?" Daphne asked.

Yas jumped up and down with her hand raised. "Ask me, I know."

Daphne nodded. "Okay, you smart one. Who else is here?"

"Two girls, an uncle, and someone else," Yas answered.

"Do they have names?" Daphne asked.

Yas drooped. "I forgot them," she said.

"Come, and I'll introduce you," Elizabet said.

Daphne changed Ardeshir into a fresh cloth diaper and then followed Yas and Elizabet into the main gathering area of the home. "This is where our believers' gathering will happen," Elizabet said. "As more come to understand The Way, we will grow and perhaps spread out through this whole land." She moved toward a hallway. "I'll get the others. Sit and wait here."

Daphne vibrated her lips and blew into Ardeshir's tummy as he laughed. As she bent over, someone set their hands on her shoulders and squeezed.

"Praise Adonai!" the woman said. "You are alive, and your son with you." A huge hug followed, and she knew it was Atossa only because Adrina stood close behind grinning from ear to ear.

Loud whoops echoed throughout the room. "I see you two already know each other," Elizabet said.

Hananel hobbled into the room on his crutch, and again cries of joy redoubled. No sooner had the three of them entered into a group hug than Samuel and Nabonidus strolled in. Daphne took one look and broke down sobbing. It was too much. Adrina, Atossa, and Hananel stepped aside, but Yas rushed in as Daphne fell to her knees.

Yas hugged Daphne protectively and said, "My momma needs me."

Nabonidus approached and crouched beside them. "Whom have we here?" he said.

Daphne wiped her eyes and nose on her sleeve and moved into his arms. "This is Yas, and the boy is Ardeshir. You left me with no one, and now I bring you two children to claim as your own."

He chuckled. "I'm sure there is a big story behind these two little ones," he said. "And I'm sure there is also a big story behind all that has happened with you and with each person in this room."

"The angel of the Lord encamps around those who fear Him," Samuel said. "We need to have our first gathering of Yeshua's followers in Persia. Come, kneel with me, and we will praise His name. Then we will share a fellowship meal and hear your stories."

Nabonidus rested with his back against the wall, watching Yas and Ardeshir sleep. "She's quite the firebrand," he whispered to Daphne who sat beside him. "Our son is all I could hope for, but you have blessed me with double joy."

"You kept your story short in our sharing time in there. What else do I need to know?"

Daphne laid her head on his shoulder. "Hananel pretended to be my cousin from up north, and they called me Humaya. You heard how I made friends with the watchman's son, and you heard how he died trying to save my life. The priest heard the boy calling me by that name, and after I lost my memory in the accident at the market, that is who I thought I was."

"How long were you at the Temple of Fire?" Nabonidus asked.

"Time passed so slowly. The priest told me things, but he couldn't answer my questions. His mistress, Vashti, was a priestess who taught me the way of the shrine but mostly kept me sweeping. We met a wounded militiaman in the market who told us about a big black demon who had destroyed his army."

"That would be me," Nabonidus said.

"Yes, that would be you." Daphne stroked his arm and traced a scar up his wrist. "I went looking for you but got caught in a battle between an Arab caravan and some bandits. I met Hananel but didn't realize I knew him. He brought me to Atossa and Adrina, who were running from someone trying to persecute them."

"How did you get separated?"

"Not so fast." She took a deep sigh. "We somehow offended a nobleman who wanted our space, and Hananel tried to appease him. When he didn't return, we had to run to hide in a forest. We stayed with a Greek innkeeper, and that's when your sister showed up with her guardians, who kicked us out of our space."

"I'll have to talk to her about that."

"She already knows. She gave me a ride to Susa, but we were trapped by the rebel soldiers and had to run through another forest. A hunter found us and hid us in his home. That's where Ardeshir was born." She wove her fingers through his. "She's the one who came up with the name Ardeshir in honor of your uncle. While I was washing one day, your sister left with the baby. One of the hunter's boys had betrayed us, and one of her guardians came to collect her."

"I can't imagine how angry you were," he said.

"I chased them to a town, but they weren't there. I went back to Susa to the Temple of Fire. That's where I saw you wrestling in that pool after Vasilius pushed the leather carriage into it."

"Wait! You know Vasilius?"

"He helped me take back the baby, and we ran. While we were hiding, Yas showed up and claimed me as her momma. While Vasilius was out gathering food for us, the hunter there showed up and decided to sell us in a slave market." Daphne leaned over and moved the blanket under Yas's chin. "Vasilius caught up and killed him. He told me that no one would believe that Yas was my daughter, because I was as dark as dusk and she was as light as dawn. That idea was like a code that helped save my life later."

"So where is Vasilius now?"

"We had to run, and he went to find you while I went to find Hananel and the girls. Having Yas with me helped keep me from trouble at the security checkpoints because no one was looking for a mother of an eight-year-old girl." She rose to her knees before him. "A man dressed like a rebel found us, shared the code words from Vasilius, and told us about the fish. We followed them here."

Nabonidus grabbed her wrist. "He didn't follow you here, did he?"

Daphne wrinkled up her nose and furrowed her eyebrows. "Why do you care? He helped us."

"That man really was a rebel," Nabonidus said. "It was a trap. They were using you to get to me. Does this mean Vasilius really is working for the regent?"

169

XII

FOR THE NEXT seven days Nabonidus paced from window to window. "How long do you plan on doing this?" Daphne asked. "Samuel erased the fish after we arrived, and the man said he wasn't with the rebels. He was only pretending."

"Those people will lie," Nabonidus responded. "They'll say anything to get to me and make me the King of kings."

"By now, they must know you're not interested," Daphne said. "They have your sister. All they need to do is to find someone to marry her and produce an heir."

"I should never have left her," he said. "Who knows what those wretched Magi might do to her? Maybe I should go back to the regent and lead his men to rescue her."

"What is wrong with you?" Daphne asked. "Hananel, Adrina, and Atossa want to spend time with us, and you've got us locked up in our room. You've been a gladiator, facing down the bloodthirstiest champions in the empire, and I've never seen you afraid like this. Your little girl needs to know her father, and you're scaring her by your paranoia."

"You go talk to the others," Nabonidus said. "I'll keep watch. Has Elizabet come back from the market? They could be questioning her, following her, using her to find me."

"Maybe you and I need to get some fresh air one day and get to know each other again," Daphne said. "You're not the man I married—at least not that I can remember. Even Adrina and Atossa say you've changed. It almost seems that the enemy inside you is more dangerous than the enemy outside you."

"You don't know these people," he said. "If they got to Vasilius, they can get to anyone. It's just a matter of time. You'll see. Go, keep Yas and Ardie safe, but watch out! One of these servants may be gathering information for the outsiders."

Daphne closed the door behind her and joined the others in the main room. Adrina was rocking Ardeshir, and Yas was bouncing on Samuel's knee. While acknowledging the glances from the group, Daphne said nothing. Finally, she asked, "So what are we all talking about in here?"

Samuel stopped bouncing Yas. "Hananel was about to tell us how he injured his ankle," he said. "Go ahead, Hananel. You were held captive by the nobleman in his chariot racing through the mountain pass with the Magi's militia all around you."

Hananel nodded. "Yes! We were traveling through the pass in the Zagros, and we came to a place where there was a narrow path and a huge drop-off. My hands were tied, but I could move." He pantomimed standing in a chariot bouncing with his wrists tied together. "I thought I saw a grassy ledge a few feet from the road just before the huge drop-off, so I jumped over the edge of the chariot."

"What happened next?" Adrina asked.

"I thought I'd jumped far enough but my foot caught on the axle and slipped between the spokes. I could feel it breaking, but there was nothing I could do as the horses raced on. The nobleman was yelling and the charioteer was trying to stop the horses, but I was caught."

"I can't imagine how painful that was," Samuel said.

"It happened so fast I hardly noticed the pain at first," Hananel said. "Then my foot came free, and I toppled over the edge and down the large drop. I had missed the grassy ledge."

"How did you survive?" Atossa asked.

"There was a bend in the river right at that place, and I landed in the water. I hit my shoulder hard on the bottom and almost drowned when the air got knocked out of me. Somehow, I had prayed out to Yeshua as I fell, and I made it to the surface and caught my breath."

"Didn't the nobleman stop and catch you?" Samuel asked.

"No! He probably thought I died in the fall. He kept right on going."

"How did you find your way back to Susa?" Daphne chimed in.

Hananel sat on his chair and propped his leg up. It was obvious to everyone he had no foot attached. "I pulled myself out of the water and lay there through the day. The pain was too much for me. I could only pray." He bowed his head. "A shepherd appeared out of nowhere, and he dragged me to the road. He waved down a passing carriage and paid for my transport. I passed out on the way and woke to find myself in a physician's tent with my foot sawn off."

"Can I see?" Yas piped up.

Hananel peeled away the wrap around the stump that was left from his leg. "Let this be a lesson to you," he said to Yas. "Never jump out of a moving carriage."

"How did you find us?" Samuel said.

"Two of the men in the physician's tent put me on a stretcher and told me that I would have to beg to pay my way. I was left in the market all day for ten days, and then a man in a blue cape told me that I should look for a fish. I didn't know what he meant, but one day as the two men carried me to the market, I saw a small fish carved on a post."

"How did you figure out what the fish meant?"

"I didn't at first, but then Atossa and Adrina came down the path looking for fish. They were so focused on the fish that they almost didn't see me. We paid a man with a cart to drop me close enough so that you could find me at the last sign."

"So do you think Yeshua is doing something special?" Samuel asked. "I wish Elizabet had heard all this. I wonder where she is."

When Elizabet hadn't returned by midafternoon, Nabonidus slipped out the back door of the shelter and headed for town. The snow had stopped but lay ankle-deep in the clear spaces. He gave little thought to the reality that it was going to be hard to disguise a mountain of a dark man among the population of average-sized light-skinned people. He avoided the main pathways and slunk through trails until he reached the trees behind the inn.

Two Arab traders in their distinctive robes and head coverings occupied the alley in animated discussion. A young man from Gaul or Britannia laughed with a group of young women who appeared to be locals. A trader of oriental descent unloaded a cart of supplies outside the back door. A slave from Egypt used a board to scrape away the snow from the cobblestones in front of the inn.

As the trader wrestled a large bundle off the back of the cart, the large innkeeper pushed through the back door leaning on a cane. A large dark bruise nestled where his left eye should have been. A gash ran across his right cheek. The rebel warriors had communicated their displeasure for his part in Nabonidus's escape.

When another servant helped the oriental trader carry the large bundle inside, Nabonidus stepped out from the trees and stood behind the innkeeper. "Stay where you are," he said. "Then you don't have to say you saw me."

The owner grunted. "I should have charged you twice as many gold shekels," he said. "There's one of the rebels disguised as a guest in my inn and in every other inn in Susa."

"I'm looking for the woman, Elizabet—Samuel's wife. She went missing yesterday."

The innkeeper reached into the cart and lifted a bag of onions. "It seems that the damage to my inn from the search by the rebels will require major repairs. They found the tunnel, and they're waiting for you at the other end. I wonder how I will fix everything so that it's even better than it was."

Nabonidus pulled out the coin purse tied by a string around his neck. "I can give you three gold shekels—that's all."

The innkeeper shrugged. "It's a start." He hobbled with the onions and set them by the door, where the servant took them inside. "This woman you speak of—Elizabet. She was at the market at midday yesterday. I saw her standing under the potter's canopy talking with another woman." He hobbled back to the cart and lifted a woven basket of dates. "I always did like these," he said. "That's the last I saw of Elizabet. You should ask the potter what he knows."

"With all these rebels hiding in this town, there's no way I can march into the open and ask questions."

The innkeeper scratched behind his ear. "Let me think. Perhaps if I sent a servant over with a shekel to ask that potter to pay me a visit, then we could meet back here in a while." He held his hand out behind his back.

Nabonidus reluctantly placed another shekel into his hand. "This is my food for today and tomorrow," he said.

The innkeeper chuckled. "I think you and I both would survive without food for a day or two. Wait in the trees." He stepped back inside and left the rest of the cart to be unloaded by the servants.

Snowflakes drifted lazily from the skies by the time the potter and the innkeeper stepped outside the back of the inn. Nabonidus joined them. The innkeeper moved back inside. "What do you know of this woman, Elizabet?" Nabonidus asked the potter.

The potter backed up against the wall of the inn and held out a calloused hand. "I have a hungry family, and with all this snow the business is not so good."

Nabonidus pulled out his coin purse once again, grateful to a sister who had been generous with him. "I can give you a shekel out of pity for your family," he said.

The potter bit the coin and nodded. "The priest from the Temple of Fire overheard Elizabet talking with that woman who talks so much. They were talking about starting a gathering for followers of Yeshua. He commanded two of his bodyguard to arrest her."

"Did they take her back to the Temple of Fire?"

"I think so," the potter said. "The linen merchant next to me said that the priest is known to have offered sacrifices to both Ahura Mazda and Angra Mainyu both—to the god of light and the god of darkness. The human sacrifices are to Angra Mainyu."

"When does he offer these sacrifices?" Nabonidus pressed.

"Usually at the height of the full moon."

"The full moon is tonight!" Nabonidus said. "I've got to stop this."

Samuel walked quickly into the house and gently shut the door behind him. Daphne was scrubbing vegetables in a basin nearby. "No one goes outside!" he said.

"What's wrong?" she asked.

"There are rebel soldiers hiding near the tunnel where your husband emerged," he said. "I think they suspect he may be in the area."

Daphne rose and peeked out the window between the curtains. "I see one man crouching by a hedge," she said.

"There are two more waiting in the trees behind him," Samuel said.

"Nabonidus disappeared a few moments after we were wondering why Elizabet was away so long. I think he went to find her at the market."

Samuel joined her at the window and then sat on a bench nearby. "Your husband is a big man. It might not be easy to stay hidden when the rebels know he's close. I thought Yeshua was bringing us a special group of people to start His gathering, and now you may lose your husband and I may lose my wife."

"We should pray!" Daphne said.

The others in the house gathered to join in, and darkness had descended before they rose for the evening meal. "Do you want us to go and look for them?" Atossa asked. "No one will trouble two women who know their way around."

"No!" Samuel said. "We have prayed, and now we trust them to Yeshua. If more people leave this house at this time of night, it will only raise more suspicion."

A pounding on the door startled them all. Daphne pulled Yas close and moved into her room with Ardeshir. She kept the children behind her and peered out a crack in the door. Samuel answered while Hananel, Atossa, and Adrina sat around the room. "Peace to you!" Samuel said. "Are you lost or in need of accommodation?"

"Stand back!" a harsh voice demanded. "Where are the men in this house?"

Samuel stood back. "There are two of us."

The rebel called over his shoulder. "Not here," he said. The door closed and the soldiers moved on.

"Susa seems to be the conflict point between the Magi and the regent," Hananel said as Daphne returned to the room. "I'm sure there is going to be more trouble before this is all over. Both sides want to find Nabonidus for one reason or another. I wouldn't want to be him."

"I can see why there's this conflict over him," Samuel said. "He's got the Maimonides name. If the Magi control him, then the Parthians keep hold over the empire. If the regent gains control over him, then the Elamites can regain their hold in this part of the world." He distributed a plate of dates, figs, and grapes, carrying the plate from person to person. "Nabonidus has been gone too long now. I'm afraid something bad has happened to Elizabet."

The evening shadows lengthened across the plaza, elongating the shrine for the Temple of Fire to form a dark path from the women's quarters to the inferno, where flames, sparks, and smoke billowed into the heavens. The shadows defied the senses and the light itself. Chanting priests in dark cloaks and masks moved in hypnotic circles around the sacrificial altar. The gates had been locked against all visitors, and Nabonidus had hurdled the hedge by the residence to scramble up on the flat roof. Pigeons launched into the sky on his arrival.

"What do you see?" a guardian asked out front.

"Pigeons!" another voice answered. Footsteps marched around the cobblestones, swept clear of snow. "There's nothing here. Without any snow I can't tell if someone was here."

"Should we check the roof?"

"It's almost impossible to get up there without using the stairs here. It's probably some aggressive male pigeon driving off his competition."

"Yes! I'm not so sure about what is happening here. They've drugged that woman and dressed her up like a moon goddess. I've got an uneasy feeling that those flames might be meant for her."

"These priests and their bloodthirsty rituals. Better them than us trying to keep the gods happy. Who knows what any god wants from us?"

"Why don't you check the gate by the Circle of Heaven pool, and I'll guard the front gate? With all this rebel activity, we should have had another dozen security men here. At least with the clear sky we're not going to get any more snow tonight."

Nabonidus waited until the footsteps faded and then slipped down into the shadows of the residence, away from where the flames lit up the plaza like a noonday. The chanting sent caterpillar-like chills racing up and down his spine. And then he saw her. She didn't look at all like Elizabet. The scanty costume, the gaudy mask, the knee-high fur-lined boots.

She was escorted by two costumed nymphs who manipulated her limbs into a seductive prance toward the festivities. If he hadn't paid heed to the potter's concerns, he would have been tempted to look elsewhere. Even if this wasn't Elizabet, she was a woman, like Sasina, being manipulated against her will by powerful forces.

He noticed two brooms leaning against the wall and picked them up—one in each hand. He loosened his wrists, ready for action. Wrestling down the fear reaching for his throat, he twirled like a fetish with the brooms extended toward the entourage. He raced in dizzying circles around and around the perimeter of the caped worshippers.

The priests applauded the unexpected flourish to their festivities and stepped aside to allow the group closer to the furnace. The nymphs lifted the woman over their heads and danced in circles closer and closer to the shrine. The high priest from the Temple of Fire let out a shrill scream. "Oh, Angra Mainyu! Accept this sacrifice, and leave us in peace to do good through the year to come." He unsheathed a razor sword from beneath his cloak and lifted it toward the moon.

And as the nymphs and priests focused on the sword descending to make its deadly cut, Nabonidus jumped forward and deflected the blade with a broom. With his foot, he kicked the priest toward the furnace and snatched the woman as she fell toward the ground. The priests stood like statutes as he sprinted away toward the residence with the woman safely cradled in his arms. He barged through the hedge and was halfway to the forest before he heard the guardian screaming for him to stop.

The moonlight spread out the trail like a golden pathway, and he hardly slowed as he raced away. Elizabet was too drugged to be able to run, and if he didn't find a place to shelter and hide, the guardian would soon overtake him. After several twists and turns and two forks in the trail, he settled for stepping off the trail into a thicket of bush, lying low, and keeping his hand firmly over Elizabet's mouth.

A short time later he heard two voices calling to each other as they walked down the path. It was the two guardians he'd heard by the residence. "Pierce the bushes with your sword now and then," the first said. "I can't believe how fast that black demon could run. Do you think it was Angra Mainyu in person, claiming his own?"

"If it was, he's probably devoured the wench by now," the second responded. "There's no way we're going to find that monster. Those priests can find someone else to sacrifice. I'm not putting myself into the jaws of that killer."

"If we walk back slow," the first guardian said, "perhaps rip up our clothes a little, and explain how the demon ate the wench before us, the priests may still reward us for our service. Maybe if things don't go well, we can join the regent. I hear he's raising an army big enough to take on the Magi."

As the guardians turned, Elizabet let out a whine. Nabonidus covered her nose and mouth firmly. She tried to move her limbs, but Nabonidus held her firmly.

"What was that?" a guardian said.

The night crawled by, every sound jerking Daphne up to her elbows as sleep refused to come. She'd been separated long enough from Nabonidus. He simply had to play the hero, and her nerves were shot waiting for the peace they had come to Persia for. Now, there were two children needing a father, and being a single mom was not in her dreams.

Adrina appeared at her door. The moonlight bathed the room enough to highlight the anxious frown on her face. "Can I join you?" she whispered. Yas stirred and mumbled in her sleep.

"Let's go into the common room," Daphne whispered back. She donned her robe and followed Adrina out of the room. The others were already gathered. "I see none of us can sleep," she said.

"I made something to keep our stomachs quiet," Atossa said, holding out a platter of food. "The roosters will be crowing soon. If Nabonidus and Elizabet don't get home by dawn, we're going out to look for them."

"Who's there?" the guardian called again. "Over here!" he called to his colleague. "I heard something over here."

"Probably a hare," the other called back.

Nabonidus held on tight to Elizabet until the guardian was steps away. "Shhh!" he whispered, trying to keep her still. "Don't make a noise."

The guardian thrust his sword into the bushes a step away. "Die, you demon!" he said. "Die!"

"See anything?" the other called.

The moment the guardian hesitated in order to answer, Nabonidus sprang out of the bush with a roar and flattened him. The edge of the guardian's sword sliced across his thigh and nicked his shoulder. In a moment the soldier was still. The other rushed toward the action but then, seeing Nabonidus rise out of the bush, turned and fled.

Nabonidus slung Elizabet over his shoulder and started for home. One touch of his arm and leg told him that he was losing blood too quickly. He set his sights on the inn. If he could get that far, perhaps he could get the help he needed. The forest blurred before him as the moonlight lured him on. The weight on his shoulder got heavier. His foot dragged. The moonlight disappeared.

The potter's servant met Daphne, Atossa, and Adrina as they neared the town plaza. "Come, quick!" he urged. "The dark man is hurt bad."

Daphne lunged forward and grabbed his arm as he turned. "What happened? Where is he?"

"He's at the inn," the servant said. "He's been cut with a sword or something. The baker found him on the path with a woman this morning. They were lying in the snow unconscious. The innkeeper sent for a physician."

The quartet raced toward the inn. "How's the woman?" Adrina asked.

"I don't know," the servant said. "The innkeeper's servant asked me if I knew how to find you because of the man. I only knew the area you lived in, so it's good you showed up when you did."

"It's the mercy of the Almighty," Daphne said.

When they reached the inn, the innkeeper stood out front keeping a crowd from getting closer. "I don't know who tried to kill him," he was shouting. "The physician is trying to keep him alive, but he's lost a lot of blood."

Three servants inside were on their knees wiping up a trail of blood on the tiles. "Watch your step," one of them said. "There's a lot of blood here. I don't know how he has any more to give."

Daphne raced past him and pushed her way through a few more servants in the hallway of the inn. One pointed the way to a room in the back. Outside the door, Elizabet lay on a mat beside a woman who was wiping her head with a cloth. The blanket half-covering her showed a much too revealing costume.

"Elizabet," Daphne said, on her knees. "Praise Yeshua! Are you okay? What happened?"

Elizabet's eyes fluttered, and she extended her hand to take Daphne's. "The priest from the Temple of Fire took me. He forced me to drink something. They were dancing around a fire, and I was flying—and then something dark."

"Now, now!" Daphne said, patting Elizabet's hand. "You're safe now. How did Nabonidus get hurt?"

"He saved me," Elizabet said. "We were in the forest. They were chasing us. Then we fell."

Adrina nudged Daphne. "We'll stay with her. You go be with your husband."

Daphne rose from her knees and nodded her appreciation. The door was ajar, so she poked her head around the corner and saw the physician stitching her husband's leg. He lay on the bed in nothing but a loincloth. He looked dead already. Blood soaked the bed.

She stood behind the physician. "I'm his wife," she said. The words had to be forced out with all her strength controlling a thumping chest, weak knees, and shaking hands. She cupped her chin in her hands to steady them.

The physician moved to suture the wound in Nabonidus's shoulder. "I see he's been in the arena," he said. "If I was one of those arena surgeons, I probably would have chosen to dissect him by now. He's a big man with a lot of blood, but I'm not sure we found him in time."

"Has he said anything?"

"Not really. He mumbled something that sounded like Yesh, but I don't know what that means."

"He's praying to Yeshua," Daphne said. "He fought in the arena for Yeshua."

"So he's a cultist!" He sat back a moment and then applied his needle to the wound again. "Normally, I wouldn't waste my time on those who pervert the gods around here, but the innkeeper is paying good money and who am I to argue with good money?"

"When will we know if he will live?" Daphne asked.

"Only the gods know for sure," the physician said. "He probably should have been dead already. If you can watch him for a while, I need to take a break. I sewed up everything I could reach, but I don't know how bad he is on the inside."

"If you can take a rotation with the rest of us, I think we can share the load of looking after him," Daphne said.

When the physician left, she beckoned for Adrina and Atossa. "Please see if you can find out how long Elizabet needs to be cared for here; then go find Samuel. Between us all, we will need to watch over Nabonidus, the children, and Elizabet. This is where we really need to be a community for each other."

The first thing Samuel did upon his arrival was to arrange for Elizabet to get into modest clothing. He laid his head on her chest and cried as she patted his shoulder. "Now, now," she said. "The big man saved me. The enemy can't win when we have Yeshua. He brought His gathering together just in time to take care of us."

Daphne longed for a love that would last through time like theirs.

Nabonidus turned feverish by the next morning, and there was little she could do as he thrashed and moaned, apart from soaking his head and body with cool cloths. "Yeshua, Nabonidus is Your champion," she prayed. "Without You fighting for him, he cannot win this battle. You who healed the lame and raised the dead—raise this one who follows You."

For the next two days, she stumbled between the children at home and her husband in the inn. The physician was clear. "His breathing is raspy and labored. His strength is leaving him. He cannot last through the night."

The innkeeper continued to supply them with food, drink, and fresh towels. He was tireless in his encouragement and support. "You must keep praying," he urged.

Samuel arrived for his shift with a small vial of olive oil. "The brother of Yeshua once told us," he said, "that when we face a sickness like this, we should anoint the body with oil, confess our sins, and bring this one into the hands of the Almighty." He poured oil on the wounds and on the forehead of Nabonidus, and the two of them and Hananel interceded through the hours of darkness. Sweat continued to pour from the body, before them as they applied cool cloths.

The physician arrived at dawn. He laid his hand on Nabonidus's chest and forehead. "It won't be long now," he said.

The dance of angels exceeded anything Nabonidus had ever dreamed of. The carousel of priests around the Temple of Fire had been as dark in its dance as the angels were in their light. The shrine's fire burned within and without him as he fought to escape the reach of the flames. In the middle of the furnace, faces faded in and out—Daphne, Elizabet, Atossa, Adrina, and others.

A figure of peace walked among the flames, speaking quiet to his racing heart. The same figure he had seen among the lions, among the Magi's daunting forces, among the chilling waters of the river. The figure cradled his son and smiled. As the man rose to leave, Nabonidus set his heart to follow. He knew it was Yeshua.

And then an agonizing cry pierced the darkness around him. A cry that made Yeshua stop and turn. He looked with compassion into the darkness, and a tear trickled into his beard. "Stay!" he said. "I will never leave you or forsake you. For now, others need you." Yeshua laid his hand on Nabonidus's forehead."

And then Nabonidus was awake, sitting bolt upright and staring into the startled eyes of his wife. "Hello," he stuttered. "Imagine seeing you here."

"Are you okay?" she asked.

He opened his arms, and she moved in quickly for a hug. "Wow!" he said, holding her tight. "It's good to be loved. Now, where are my children?"

Yas huddled by the door, hugging Daphne's arm, as Ardeshir stared up into the face of his father. "He's safe," Daphne said to Yas. "You don't have to hug him right away, but if I'm going to be your momma, then he will be your poppa."

The girl pushed behind Daphne, peeking out at the giant dark man wrapped in bandages. "Why is he never home if he's going to be my poppa?" she asked.

Daphne rubbed the back of Yas's head. "He'll be home more now. He just had to go help Elizabet with some trouble she was in."

At that moment, Elizabet pushed through the door. "Well, if it isn't my champion," she said. "Samuel told me how he found me and what you told him about the priests at the Temple of Fire. I've had nightmares, hearing chants through my sleep, but I also know that Yeshua was with me."

"Yes, he was," Nabonidus said. "I saw Him there as well, during my fever, walking through the flames. There is no power in the heavens or on the earth able to defeat Him. I believe the gathering place for believers will stand the test of time just like the one in Ephesus."

"I hear you're ready to come back home," Elizabet continued. "Samuel and I worked with the girls to clean up the two extra storage rooms out back, and we've decided that your family would do well there if you'll make them your own. We'll build a few more rooms for Adrina, Atossa, and Hananel so we can take in others to our growing community. The enemy will have to do more than this to chase us out of here."

"Be careful," Daphne said. "We've seen what the enemy is capable of in Ephesus. This is a small taste of that." She put sandals on Nabonidus and helped him to his feet.

He accepted a pair of crude walking sticks to help him out to the donkey cart that would transport him home. "I promise you all that I will be off of these things and doing my share of the work as soon as I can," he said. "No more stupid mistakes taking on warriors in the dark."

Daphne walked alongside the cart where Ardeshir lay swaddled in his father's arms. Yas sat on the seat as far as possible away from Nabonidus. Daphne held her daughter's hand and taught her songs she had learned with the children at Ephesus.

Yas squeezed Daphne's hand and whispered into her ear. "Is he going to sleep in the same room as us?"

Daphne whispered back. "Is that going to bother you?"

"Maybe he can sleep in the other room with Ardie. We can have the boys in one room and the girls in the other."

"This is bothering you, isn't it?" Daphne squeezed her knee reassuringly. "I'm here with you."

Yas patted her new mother's hand. "If you stay close to me, I'll be okay."

As they reached the last path toward Samuel and Elizabet's home, Daphne saw the flash of a blue cape through the hedge.

XIII

NABONIDUS PUSHED HIMSELF out of the cart to stand on his own two feet. He reached for the two canes to prop himself up. Three men in blue capes barred the path, swords drawn. "We heard you were back in Susa," the leader said. "The regent sent us to start a talk with you. Vasilius is imprisoned in the arched house. He will stay that way until you agree to stand for the throne." He examined Nabonidus's strength with a frown. "It appears you can hardly stand, never mind stand for the throne."

"My leg and my arm were slashed badly," Nabonidus said. "I nearly died. I will never again be in shape to fight for the regent or for anyone else. I wish to be left in peace with my family."

"The regent will be disappointed. He didn't want to send someone as valiant as Vasilius to the lions, but that stubborn fool insists he will only serve under you." He set his sword point into the slushy snow between his feet. "There are few who live through your options," he said. "You can disown your own family, marry your sister, and take the throne as King of kings for the Magi, or you can bring your whole family and fight with the regent and our army to take what is rightfully ours."

"What happens to my sister if I fight with the regent?" Nabonidus asked. "She is still under the control of the Magi."

The soldier grimaced. "Unfortunately, for her, she will have to die. While she is alive, she can produce another contender for the throne, which will create massive instability for the whole empire." He raised his sword and bowed. "It is no fault of your own you were born with royal blood. The fates have called you to your place, and though you resist, they will have their way."

"Return to the regent," Nabonidus said. "Tell him of my condition. I can hardly walk. Tell him if he is so determined to have me take my place then he must allow me time to heal, to pray, to discern the will of my God."

"Why do you need time to discern the will of your god?" the soldier asked. "Call a priest, kill a pig or a pigeon or a dog—whatever you do. Ask him to study the entrails, to chant, to tell you what the will of the gods might be. A few coins in his palm, and he will see things exactly as we wish."

"That's not the way it works with Yeshua," Nabonidus said. "I am not returning with you if it costs me my family or my sister. Vasilius will have to decide for himself whom he will serve. He has proved to be a loyal comrade worthy of respect." He hobbled toward the three soldiers. "I assume that if you kill me, the regent will not take it well. Perhaps you too wish to sleep in peace another night. Go and tell him what I've said."

The three rebels parted as Daphne, carrying Ardeshir with one arm and holding Yas's hand with the other, escorted the children behind Nabonidus. Elizabet sat trembling in the cart with the driver.

"We'll be back with others," the rebel leader said.

"We'll be waiting," Nabonidus said over his shoulder. "We'll be waiting."

"What is that?" Yas asked Daphne as they stood in the marketplace at Susa. She pointed toward a golden statue half her size. It had the wings and head of an eagle and the body of a lion.

"This is a gryphon," declared the proud artisan standing beside it.

"Did you make it?" Yas asked.

"Yes. I sculped it from pure gold. Also, this small chariot, this dragon, and this tiger."

"Why do your creatures all look so fierce?" she asked.

He chuckled. "They are powerful symbols of our Persian peoples. The gryphon is a symbol of the people in my hometown, Persepolis."

"We're here to buy some of the carpets for our new rooms," Daphne said. "Your skill for detail is incredible. With so much gold out in the open, aren't you afraid of bandits along the way?"

The artisan nodded his chin toward a group of men huddled around a fire. "Those men, and a dozen more, guard me along the way. We only travel in caravans, and we are wise in how we move from place to place. Only twice have we had to fight off bandits since we started in Egypt." He picked up a gold-handled knife. "Of course, these bandits know the penalty if they are caught. They would be skinned alive and thrown to the dogs."

"That's enough!" Daphne said, pulling Yas away.

The carpet weaver stepped closer. "Come and see my samples. From the finest wool in Persia. You tell me the size, the pattern, and the weave, and you shall have your dreams come true." The man patted Yas on the head. "I have a daughter your age who works with my wife and the women of my village to make the carpets."

"Do your sons help in the work?" Yas asked.

"Of course not," the man said. "My sons are tutored by an Armenian in reading, writing, and astronomy. They also sculpt in metal and wood and train in the art of war." He laid out a large carpet for inspection. It had an intricate pattern. "Among my class of peoples, our boys are raised by their mothers and their mothers' sisters until they turn five. When a boy is five then he is given to the king's court to be trained in all the arts and warfare. I hardly ever see my sons." He pulled another carpet from a pile and stretched it out on the first sample. "I once saw my sons marching with a thousand boys in their class. Every one of them wore the same uniform. I knew my sons were there but I could never identify them."

"That must make them very sad," Yas said. "When I didn't have a momma or a poppa to hold me, I was very sad."

"It is an honor for a family to give up their sons," he said. "My brother made it into the Immortals. He could fight against a whole army by himself with a sword, a lance, a bow, a shield, and a sheath of armor plates over his body. I once saw him destroy a dozen men without even a wound to show for it."

"I think we've had enough for one day," Daphne said. "My daughter needs to find out her place as a woman without thinking about what the men are doing."

"Did you know that one of Persia's greatest warriors was a woman?" the weaver asked. "Under King Xerxes, there was a Greek queen named Artemisia of Halicarnassus. She commanded her own warship at the battle of Salamis. A woman can do almost anything she wants in this empire."

Daphne pulled Yas away from the merchant. "I'll be back another time when I know what I need," she said.

As she rounded the corner, another merchant stood in her path. This merchant wore tight-fitting animal skin trousers, a thick jacket strapped tight, and a fur hat on his head. He withdrew his hand from a pouch at his waist. "Fresh pearls from the orient at the far end of the Silk Road," he said. He held out his palm where a dozen pearls nestled. "If you aren't ready for pearls, then take a look at my silk. Brought to you at great risk."

"What did you trade for those pearls?" Daphne asked.

The merchant arched his eyebrows and slipped the pearls into his pouch. "The Han demand the best of our spices, perfumes, and fruits. On my last trade mission, we took lions, gazelles, and glassware from Rome."

"I don't think we need pearls or silk today," she said.

"What about a bronze statue?" he said, pulling aside a blanket and unveiling four life-size bronze statues.

"Who are they supposed to be?" Yas asked, reaching out to touch one.

"This is Alexander the Great, this is Artaxerxes, this is Nebuchadnezzar, and this is his son Nabonidus."

"My poppa's name is Nabonidus," Yas said.

"Oh, really!" the trader said. "Now if he was a Maimonides that would be a perfect name to have," he said, chuckling. "I hear there's a Roman general looking for a meeting with a man like that." He stepped closer to Daphne. "Rome is at war with Parthia right now over Armenia. The leadership in this empire is unstable, and we need someone to unite and lead us all."

"Thanks for letting us see your wares," Daphne said. "I've got a baby waiting at home. My husband is not the man you are hoping for."

"If you get a visit from a Roman messenger some night, don't be surprised," he said.

"Would you at least consider being a satrap over us?" Samuel asked Nabonidus in the living room of their home. "Think how much influence such a governor would have to advance the news of Yeshua. You could set up laws to protect His followers, and we could establish many gatherings for those who seek truth. The most important value in Persia is truth, and we can show them the One who is truth itself."

Nabonidus chewed on a roasted pheasant leg as he listened. "I came to this land to find out my identity. I believe I have done that but at a heavy price. I would like to share the good news of Yeshua quietly from home to home so that others can hear it for what it is—not because of who I am."

"But imagine how you could unite us all," Samuel said. "Your sister is honored by the Magi, you have gained credibility with the rebels, and you know the mind of Rome from your time there."

"I don't believe that governing authorities are the best way to promote the truth of Yeshua," he said. "If followers of Yeshua become rulers, then the people who oppose their ideas will use their energy to turn on the truth of Yeshua. You can't legislate goodness."

Hananel hobbled into the room on his crutches. "What is this I hear about Yeshua's people becoming rulers?"

Samuel adjusted a pillow on a chair and helped Hananel settle. "Nabonidus thinks it is better to share the gospel quietly, person to person, rather than to dictate it through government channels. He says you can't change people's hearts by making laws. He refuses to step forward even to become a governor."

"He has a point," Hananel responded. "I just came from the market and spoke with one of the royal messengers. He says the Romans have manipulated the monarchy in Armenia to have their way. There is a lot of intrigue among the Parthians and Elamites as they try to regain power."

"I have seen the heart of both sides," Nabonidus said. "I don't want to be among the manipulators or among the manipulated. One of my true regrets is that I put the issue of my identity over that of Yeshua in this land. Too many people have paid with their lives because others thought they knew their plans for my life."

"So are we left to talk about the price of chickens?" Samuel said. "We are men who must prove our worth by what we do. Can you sleep through the night knowing that you have the power to change what is wrong?"

Nabonidus rose from his stool and poured a glass of grape juice. "I don't believe I have the power to change what is wrong. The thing that is wrong is in the heart of every man, woman, and child. Only the Almighty can change the heart."

Samuel raised his hands in frustration. "So you are saying we have to sit like logs decaying on the side of the path? Doing nothing, saying nothing?"

"Not at all," Nabonidus said. "We must pray, preach, proselytize. Yeshua will let us know when it is time to act and what we must do to act. We must be quiet before Him."

Hananel chuckled and raised his glass. "All this from the mighty champion, the victorious gladiator, the man who wins his way by imposing his will on his enemies."

"One thing I've learned since arriving in this land," Nabonidus said. "I don't have any control over what will happen next. I am tired of bloodshed, but I know that the path to power is covered in blood. Too much of mine has already been shed."

Atossa stepped into the room. "Nabonidus, you have a visitor."

Daphne arrived home with Yas to a chorus of angry voices. She circled the house to enter from the back. Adrina and Atossa huddled together, crouching outside the back door.

"What's happening?" Daphne asked. "Where is Ardeshir?"

Atossa turned and beckoned her close. "Elizabet took Ardeshir to the tunnel, and she's waiting there for us. A Roman messenger disguised as a Parthian is in there trying to convince Nabonidus to be an emissary for Rome. Samuel and Hananel think it is a good idea, but Nabonidus refuses to even consider such a thing."

"Not only that," Adrina added. "Vasilius arrived, and the men had their swords drawn until Nabonidus calmed them down. We knew this was not the time for women to be interfering."

"Is Poppa going to be okay?" Yas asked.

Daphne cradled the girl's head against her chest. "Poppa will be fine, little one. We need to pray that Yeshua will bring him wisdom and give peace to this house."

"Vasilius says that the regent is dying," Atossa said. "They are saying that if your husband returns with Vasilius to take over control of the Elamite satrapy and if he allies himself with Rome, they can overthrow the Parthians and gain a way to the throne. He wants no part of it, and they have threatened him."

"How did all these people even find us?" Daphne asked. "I thought we were hidden away from everyone out here." She ran her fingers through her daughter's hair. "All I know is that I came to this land to be at peace with my husband and to share the good news of the peace of Yeshua. All we've known is pain and conflict. Is this the path that Yeshua has for His people?"

Atossa and Adrina rose and wrapped their arms around Daphne and Yas. "We need to pray. There is nothing else we can do."

Standing between the two disguised Romans was unnerving. Vasilius maintained his role as a rebel ally while the newcomer feigned identity as a militiaman allied with the Magi. Both men stood eye level to Nabonidus, but Vasilius had broader shoulders and longer arms. The newcomer, Octavian, constantly flexed his wrist, ensuring that the sword in his hand always appeared in motion. Vasilius stood immobile as stone, giving the deadly appearance of a statue ready to strike with his dagger.

"I will say this one more time," Nabonidus declared. "I am not ready to become the King of kings." He held his hands out toward the men and backed them away with his commanding presence. "For one thing, there is so much intrigue in this land that whoever is on the throne will likely be dead within a few moons. For another thing, I have a family, and I came to this land for a mission of peace to share good news about Yeshua."

Octavian raised his sword to waist level, pointing at Nabonidus. "If you had stayed in Ephesus, I myself would have fed you to the lions for such heresy. In this land, where they worship anything and everything, the only thing I worship is the golden shekel." He reached into a purse tied to his waistbelt and pulled out a coin. "Right now, it is the emperor who covers my palm in gold, and he covers it so that I will find the right emissaries to advance the cause of Rome. All my sources say that you are the right one for what Rome needs."

Vasilius stepped away and lowered his dagger. "Rome might offer you gold, but I can offer you power that will let you control all the gold, silver, silk, and ivory you could ever desire. The regent is even now waiting to command all his forces, including me, to support your cause. Once he dies, there is no certainty as to who those forces might support."

Nabonidus lowered his arms. "There will be no champion on this. If I choose one of you, the other will strike me dead. Now that I have discovered my true identity, I wish I had never known it and that I had stayed hidden, sharing the good news of what is truly true."

Vasilius sat down on a stool. "So here we are. Outside this home stand two dozen cataphracts charged with one mission: to bring you back where you belong." He pointed at Octavian. "Over there stands one man, greedy for his own gold and nothing more."

"And somewhere near here," Nabonidus said, "stands a woman who wants nothing but her husband to be at home, to love his children, and to bring peace to their home."

Vasilius rose again and looked toward the back door. "That woman may not be standing as close to this place as you think," he said. "The regent hoped you would come peacefully and chose to invite your family ahead of you to be sure. He knew you would be happier if you had a cause worth fighting for."

Octavian raised his sword and swung the point in small circles. "There is only one error in what this unworthy son of Rome is saying." He whistled sharply. The door swung open and two men dressed like commoners pushed Hananel and Samuel into the room. They held daggers across the throats of the followers of Yeshua. "The leadership of your cult will die if you do not come with us. The men he promises outside are half of what he claims."

There had been no chance to scream a warning. The men had covered the mouths and noses of Daphne, Yas, Atossa, and Adrina before they'd even been aware of the kidnappers. The temple they were held in was far more fortified than the Temple of Fire. The Greek columns under the portico, combined with numerous arches, marked it as a blend of east and west. Terracotta figurines lined the perimeter.

The women were tied to posts, hands behind their backs, in the center of a courtyard at the heart of the temple complex. Gags covered their mouths until the leader of the troop approached Daphne and ripped hers off.

"So this is the consort behind the mighty Persian who seeks the throne." He ran his fingers down her cheek and under her chin, lifting it up to force her to look at him. "I see the fire in your eyes," he said. "I think you're the one I'm going to ask for from the regent when all this is done." She turned her head sideways and he slapped her hard. "Fire I can handle," he yelled. "Disrespect, I will not." He turned toward Atossa and Adrina. "These two should make a nice dessert," he said, running his hand under the chin and down the neck of Atossa.

"Stop!" Daphne said. "Let the others go! You want my husband. He will come for me, but let the others go."

"Maybe I'll keep the little one for my men," he said, bending down to rest his hands on Yas's shoulders. "You look like the perfect child to help feed hungry men." Yas spat in his face.

"No!" Daphne said. "If you have to take us, at least release the child. She cannot help you or hurt you. In the name of Yeshua, release the child!"

The commander arched back with his hands raised as if she had roared in his ear. He shook his head, seeming confused, then turned and walked away. A few moments later, a priestess of the temple shuffled into the courtyard and walked to Yas. She untied the ropes and said, "Follow me!" When Yas turned to Daphne and resisted, she grabbed the child's wrists and dragged her screaming from the courtyard.

"Where are you taking her?" Daphne called. No one answered.

Adrina and Atossa trembled in terror, tears streaming down their cheeks. "What will become of us?" Adrina asked. "What will they do with Yas?"

"Yeshua, help us!" Daphne screamed. "Yeshua, help us!"

The pillars of the temple shook and bits of mortar fell from the ceiling. A roaring rumble tore through the heart of the earth.

The earthquake knocked Octavian off stride as he reached for Nabonidus. The three clay lamps on the mantle shattered on the floor, and the spilled oil burst into flame. The former gladiator rolled away from the Roman and tossed a stool into his feet, causing him to tumble to his knees in the midst of the flames.

Vasilius dove for the floor, rolled, and hurled his dagger into the neck of the warrior holding Samuel. Before Octavian could regain his balance, Vasilius kicked him in the jaw and knocked him unconscious. Snatching the fallen warrior's sword, he thrust it up and under the armor of the man who had allowed Hananel to tumble away from him. As he got to his feet, he surveyed the chaos. Two men lay dying, one lay unconscious, and two struggled to their knees amid a room on fire. Nabonidus slipped away.

Nabonidus took advantage of the chaos in the darkness outside. He huddled in a hedge and allowed his eyes to adjust to the dim moonlight. Warriors shouting to comrades betrayed their location, and he slipped past them with little challenge. Vasilius could be heard shouting, "Spread out! He can't be far. We can't let him get to the sun temple before us."

Near the perimeter, Nabonidus found a young man left responsible for the horses. The sentry sat by a fire staring into the flames as if hypnotized. He paid little attention to the shouts in the distance.

Nabonidus crept up behind him and with his fist knocked the sentry senseless. He snatched up the man's dagger and grabbed the reins of the horses, ripping them away from the bushes they were tied to. He secured the soldier firmly on the back of one horse and mounting another, he led the warhorses away.

Vasilius shouted in the darkness. "You'll never find them in time."

As Nabonidus attempted to trot, several of the horses slipped away from his grip. He held the others firmly until reaching a small stream about belly deep on the horses. He crossed and then, releasing his hold on all but the one bearing the soldier, he shouted at the animals until they ran south away from Susa.

There were a hundred temples in a place like Susa. Perhaps a dozen dedicated to the sun. Unless Vasilius had misdirected him with his shout about the sun temple, he had little time to spare. Dismounting, he stooped at the stream and scooped up some ice-cold water. He flung it into the face of the unconscious soldier. He gained a moan.

Untying the young man, Nabonidus dragged him to the stream and dunked his head in the water. He pulled the man up choking and spluttering. "When you're given a task, even if you think it isn't important, then you need to do it well," he lectured. "Now, where did the others take the women?"

The young man struggled to catch his breath and stop coughing until Nabonidus pounded on his back. "Okay, okay!" he said. "The sun temple south of Susa. On the way toward the regent's camp."

"How many women were there?" Nabonidus said.

"Four!" the soldier said. "No, three. One was a girl."

Nabonidus tied the man back on the horse and began to gallop. He didn't slow, even when the man fell off the mount. Instead, he secured the reins of the mount around his wrist and pushed the horses harder.

The pillars they were tied to disintegrated behind them, and the three women stood alone in the courtyard. Yas raced back into the middle of the space as the roof and walls disintegrated around them. Shouts echoed through the rubble, but no one else appeared. A great gash opened in the floor of the courtyard and grew into a chasm right under the crumbling walls.

Adrina pulled at Daphne who was hugging Yas. "Come!" she yelled. "Yeshua has opened a way for us." She grabbed hold of Atossa's hand and ran toward the newly created ditch. "Follow me!" she said, as the others scrambled down the embankment after her.

When Daphne surfaced with the others outside the wall, she stood in the forest grove shaking. The edifice in front of them continued to tumble as cries of pain and terror filled the night skies. Small fires grew in various parts of the complex.

As they huddled together a stream of soldiers emerged and surrounded the place. A dark cloud covered the moon, immersing the landscape in pitch black. Only the fires provided illumination.

"We've got to go before they find lamps and start searching for us," Daphne said. "We'll have to trust Yeshua to guide our feet along the trails."

Holding her hands out front to feel for branches and bushes, and snaking her feet along tentatively in front of her, Daphne moved steadily forward with Yas holding tightly to her waist. "Momma, I'm scared," the little one said.

"Me too!" Daphne answered. "Yeshua will help us."

The sounds of the temple mayhem had almost faded behind them when Daphne heard the sound of hooves ahead of them. "Horses!" she said. "Hide."

The noises coming from the sun temple seemed especially chaotic for the middle of the night. Nabonidus hoped it was not evidence of a sacrificial ritual involving unwilling participants. A dark cloud had covered the moon, but firelight flickered throughout the complex.

He dismounted and surveyed the scene. There were a dozen or more soldiers and priests scrambling in and out. Then he noticed the slanted walls where a fire burned especially bright. The carpets and wall hangings inside must have caught fire. Perhaps there was a way to rescue the women in the middle of the chaos unless the rebels were burning down the edifice with Daphne and the others inside.

The back side would be an easier approach. He led his horses away and then mounted one to surge through a trail in the dark. The horses would find their way when he couldn't. As he strained to see through the darkness toward the temple, a human sound nearby caught his attention. He stopped the horses, dismounted, and lay flat on the ground.

"Are they gone?"

It was the voice of a young girl. A priestess from the temple?

"Shhhh!"

Someone knew he was here. He rose and gave a firm pat to one of the horses. It moved on down the trail. He lay flat again.

"I think they left."

He waited.

"Ouch!" someone said softly. "I knelt on a thorn."

It sounded a lot like Adrina. He waited longer.

The shouts from the temple grew closer. The soldiers were coming.

"The soldiers are coming! We need to run."

It was Daphne. No question. He stepped toward the voices. "Daphne! It's me."

Yas, Adrina, and Atossa all screamed in unison until Daphne calmed them. "Shhh! It's Nabonidus. Quiet."

It was too late. The soldiers had heard.

"Stay here!" Nabonidus ordered. He shuffled down the path, retrieved the horses and rode them back. "Get on," he said. "Daphne, you take Yas. Adrina and Atossa, get on the other. Where's Ardeshir?"

"With Elizabet," Daphne answered. "He's safe."

Nabonidus helped them mount. "I'll try to distract the soldiers," he said. "Meet me at the pool near the Temple of Fire. Hide behind the white building. Go to the end of this trail, turn up the hill and then around the forest until you see a stream. The temple is not too far on the other side." He gave the horse a firm pat and tried to feel his way down the pathway toward the soldiers. They were crashing through the bushes in his direction.

Daphne heeled her lead horse up the hill toward the Temple of Fire. When would this ever end? No sooner had she and Nabonidus come close to realizing their dream than chaos interrupted. Could there be darker forces at work in undermining all they hoped for? How did Nabonidus end up being a political pawn at the mercy of unscrupulous forces?

At the crest of the hill, she reined in the horse and waited as Adrina and Atossa caught up. "Momma, I want to get off," Yas whined. "This horse hurts."

Daphne pointed toward a small flickering through the trees. "Do you see that light? We just need to ride close to there, and then we can get off."

Atossa reached out and snagged Daphne by the elbow. "I think we need to pray for your husband and for us," she said. "We don't know what has happened to Hananel, Samuel, Elizabet, or Ardeshir. We need Yeshua to take care of us all."

"I think that earthquake was part of the way He has already taken care of us," Daphne said. "Before we pray, I need to ask Yas a few things."

"What, Momma?" the girl asked, leaning back against Daphne.

"Where was the woman taking you, and what did she want you to do?" Daphne asked.

Yas shrugged her shoulders. "She wanted me to go with the soldiers somewhere," she answered. "I didn't want to go, but she hit me and then you yelled Yeshua and the ground swallowed her and everything shook and I ran to you and it was dark."

"You did good," Daphne said.

"Did Yeshua save me?" Yas asked.

"Yes! Yeshua saved you," Daphne said. "And when you are in trouble again, you call to Him, and He will come to you." She pulled the horse to a stop and swung down onto the ground. "Come, now, we can walk from here. First, let's pray."

Rather than a direct confrontation, Nabonidus bush-barged around the advancing soldiers and watched their torches from a small hill near the sun temple. Daphne and the others would be safe if he could draw the force away from their current search pattern. He cupped his hands and shouted into the darkness. "Over here! You're going the wrong way. Over here!"

The torches stopped, and the voices in the bush silenced. They were trying to discern direction. He shouted again. "Hurry! Over here."

The half-moon slid out from behind the clouds and bathed the temple in a silvery sheen. Before the soldiers moved closer, Nabonidus slid around the perimeter of the grounds and took up a position behind the temple. "Over here! Hurry!" he called.

Two soldiers emerged from the temple ruins and rushed toward him. He crouched low and raced down a trail, arriving at a clearing where the horses were tied. Without hesitation, he slashed the reins tying the horses in place, led one of the animals toward a roadway, and galloped away.

XIV

"WHAT DO WE do now?" Atossa asked as the women and Yas crept into the shadows behind the monument fronting the Circle of Heaven pool. The moonlight now washed through the shadows of building, tree, and bush to expose their refuge.

"Nabonidus said to wait for him here," Daphne answered. "This is the last place I want to be on a night like this."

"Do you think Ardie is scared without us?" Yas asked. "I think we should be going home."

"Shhh! Someone is coming," Atossa hissed. "Get down until we know who it is."

The four of them lay flat on their bellies, necks arched to see under the hedge in front of them. The large man in the shadows tempted Daphne to rise, thinking it was Nabonidus, but she stayed in place. When he quick-stepped into sight across the marble plaza, there was no doubt who it was. Vasilius! He moved to the rear of the building and explored the window where he had helped Daphne escape before. It was now barred shut. Without trying further, he slipped around to the side of the building. Would this nightmare never end?

No sooner had Vasilius crept around the building to the front than Nabonidus stepped into the space near where they hid. "Daphne," he called.

Daphne put a hand on Atossa's shoulder to keep her down and stood slowly. "Here!" she said.

"Come! Hurry!" Nabonidus said. He stepped into the shadows, and Daphne grabbed Yas by the hand and followed. Twenty paces into the shadows Nabonidus stopped them and crouched down again. As he did, Vasilius returned with one of the priests from the Temple of Fire.

"I know they were here," Vasilius declared. "This is the only place he would think of to send them for safety. I saw the horses." He raised a torch and looked around the small glen. "Go, get my men. We'll search this place from end to end. You'd better not be hiding them."

Nabonidus took Daphne by the hand and led her further into the darkness of the forest. The moonlight hardly penetrated the leafy canopy. Daphne held Yas's hand, Yas held Atossa, and Atossa held Adrina. All went well until Yas tripped over a tree root and fell to her knees. She started crying. Daphne clamped a hand over her mouth and held her tight as the others collectively held their breath.

"Shhh!" Daphne said. "Horses!"

Sure enough. Moments later, hooves clattered by on the stony roadway nearby. The riders carried torches. "Which way would they go?" a rider asked. The group continued on past.

"Stay!" Nabonidus whispered. "Watch!"

Minutes later, Vasilius and the temple priest crunched by on the path a few strides away. "I was sure they were here," Vasilius said. "That little one should have given them away by now. Go check the residences one more time, and I'll wait by the front gate for the scouts to report back. We've got to get Nabonidus back to the regent before he dies."

When the two men passed out of hearing distance, the five of them crouched and moved deeper into the woods. When they arrived at the next bend in the road, they scrambled across it and climbed up into the hills. From their vantage point at the top, Nabonidus looked back toward the temple grounds. Horses and men formed an increasingly tight cordon around the perimeter with torches adding to the moonlight.

"It's a good thing we got out of there," Daphne said. "Where are we going to go from here?"

"To the regent," Nabonidus said.

"What?" Daphne blurted. "We've spent all this time avoiding the rebels, and now you're going to walk right into their camp?"

"It's about control and power," Nabonidus said. "He wants control and power over me, and I don't want him to have it." He pulled Daphne up by the elbow and waited for her to help Yas up. "It would have been easier if we could have ridden there in comfort, but there's a price to pay for getting things your way."

"Can you go back and take some of the horses?" Atossa asked.

The horses had been gathered together near the main gate of the Temple of Fire shrine. The fire was blazing and several men stood near warming their hands. Small drifts of snow clumped up against the hedges and glistened in the moonlight. Four women swept the cobblestones while two priests chatted with the soldiers. It seemed an impossible task to get to the horses. "I think we'll have to find another way," Nabonidus said. "For now, we need a place to hide until it's safe to travel."

Nabonidus pushed the pace south as the first fingers of dawn wriggled their way across the peaks of the Zagros Mountains. Yas was nestled snuggly against his back as he carried her. It was the first close contact he'd had with his daughter. She hadn't even resisted when Daphne insisted she get a ride. The women were stumbling enough after the all-night hike.

"I thought you said they'd be riding by before dawn," Atossa said. "My feet are numb and wet, and the pain in my back is too much. Why can't we go home instead?"

Nabonidus stopped, shifted Yas higher on his back, and then looked west. "We'll be at the crossroads soon. A carriage will stop near here and take three of you home. Daphne needs to come with me."

"We're not going without you," Adrina said. "Yas will never agree to travel without Daphne. Walking into the regent's camp is putting Yeshua to the test—forcing Him to protect you when you're being foolish."

"It does seem that way, doesn't it?" Nabonidus said. "I assure you that this is not the step I prefer, but I think it's the one I need to take."

"You had better bring Daphne back," Atossa warned, "or you can head back to Ephesus and take your chances on your own. We've had enough of you trying to find your identity. You have a family you need to take care of now."

"Something's coming," Daphne warned, pulling on Nabonidus's arm. "We need to hide."

"At this time of morning, it's probably a camel caravan of Arabs," he said. "They'll be trying to reach the caravansary on the other side of the crossroads before it gets too busy." He backed off the road and nudged the women toward a small opening in some waist-high grasses. "Just in case, let's give ourselves a chance to hide."

A camel did appear, and Nabonidus stepped out from the grass onto the side of the road. The rider made frantic motions to move back. Nabonidus stepped away and watched him. The Arab made hand motions indicating soldiers were following. The moment he understood, he herded the others deeper into the brush. "Hurry! There are soldiers on horseback coming," he said.

They sheltered in a shallow ravine, lying flat in the mud. "It's cold," Yas complained.

"Shhhh!" Daphne soothed. "After the soldiers go by, you can ride on your poppa until we can get you a ride home. Tonight, you'll be able to get a warm bath, clean clothes, and a fresh bed. Won't that be good?"

"Are you coming?" Yas asked.

"We'll talk about all that as soon as the soldiers pass. Right now, we need to be very quiet."

The clop-clop of hooves sounded nearby. A voice called out. "Sir, travelers have stopped here recently. Do you want me to check this out? It could be them."

Another voice called back, "They're traveling with a little girl and three women." Vasilius! "They would never have made it this far on foot. If they got help, they could be at the inn ahead."

"It will only take a moment, sir!" the first man said. "There appear to be several of them."

"Come!" Vasilius ordered. "There's no need to waste time on every little pilgrim taking time to relieve themselves. We'll camp out at the inn and see what kind of traffic comes by over the next day or two."

"Doesn't the regent want us back today?" the second rider asked.

"Only if we have Nabonidus in chains," Vasilius said. "None of us want to hurry back in order to be shamed by an old man who can hardly stand on his own feet."

A dozen cataphracts on horseback passed, backs straight, lances poised. Nabonidus watched them weave around a caravan of donkey carts moving up the road toward him. Still, he waited. "Remember how many horses there were in the courtyard last night?" he whispered to Daphne. "There's more coming." It was a notorious trick to send a preliminary force to lure the quarry out of its refuge, only to be scooped up by a follow-up group. As the donkey carts passed in front of them, another dozen horses trotted by. Some things never changed, regardless of which fighting force operated.

A short time later a caravan of camels passed by. Nabonidus stepped out and signaled for the Arab to stop. "I have women and a girl who need a ride to the crossroads," he said. "A gold shekel will be your blessing for this small favor."

"Such a great gift for such a small favor," the Arab said. "A silver shekel would make any man happy on a day like today."

"These women have walked all night to escape trouble," he said. "A gold shekel will help you with warmth and clean clothes for them. The girl especially will need to be guarded until she can take the carriage to her home past Susa."

"As a favor for a friend," the Arab said. "The gold shekel will do all you desire. I will take good care of it for you."

Although Yas resisted being loaded onto the back of a camel when she realized that Daphne wouldn't be riding along, she settled on when Adrina clambered on behind her. Atossa settled on another camel in front of its rider. The Arabs wrapped the three in hooded robes and thick sheepskin coverings. "We'll be there as soon as we can," Daphne promised. "Be a big sister, and take care of Ardeshir for me."

As the sun bathed the treetops and slush-covered roads, the camels swayed down the path toward whatever lay ahead.

Daphne's teeth were chattering as she and Nabonidus crouched behind the inn's hedge at the crossroads. The chaos of camels, donkeys, horses, and oxen milling about the feedlot as their owners took advantage of the roadside hospitality kept any security forces preoccupied. The rebel soldiers departed and headed south.

The two fugitives crept into the rear entrance and slipped into the dining area. They ordered lamb stew and flat bread, sitting in a dark corner watching the entrance. No one looking for them entered. Nabonidus booked a room, and the two of them washed up and snuggled in a warm bed. It had been a long time.

"I hope they all made it home okay," Daphne said, laying her head on her husband's chest. "I'm hurting bad and need to feed that boy. I need to be with him." She ran her fingers across his lips. "Yas was not happy at all. I hope Ardeshir is okay. It's a lot to expect of Elizabet."

Nabonidus stroked her hair, listening. "Sometimes I forget we have children in need of us. I thought we'd settle in peacefully, have our family, confirm my identity, and share the good news of Yeshua. None of that seems to be happening in the way I planned."

"Please tell me this is our last adventure. I came to this country just wanting to be with you, and we've been apart more than ever. I can't keep going on this way."

"I'd have gone back with the others," Nabonidus said, "if I thought the regent and the Magi would leave us alone. You're here to keep me focused and to make sure I do get home. My son needs a father, and I want to give him one."

"How are we going to find the regent before he finds us?" Daphne asked. "I'm sure he'll have spies or informants letting them know we're here already."

Nabonidus parted the curtains a crack. "In a moment, I'm going to go out and purchase cloaks and canes and hats that will help us with disguises. I used to know a Roman who was a master of disguise. By pretending to be an old blind man, he kept people from paying any attention to him."

"I think you're a little too large to fool anyone that you're someone other than who you are," Daphne said.

"People expect to see two of us together," Nabonidus said. "By separating, bending over with a cane, wearing different clothing, and appearing where we're not expected, it is amazing how even someone like me can disappear in a crowd."

At first light, Nabonidus bartered with a carriage driver to take them south toward the rebel camp. They arrived separately and found their places—one at the front and the other at the back. Most of the caravan traffic and other carts were loaded down heading for the harbors where goods would be sent all over the world. A fresh layer of snow covered the road, and walking the distance didn't make sense.

The two travelers alighted from the carriage just after noon. Nabonidus took off his own scarf and wrapped it around Daphne's neck, tying it snugly. "We'll go over a few hills into the back of the property so that none of his sentries along the road see us," he said. "That wind is cold enough I hope most of the men are inside today."

Daphne stuffed her hands inside the folds of her wrap and followed in the footprints Nabonidus stamped out for her. The snow on the hills reached halfway up her shin and almost overtopped her sheepskin boots. The two of them crested a hill and stood behind a large cedar at the top. The main building on the large farm had arched doorways. "I can't believe those lions you told me about could survive in weather like this," she said. "Don't they have a warmer place to keep them?"

Nabonidus pointed toward a small section of upturned earth in front of the horse barn. "I think there's a small tunnel in the pit where they can lie down and keep each other warm. Someone still has to feed them, so I'm sure they aren't hibernating like bears. We'll go in behind the barn and decide what to do after that."

"You mean you're not going to march in where the regent is and let him know you don't want his job?"

Nabonidus chuckled. "If only it were that easy. That old man has a plan and doesn't take no for an answer."

Amazingly, no one appeared until they reached the arched building. Nabonidus hurried Daphne in through a back entrance. Loud laughter echoed down the hallways illuminated by three clay lamps. The farther they walked, the warmer the space became.

The kitchen area buzzed with servants and chefs preparing for whatever feast was ahead. The clash of steel on steel came from the main gathering space. Nabonidus grabbed Daphne's hand and pulled her along. Ducking through a thick curtain, they entered a darkened room covered from ceiling to floor in rich Persian carpets. The muffled sounds of the celebrants could be heard as a faint hum.

Nabonidus pulled aside a curtain and stepped into a dark space behind the main hall. A familiar voice addressed the audience. Vasilius! "By now, we know that Nabonidus is getting closer. Once he realizes we have his daughter and her two guardians, he will do anything we ask. We are hoping to find his son soon."

The regent's voice quavered in response. "What makes you think that he's not already here while you and your men are sitting here filling your faces and falling asleep in the warmth of my hospitality?"

Vasilius replied. "The innkeeper let us know that Nabonidus and his wife arrived after leaving their daughter and the two guardians with our Arabs on their camels. He believes they should arrive sometime later today, but our men haven't seen anyone matching their descriptions on the public carriages or private caravans. Can you believe that old gladiator paid a perfect stranger to take his own daughter?" The muffled laughter rumbled through the carpet.

Nabonidus stepped through the carpet and appeared behind the regent's throne. With a double chop of his fists he felled the two cataphracts standing on either side of the old man. Before anyone could move, he lifted the old man above his head and held him there. "While I appear to you as a fool," Nabonidus said, "the life of the regent is now in my hands. I offer you his life in exchange for the lives of those you hold."

Vasilius, sitting on a gilded couch nearby, raised a glass and smiled. "He has arrived, just as we told you. We have played the fool, and he has walked right into the trap." He got to his feet. "This time he even brought his wife to save us the trouble. Perhaps now we can share the ruse." He motioned for Nabonidus to step forward. "In your hands is an old pawn who plays his part well, nothing more. Whether you dispose of him to the lions or the snow, I care little. You see, I am the true regent who woos you to take up the cause of Elam." He raised an arm, and two archers stepped forward; bows drawn. In a heartbeat, dual arrows slashed the air and pierced the old man.

Nabonidus, outmaneuvered and outplayed, lowered the convulsing old man to the ground and slouched back on the throne behind him.

"Why do you need me?" he said. "You have the loyalty of your men, the control of this region, and the passion of your cause. I desire none of it."

Vasilius paced in front of his gilded couch. "The path to the throne for the King of kings is through the line Maimonides. All the people know this."

He sipped from his golden goblet. "We know the Magi and the Parthians control your sister and could produce an heir through her. We Elamites are the rightful rulers of Persia but don't have the strength to wrest power back. Our only hope is to produce a more worthy heir."

He knelt beside the old man and closed the old man's sightless eyes. "We tried to work through your uncle but he refused to side with us against his own niece. When we heard you had arrived, we knew that the son of a Maimonides would be welcomed even more than the daughter. It seems that our creative attempts to win your loyalty have failed, and that now we must prove the strength of our intent."

He stepped to the side and the two archers, surrounded by a dozen cataphracts with lances drawn, aimed their weapons not at him but at Daphne. "As you no doubt overheard, we have your daughter and her two guardians. Soon, we will have your son. We leave the choice to you." He picked up a golden scepter and extended it to Nabonidus. "Either we crown you as our contender for the throne, or we kill you and your wife and raise your son as the rightful heir. No one else in this room can make that choice except you."

Nabonidus knelt with his head bowed. "I desire first to tell you about the true King of kings whom the leaders of this land once anointed as the true heir of all things."

"Speak!" Vasilius said.

"His name is Yeshua," Nabonidus said. "A caravan of Persian king-makers rode to the land of Judah in line with what your prophet Balaam had predicted many years ago. They followed a star appearing in the heavens of this land until they found Him. They gave Him gifts of gold, frankincense, and myrrh." He lifted his head, looking up. "I have come to kneel before this King of kings and the kingdom He is building with people from every tribe and tongue and nation. To take His place in this land or any other land would dishonor the One who made us all for His purposes."

Vasilius stepped forward and grabbed the lance from the hands of one of the cataphracts. "Stop it!" he shouted. "I've heard enough. You have chosen to feed the lions with the women who are closest to you. We know they can't stomach you, but today you will regret the lives who have died before you."

Nabonidus stayed on his knees as the men grabbed and tied up Daphne. He stayed on his knees as others tied him. He rose without resistance as the warriors prodded him out the door and onto the snowy path toward the pit. Silence cloaked the land.

"Bring out the other women!" Vasilius commanded. Several Arabs stepped out from the horse barn with Adrina, Atossa, and Yas all gagged. The terrified look in Yas's eyes was haunting. Tears ran down Atossa's cheeks. Adrina did her best to resist and slow the forced march. Two dozen cataphracts stepped aside and gathered around the edge of the lions' den.

When the captives reached the edge of the pit, Vasilius nodded to one of the archers. The man clanged on a bell. A low growl rumbled through the pit below. Two of the beasts appeared, looking up in expectation. Yas shook, falling to her knees before being yanked back to her feet. Vasilius thrust a lance into the ground at his feet. "In honor of your right to rule, I give you the privilege of choosing the order in which the lions eat. Now you know, I was the one who fed them Sasina—the woman you refused to choose. This time, it is your turn."

Nabonidus nodded at the Arab holding Yas. The man stepped forward with the girl and Vasilius stepped back. The little one wriggled and screamed through her gag. As the Arab reached the pit, he wrenched the lance out of the ground and hurled it toward Nabonidus. The former gladiator caught the projectile and charged toward Vasilius.

Surprised but not defenseless, Vasilius dodged back and grabbed a lance from one of his cataphracts. Every warrior, honoring the tradition of combat, stepped aside as Nabonidus and Vasilius faced off. The clang of lance against lance resounded. The Arab dragged Yas from the arena and disappeared into the crowd.

Each man fought for solid footing in the muddy terrain around the pit. Lunging and dodging inches from sharpened iron, they parried. Vasilius wore his pleated armor vest—Nabonidus only his sheepskin. The self-revealed regent backed the former gladiator toward the pit.

Feigning a slip, he allowed Nabonidus to thrust dangerously close to his shoulder before lunging upward toward his opponent's neck. Nabonidus twisted desperately and the blade sliced across his bicep. The razor tip opened a bloody gash that reddened the little patch of undisturbed snow.

Vasilius repositioned his lance and swung it like an axe at Nabonidus's knees. Despite his heavy clothing, Nabonidus hurdled over the weapon and swung his own lance. The blade bounced off the armored chest of Vasilius and left Nabonidus off balance.

Vasilius brought the shaft of his lance onto the back of Nabonidus's head, felling the giant to his knees, a stride from the edge of the pit. One of the lions stretched on its back legs, jaws open. A vicious roar vibrated out of the depths of the earth.

Nabonidus rolled as the enemy's spear point stabbed inches from his ribs. In his roll, his left hand thrust into space, feeling the hot breath of the lion. Using his own lance for leverage, he bounced up. On his feet again, he parried off a series of vicious blows as he pushed to create space away from the lions. Several roars now emanated from the pit as the beasts anticipated something from the chaos above.

Vasilius worked his opponent's injured right side, jabbing at the weakening limb. Twice, he caught the thin material covering along the right arm, ripping away at the gladiator's sense of security. His own armored vest seemed to embolden him to push the boundaries of safety.

Twice the men parried the shafts of their lances so that they stood face to face, weapons crossed in front of them. Nabonidus proved stronger in the contest of brute strength and used the slight rise at the edge of the pit to leverage his push and gain several strides of space away from the jaws of the hungry maneaters. "You should have sacrificed the girl," Vasilius said. "What is an orphan to you? A leader has to know when to let go of those who won't benefit the cause." His feet slipped back in the mud, but he maintained his balance, leaning hard against Nabonidus. "It looks like you are proving to be one who doesn't benefit our cause anymore."

"I fight for Yeshua!" Nabonidus snarled. "I fight for truth. I fight for the life of all who matter." He pushed harder.

Finding solid ground again, Vasilius stepped away from Nabonidus's push and forced the former gladiator to stumble forward. Withdrawing his lance, he grabbed the shaft with both hands and pushed hard against Nabonidus's ribs. With space opened, he jabbed the blade up toward Nabonidus's gut.

Vasilius's spear point found only air and his own feet slipped, leaving him flat on his back. He rolled away from the blade, which bounced off the back of his breastplate. On his feet again, he faced the fiery eyes of an enemy fighting for more than life. The thrusts coming at him were quicker, deadlier, dangerously close to his neck, knees, and arms. He fought harder, still confident in his training and experience but visibly wary of the power unleashed against him.

The two giants came together again, and Nabonidus pivoted Vasilius, step by step, toward the pit. The lions were ravenous now, smelling blood, lunging toward the top of the enclosure. Vasilius leveraged himself against the lip of the den in much the same way Nabonidus had done. For a short time, the two stood deadlocked, breathing heavily, eying each other, gritting teeth, determined not to give another inch.

And then, a deadly clawed paw rose above the lip of the den and swatted the back of Vasilius's leg. Seizing the distraction, Nabonidus kicked at his knee, buckling it. With his own knee, Nabonidus pushed into Vasilius's gut and leveraged his lance to push his opponent backward.

The regent grunted as his foot gave way, and he tumbled into the yawning chasm. The beasts were on him before he reached the floor of the pit but he rolled away, thrusting with his lance. Two of the big cats recoiled as the spear head pierced them, but now all six cats circled the prey warily. They were hungry hunters maddened by blood. The attack was on.

Two of the cataphracts raced to the edge of the pit and hurled lances into a pair of lions. Another cat went down under Vasilius's lance, but the moment he drove his spear into the heart of a lion the other three were on him, tearing at his legs, his arm, his throat.

Nabonidus looked away as other warriors hurled their weapons into the pit. The snarls, growls, and roars ended but none of the men jumped into the pit. The regent was beyond rescue.

One of the cataphracts knelt before Nabonidus. "We are at your service. You have earned the right to rule."

Nabonidus stood still as Daphne ripped a strip off her tunic to wrap his arm. He looked over the men standing in the mud. "Release the women, and go back to your families," he said. "Know that you live today because of Yeshua and His mercy for all people. This place will become a home for orphans, widows, and those who have no place to call their own. It will become a center from which the good news of Yeshua will spread."

"But what about the throne for the King of kings?" the cataphract asked.

Nabonidus embraced Daphne and Yas and nodded toward Adrina and Atossa. "We will know when the King of kings shows himself. His kingdom will be a kingdom of peace. There has been enough blood shed from this place, so go home to your families and lay aside your swords and lances."

The men gathered around the pit for a moment of silence. "We will go," the leader said, "until it is time to fight again. Peace cannot last in a land like ours. The Magi will soon sense our weakness and come to destroy us all."

A carriage rolled into the yard, and Daphne ran toward it. "Come, Yas," she called. "Your brother's here."

"One day," Nabonidus said to his men, "the true King of kings will come to save us, and peace will be His gift for all to embrace."

OTHER TITLES BY CASTLE QUAY BOOKS

ONE SMOOTH STONE
Marcia Lee Laycock

A LIFE WORTH LIVING
THE CAL YOU NEVER KNEW
CAL BOMBAY
FOREWORD BY JIM CANTELON

CASTLE QUAY BOOKS

OTHER TITLES BY CASTLE QUAY BOOKS

A Holy Calling: Becoming A Godly Wife — Ann McCallum

Women in the Bible: Small group Bible study — Marina Hofman PhD

Castle Quay Books

Check out Jack Taylor's other books
and short stories and contact him at

jackataylor.com

Other Titles by Castle Quay Books

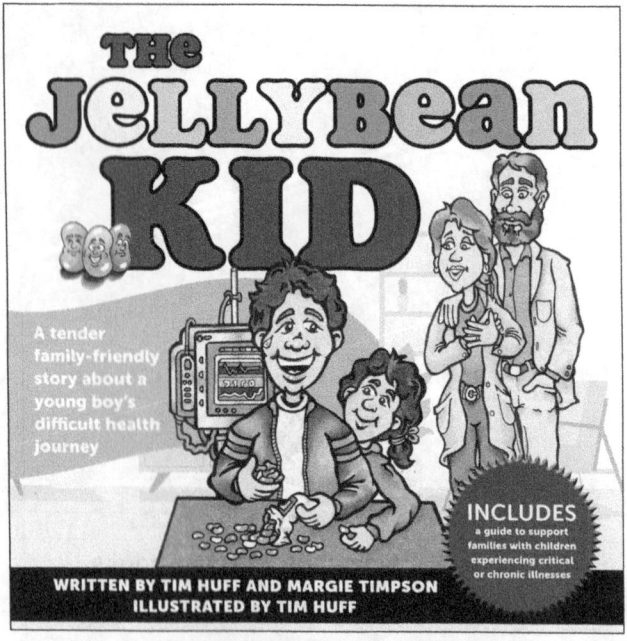

The Jellybean Kid

A tender family-friendly story about a young boy's difficult health journey

INCLUDES a guide to support families with children experiencing critical or chronic illnesses

WRITTEN BY TIM HUFF AND MARGIE TIMPSON
ILLUSTRATED BY TIM HUFF

Barclay and Berk Builders

A Parable

Retold by BEVERLEY RAYNER
Illustrated by JAMES HENSMAN

Castle Quay Books